MY FAMILY LIES

NJ MOSS

BLOODHOUND
BOOKS

Copyright © 2025 NJ Moss

The right of NJ Moss to be identified as the Author of the Work has been asserted by him in accordance with the Copyright, Designs and Patents Act 1988.

First published in 2025 by Bloodhound Books.

Apart from any use permitted under UK copyright law, this publication may only be reproduced, stored, or transmitted, in any form, or by any means, with prior permission in writing of the publisher or, in the case of reprographic production, in accordance with the terms of licences issued by the Copyright Licensing Agency.
All characters in this publication are fictitious and any resemblance to real persons, living or dead, is purely coincidental.

www.bloodhoundbooks.com

Print ISBN: 978-1-917705-17-2

For Krystle

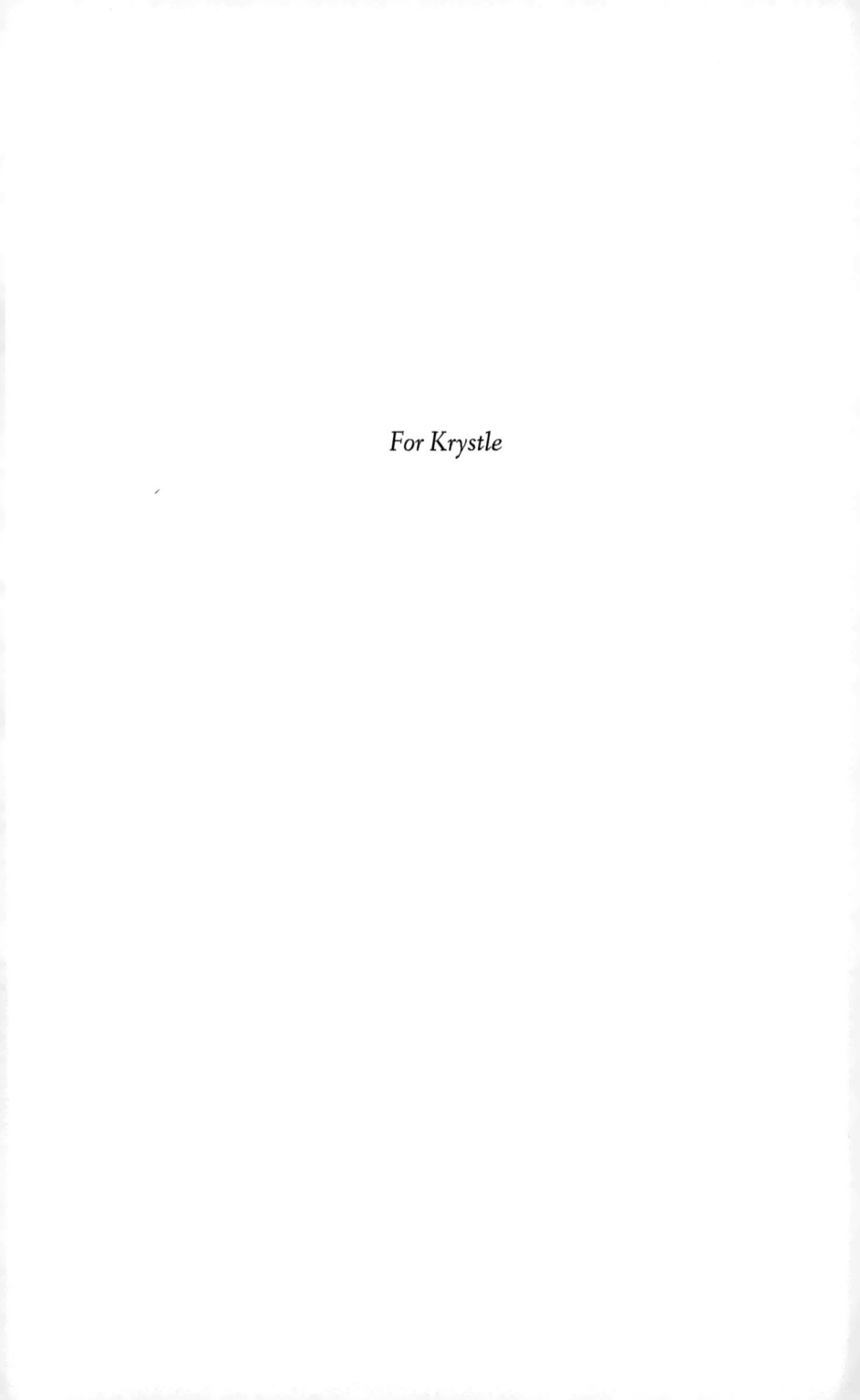

A MOTHER'S MUSINGS: READER QUESTION #47
22/09/24

Victoria Hawthorne

What is something you miss about your son being a baby?

Well, who's to say that my forty-three-year-old Dominic *isn't* a baby? Ha, joking! (Thankfully he doesn't read my blog.) But sincerely, this is a fantastic question. Motherhood is a magnificent journey, but I have often wondered what it would be like to live it in reverse: to birth a middle-aged man (without the, let's say, *ouch* factor that would cause), to see him become an enthusiastic and purposeful twenty-something, then to watch as his hormones riot and cascade into a baby-faced pre-teen and then a toddling stampede of joy and finally, the last gift, a bundle of pure happiness. (For those interested, one of my favourite writers, F Scott Fitzgerald, wrote a short story about this entitled *The Curious Case of Benjamin Button*. It was also made into a motion picture with Brad Pitt... How can that man still look dashingly handsome in all those prosthetics?)

To take a more serious view of the question, I think I miss the honest affirmation most of all. In this day and age, self-love and positive self-talk is a difficult ideal to attain. There is so much negativity. There is so much comparison. Open your phone and you will see elegant women who have their lives utterly together, who are funnier than you will ever be, whose skin is tighter, whose waists are thinner, whose minds are sharper, whose smiles elicit a deeper response. But when my little Dominic – or "Dom Dom" as he was known back then – was a cherub, I never had to question anything. When I smiled at him and he grinned up at me, I knew I had the most perfect smile anybody ever had. When I played peekaboo with him for hours, and he never tired, I knew I was interesting. I didn't need anybody to tell me. He was all I needed. When I looked in the mirror and noticed the crow's feet creeping, when he reached up and touched my face, I knew I was beautiful. Because, to him, I was an angel. That was all that mattered.

I've just taken a break. Writing about this equals, yep, you guessed it: tears! As many of you will know from my previous posts, Dominic's father left when he was a child. I'm not talking the modern "I have my adventure and you have yours but let's give this kid the best possible shot" sort of desertion, either. This wasn't the "I'll take him on the weekends and financially assist you in his support". This was the somewhat clichéd leaving for cigarettes and simply never returning.

Sometimes, I wonder if this abandonment had something to do with my dearly deserted being unable to handle the complications of a growing child. He missed Dom Dom; he missed the baby boy. I mourned when my baby became a man, but I rejoiced in it too. I accepted that my smile would not always be the most delightful thing he had ever experienced. I understood my laughter would not always be his music. It hurt, and that subtle and somehow exquisite pain only increased as he grew older, but I did the right thing. I didn't idealise little Dom Dom. I knew he had to become Dominic. But I wouldn't allow my child to keep the deserter's name. From the day he disappeared in a puff of smoke, Dominic would be a Hawthorne.

Fathers need to learn that to be a parent, you have to parent.

Sorry if that got a little morbid! (If you've experienced a similar situation, please check out my friend's blog, *Living Life Solo: A Single Mother's Journey,* in which she discusses many of these topics.)

Please remember to use promo code *MMusingsVictoria* to receive 10% off baby products at my sponsored shop, *All Care Wear.* As always, thank you for reading.

Please comment what you miss most about your baby no longer being a baby. But let's be honest, ladies, it's like I joked at the start… Do they ever really grow up?

CHAPTER ONE

DOMINIC

His was a world of secrets. He had never intended it to be that way. He had always tried to be as honest as his personality would allow, but over and over, he returned to the dark. There was a scared little boy in him crawling into the cellar as if hiding from some horror-film villain.

As he drove, far too fast, as the rain hammered against the windscreen and the whisky surged through his system, Dominic Hawthorne wanted to scream. He wanted somebody else to take over his life, not just tell him what to do, but do it for him. Often, he looked at regular people and wondered how they could possibly function in such a seemingly easy manner.

'*You're too hard on yourself,*' Eloise had often said. To know he was thinking of his wife then, in those circumstances, was another punchline to the never-ending joke that was his life. '*You have to be nice to yourself, Dominic. And that doesn't just mean taking warm baths or sneaking the occasional cigarette. It means fixing the way you speak to yourself. You are enough. You work hard. You earn a good living. You're kind and loving... when you're not in one of your grumpy moods.*'

Thinking of his wife hurt for a myriad of reasons he rarely

let himself truly contemplate. Mostly, it was the fact she didn't know who he truly was.

He turned a corner, the wheels screeching. He was racing through the Somerset countryside. He'd met Eloise in Henley-on-Thames, Oxfordshire, where both he and Eloise were from originally. He'd owned a chain of hotels and she'd been a model; when she'd looked not once, not twice, not thrice (he actually smiled, because it was one of those "ick" words that always made Eloise cringe and giggle), but four times, five, six... he'd felt like the luckiest man alive.

Their romance had been swift, their marriage quicker. Sometimes he wondered if he'd put the ring on her finger so she wouldn't have time to see just how messed up he was.

The alcohol made the car wobble, his thoughts doing the same. They'd moved to Somerset to start a slower pace of life. Weston-super-Mare was a small town on the west coast of England. The Victorians had holidayed there. Their five-bedroom house sat upon the same hill which ancient people had once made their places of permanence, overlooking what had been swamp land back then. He and Eloise had a large, gorgeous home.

Some people had judged his mother, Victoria, when she'd also moved to the West Country to be closer to her only son. But who could judge a mother's love? Who was to say it was vaguely suspicious or overbearing rather than endearing, caring, sweet?

'We have to slow down,' his passenger said.

He gripped the wheel harder. He was moaning; words were tumbling out, but he wasn't sure if they were spilling in his mind or out of his mouth. The edges of reality were becoming too tight, just as they'd been ever since he was a boy, when he sat in class and looked at his schoolmates and thought, *Is it the same for them? Is everything extra effort? Do they close their eyes at night and wish they wouldn't wake up?*

Eloise was correct in her assessment of him. Any good mood he was able to cultivate, even for a short time, inevitably leaked into the grey when his mind began to drive against itself. He felt like he was pushing a boulder uphill anytime he tried to function like a regular person. He would often shout at himself in his own head. What was wrong with him? Almost forty-four with an angelic wife a decade younger, with a big house, a successful career.

All that, and yet he couldn't let himself be happy… He had demons in him. And it hurt. Then the self-loathing would come. He was becoming old, and he still dwelled on things that should've stopped mattering a long time ago. He couldn't release the demons. He built the bars of his own prison and locked his own padlock and hoped they would go away. They never did.

His passenger cried out, 'Put your hands on the wheel – Dom!'

He was well and truly drunk. He was drunker than a skunk. Ha, ha, wasn't that cute, sweetie pie? Wasn't he a beautiful little boy? He was a *forever baby*. He grabbed the wheel of the Volvo, took another corner, the rain making patterns across the windshield as if the droplets would form words. *Pull over. This is the end. It was always going to come to this.*

'Please.'

'I have to end this,' he yelled. He wondered if he was a narcissist. Or perhaps it would be more accurate to call him a solipsist. He worked as a business professor at Bristol University, was well-regarded by both faculty and students; he sometimes lunched with the philosophy professor. She'd explained solipsism as the theory that the self is all that can be known to exist.

It fit him like a glove. That would mean that everything else, all the unspoken secrets, all the hidden hurts, all the stifled pains, none of them breathed anywhere except inside the walls of his skull. If he stopped thinking, if he let go, they ended.

'Just pull over,' his passenger begged.

'Shut up.'

'You're scaring me.'

'You should be scared.'

He almost looked at her, almost allowed himself to acknowledge what he had done. Nobody would ever understand what it was like to be him.

It was a self-pitying notion. He'd owned seven hotels. He'd employed hundreds of people. He'd sat in thousands of meetings and made thousands of business decisions. He'd made money on the stock market. He owned the best suits: Huntsman, Gieves & Hawkes, Tom Ford. More he couldn't even remember. He went to the gym three times a week; he kept himself in shape. He was a success. But he'd never felt alive.

'Please.' The whimpering came. 'Puh-please.'

But he kept on, just as he had his entire life. The old cliché about one foot in front of the other. That was all he'd ever done, taken the next step, as days turned to weeks to months to years to decades, and there he was, a middle-aged man with an outwardly perfect wife and all the luxuries a person could ask for. But inside, he was a child wishing he possessed the daring to end it all.

With the Dutch courage, he didn't even have to make a choice. But still, he focused on trying not to crash. That was why he slammed on the brakes when the fox darted out in front of them.

'Dom!'

Time slowed as the car skidded and didn't decelerate. They were spinning too fast – a tree – slam, and it was like a hard metal fist punched into his side. His eyes welled. He could taste blood.

'Dominic,' she whispered from beside him, and suddenly, the alcohol was wearing off. He'd never sobered up this quickly. His vision was failing him. What had he done? Oh, Jesus, what was wrong with him? 'Dominic. Can you hear me? I'm going to ring – Oh, where's my phone? *Dominic.*'

He coughed, his throat tightening, his eyes closing.

'There's a car. I'll use their phone. Stay with me.'

He was already gone, floating away... then he was in that dark place. He was the unloved creature he'd always been. He was staring into his own eyes, his own soul. This was the end. All his secrets would go with him. All his love. All his hate. He would've laughed if his throat hadn't been filled with blood.

CHAPTER TWO

ELOISE

Eloise sat on the toilet seat after vomiting, everything seeming far more real since the morning sickness had begun. She was two months pregnant with a child her husband knew nothing about. Smoothing her hands across her belly, she closed her eyes and tried to envision a warm and happy future. *There's an explanation, Dominic. But you have to listen to me.* She would force him to understand.

Eloise had used positive affirmations her entire life, from her first Oxfordshire beauty pageant to the highlights of her career: the Met Gala and Paris Fashion Week. She had learnt a long time ago that her mind could turn against her.

She told herself Dominic would come to support her unplanned and hard-to-explain pregnancy; their child's life would be filled with love and happiness and laughter; this beautiful baby would smooth over the bumps which she had never allowed herself to fully examine.

She stood up, looked at herself in the mirror. She had lines around her eyes; her belly was—

She stopped the trail of those thoughts. She said to herself,

My face is maturing in an experienced and elegant way. My belly is evidence that I have more to offer to the world than a stick-thin figure only attainable through self-abuse. She no longer flagellated at the altar of body idealism.

Before leaving the bathroom, knowing she would have to return to her marital bed, she took several slow breaths and mindfully connected herself to the tiles, feeling their coolness, making herself present. Maybe it was woo-woo and a little *out there*, but she enjoyed being in control of her reality.

Walking through the house, she rehearsed what she would say to Dominic if he asked why she'd been gone from their bed for an hour in the middle of the night. She didn't want to tell him of the bouts of sickness, because then he'd encourage her to go to the doctor; there might be a slip-up, a mention of the pregnancy. She'd been to the doctor already to make sure everything was okay. It was early days, but there was no doubt. She had a life inside of her. She needed to figure out how she would tell her husband.

If he asked where she'd been, she'd most likely say that she had been writing. She'd been working on a memoir about her modelling years, and she currently had a light-hearted novel about a girl growing up on a farm in the hands of an agent who seemed mildly interested. She was going places, doing things, making statements. This baby, whether planned or not, secret or not, would make everything better. She had to believe that.

The walls were lined with photos of their holidays: Lake Como, Aspen, the Maldives, Santorini, more. So many memories. In all of them, Dominic looked tall and strong, his hair seeming silver rather than grey, as if he'd turned it that way by choice, but not dyed it. As if he'd *willed* it into being in his late thirties like he was choosing the colour. She was perched on his arm, seeming birdlike, a trophy, even to herself. But she didn't mind that. She relished being someone he was proud of.

She told herself this often. *I may be a trophy wife, but I'm a fine trophy. I sparkle. I gleam.* She sometimes wished she could pluck Dominic from the photos and have him as her husband instead of the flesh-and-blood man she slept beside each night.

In their bedroom, moonlight glinted off the whisky bottle which lay on his side table. Dominic had been drinking too much lately. He was stressed with his workload at the university. She'd tried to explain that teaching, while rewarding, was something he was still getting used to. She'd seen him trying to listen; she knew his looks, knew the shape of his scowls and which ones might turn to smiles with some coaxing.

Dominic wasn't in bed. Eloise peeled back the covers as if to make sure. He never normally went wandering after drinking himself into a stupor. It was one of the only things she enjoyed about his alcohol binges; it would turn him into a hibernating bear, the bed his cave.

Eloise grabbed her phone from the bedside table and texted him, *Where are you?* She added some kisses and pressed send, remembering the time he'd teased her about leaving kisses in texts. He'd said he thought they were immature, laughing as he bantered her, then kissing her three times, once on each cheek and then on the lips, for the three kisses she'd sent him in her most recent text.

She didn't like memories like that. She shut her mind.

Biting her fingernails, she thought about the possibility that he somehow knew about the pregnancy. She opened his bedside drawer to check if his phone was in there. He wasn't usually the type to take his phone around the house, swiping, texting; he wasn't a TikTok or an Instagram Reels person. He never watched YouTube. He liked audiobooks, peace and quiet, regular old television. James Patterson novels and the occasional classic if he was feeling intellectual.

No phone in the drawer. Just two condoms in their

wrappers, staring at her like accusing eyes. How could he know about the pregnancy? Had he followed her to the doctor? She hadn't even told her sister. Her family had never been close, but in recent years, her sister had been making more of an effort, not that Eloise would ever share all her secrets.

Moving through the house, she checked his office, her office, the gym, the spare room. A certain sadness touched her as she looked over these hollow spaces. There wasn't any sign of a cot or half-painted walls or boxes holding children's toys.

Downstairs, she switched on the kitchen light, the obsidian island reflecting the light. She caught another glimpse of herself in the floor-to-ceiling windows which overlooked the garden. She stood up straighter, smoothed her nightie down. Whatever had happened, she could handle it.

That thought bolstered her until she came to the entranceway. The landline was hanging from the hook. The mirror was splintered and glistened red with what must've been blood. Dominic's mobile phone was on the floor.

Her mind sped; she stared. She tried to figure out what she was looking at. He'd taken a call on the landline, then – then what? Punched the mirror? Then he'd dropped his mobile phone for some reason and left the house.

She switched on the exterior lights and walked barefoot into their outer courtyard. The stones were wet from the recent downpour, but it had stopped, the air smelling fresh. Her beloved Pixie – her Mini Cooper – sat outside the garage. She was almost sure she would've heard if he'd left in his Volvo, but she'd been so busy vomiting and trying not to vomit any more, she couldn't be certain.

Should she ring the police? And tell them what? Her husband had punched a mirror and taken their car – the alarm hadn't gone off – he'd left his mobile behind. They'd most likely ask if they had any problems. It might even lead to the secret baby somehow if they snooped around the GP's office. It might lead to other, darker things.

Could they, *would* they do that? She took another breath, went to the landline, replaced the receiver and then dialled the button to call back the most recent number. But it was withheld. Whoever had rung her husband, whoever had caused him to punch the mirror as though he couldn't stand the sight of his own reflection, wanted to remain anonymous.

She decided she'd ring Garry, one of Dominic's friends and colleagues at the university. It was 2am, but Dominic and Garry often got carried away drinking. It was possible that Dom was so drunk he'd stumbled into the mirror instead of punching it, not realised he was bleeding and had taken the car despite his state. She'd never known him to drink and drive, but there had to be a reasonable explanation for this. She had Garry's number from their previous escapades. He sounded groggy and annoyed when he answered.

'I'm sorry, Garry. It's Eloise.'

'Is everything all right?'

'Is Dominic with you? I woke up and his car is gone. I thought maybe you were having a last-minute night out.'

'It's two in the bloody morning. We're not twenty-five anymore!'

'I know that. I just— He hasn't taken his mobile. And I think maybe he was angry. Or maybe very, very drunk. He broke the mirror on the way out. The landline was off the hook. Did you ring him?'

'No. I haven't spoken to him since Thursday. Did you have an argument or something?'

'Why would you assume that?' Had he said something? Hinted at something? Framed something in the wrong way?

'I don't know. I can't think why he'd disappear like that.'

'He's drunk almost an entire bottle of whisky,' she whispered.

'Pardon?'

Eloise was glad he hadn't heard. She hadn't worked so hard to create the image of a perfect marriage to give up ugly truths without a fight. 'I just want to know he's safe.'

'I'm sure there's a reasonable explanation.'

'He hasn't said anything to you?'

'Like what?'

'Anything that would relate to him not being here now, in the middle of the night. Gambling, something.'

'Gambling?'

'That was just an example!'

'Eloise, just breathe. Let me think.'

'Okay. I'm sorry. I don't mean to snap.'

'It's completely understandable.'

There was a long silence. 'There's nothing. Dominic is just... Dominic. You know him. Gets on with his work, bloody excels at it, truth be told. Has a few pints. Talks about you constantly, raves about you, Eloise. His model wife. His talented writer wife. It's gross, honestly.'

Eloise laughed at the sarcasm in Garry's voice.

'You want my advice?' he said.

'Please.'

'Try and relax for a little while. Before you know it, he'll walk through that door with a cheesy grin on his face and you'll forget he was ever gone. In the meantime, would you like me to ring around a few of our mates?'

'That would be helpful. Thanks, Garry.'

'Not a problem, sweetheart. I'll ring you if there's anything.'

'Can you ring me, or text me, even if there isn't? Just so I'm not left waiting.'

'Of course.'

She said goodbye, hanging up. But any notion that she could take his advice and relax was absurd. She hadn't felt relaxed since she'd missed her first period and done her first test. That was when she'd begun analysing everything her husband did, said, each of his gestures, searching his eyes for any sign of judgement, resentment.

'You need to let this go,' he'd said to her once. *'I know you want kids all of a sudden—'*

'Don't say it like that. Don't say it like it came from nowhere.'

'You told me you were fine with it being just us.'

The memory hurt to think about, but suddenly, it was like she was back in the dining room six months previously, the remains of their lobster dinner on the silverware, Dominic's eyes glassy from the Dom Pérignon. She'd giggled drunkenly and told him Dom was drinking Dom. But they hadn't been laughing when the discussion turned to children.

'You knew I didn't mean it,' she'd said. *'I know you – you can read me. You knew I'd want a baby eventually. A little bundle of joy to care for, to love.'*

'If you want a baby, then you need to find somebody else. I'll never be a father.'

'Why?' she'd yelled. *'What's wrong with you? What makes you so different to everybody else?'*

He'd stared at her, closing himself off as he had so many times before.

It was like there was a secret room in her husband's head to which he would retreat if the conversation became too serious. It was like he wanted her to remain his prize and nothing else. A pregnant woman might glow and gleam like a trophy, but only for a short while. Then reality would hit. A house full of crying. A round, fat, happy face thieving her love.

That was why she'd taken drastic action. And maybe that was why Dominic wasn't there with her then.

Perhaps he knew; perhaps he hated her. If he'd learnt the truth, she couldn't blame him. When all her affirmations and mindfulness techniques fell away, she had to admit a brutal fact. Her husband had plenty of reasons to despise her.

CHAPTER THREE

JANINE

She was groggy, her lids heavy, her mind struggling to comprehend how she had somehow ended up here. Where was *here*, exactly? She blinked, her vision blurring, staring up at a ceiling of exposed rafters. There was a mustiness in the air that convinced her she must be in a cellar.

Had the crash given her a concussion? She'd felt almost lucid in the moments after, her protective instincts kicking in when she realised how severely injured Dominic was. Why had she even agreed to get in the car with him? He'd been so visibly, revoltingly drunk.

Across the room, somebody was humming. It was sickeningly out of place. Janine tried to sit up, but her body, usually so sturdy and strong – she had almost the polar opposite of Dominic's trophy wife's build – was suddenly weak.

She felt like a little girl again, and that infuriated her so badly, she wanted to scream. That impulse, the scream, was what made her realise there was a gag in her mouth. She attempted to sit. She managed to move a few inches, then the bindings on her wrists tugged her back down to the uncomfortable mattress.

The humming continued. Janine closed her eyes.

Why couldn't she think? She had never been what people would describe as an intellectual. But she worked in an environment that could be surprisingly high stress: a personal trainer to some of the biggest divas – and occasional divos – in the Weston and Bristol area. Her clients were wealthy and expected instant, often magical results. And they weren't shy about expressing this, sometimes with a generous heaping of swear words. Janine had also competed in powerlifting competitions. She was tough; she prided herself on that.

Janine moaned, and the humming abruptly cut off. The woman who spoke sounded posh. 'The fact that you're capable of making noise is evidence of my magnanimous nature. I hope you can see that.'

Janine moaned again. She was trying to say, *Where am I, you psycho?* Even without the gag choking her, she wouldn't have been able to speak. She suspected the kidnapping lunatic had drugged her.

She couldn't remember what had happened between the crash and waking in the cellar. Dominic had been absolutely hammered, his eyes wild, his hair in disarray. Every time she'd spoken, he'd looked at her like she wasn't even there. It was like he thought he was seeing things. She'd never been fully real to him anyway; she'd been a tool for him to deal with his own crap.

'If I had any desire to kill you,' the posh voice went on, 'I could do so at any time. Instead, I have elected to administer a moderate dose of Valium. If you're experiencing grogginess and memory loss, that's why. Do you see how reasonable I'm being, Janine? Janine Jenkins; I checked your purse. Or wallet, I might say, as it was a rather manly leather specimen. Your name, however, is feminine. Perhaps it's the alliterative quality of it. Janine Jenkins... If I had to picture you based on that name alone, I'd have you long-limbed, slender, shy, high cheekbones, sophisticated. But you're like a Hobbit. Your shoulders are broader than some men. Or maybe that would make you more akin to a dwarf. Though your feet are quite large, which returns us to the Hobbit hypothesis.'

Janine wanted to spit in the woman's face. There were bigger concerns than being compared to characters from fantasy novels, namely: why was she here? What was the insane woman going to do to her?

Nevertheless, her words were offensive. Janine had deadlifted two hundred and ten kilograms the week before. That was an incredibly impressive feat, especially as she'd done it for three reps. Nobody had the right to talk down to her because her body had a purpose and wasn't just for show.

Footsteps approached Janine's bed. She managed to turn her head, but a powerful light from across the room made the figure into a hazy silhouette. Janine had to close her eyes against the harshness.

She sensed the woman standing over her. 'Now, what am I going to do with you? I confess I have been behaving in a somewhat automated manner. Until you were appropriately subdued, I was all *go go go*. But clearly, there's now time to ponder my decision. I don't wish to hurt you, Janine Jenkins. But things have come rather far, haven't they? I've never wanted to hurt anybody.'

Janine tried to bite the hand as it pulled the gag free, but she was too sluggish.

'You're not going to scream,' the woman said. 'But if you try with all your might, you may be able to speak.'

'Wuh-wuh-why?' Janine sounded as exhausted as she felt. It angered her. She wasn't weak.

'Because you survived the crash. I couldn't exactly leave you there. I have questions for you... not when you're in this current state, of course. I'll need to know what you know.'

'Duh-Duh...'

'Dominic?'

Janine managed to nod. She wanted to open her eyes; she could feel her kidnapper staring at her, but the light was too bright, even through her closed lids.

'Dominic is dead. He was a complete mess. It was frightening to look at, honestly.'

Janine shuddered. It felt like a punch to the gut. So this maniac hadn't rung an ambulance. 'No,' Janine managed to whimper. 'Duh-duh-*Dom*.' She didn't know he was dead. He might've looked like he wasn't breathing, but perhaps he was taking in just enough. Her silly, dangerous man. Maybe he could've made it if she'd done the right thing.

'My goodness,' the woman said. 'You cared about him, didn't you?'

Janine had loved him more than anything, and he had loved her more than she ever thought anybody could. But that didn't make it better, did it? This was his fault. He didn't have to pick her up. She didn't have to offer her support, her love, despite his state.

She'd made a terrible mistake getting in that car with him.

A MOTHER'S MUSINGS: MOTHER BEARS WILL DO ANYTHING!
23/09/24

Victoria Hawthorne

Motherhood is not all sunshine and rainbows. We all know this, but I think it's good to share times we have... let's say, let our mother bear get the better of us? In view of my friend Margot's recent post about her argument with a primary school teacher, I'd like to share something from when my Dom Dom was eight years old. This story doesn't bring me any pride. It does, however, put me in that awkward in-between place of finding my behaviour ugly... but knowing I'd do it again.

I was sitting at the front window, doing some knitting, as Dom Dom was riding his bike up and down our quaint little suburban street. It was circular, a patch of green in the middle, with an apple tree. Picturesque, some might say. My baby was doing so well on his bike, overcoming his natural fear, building up quite a bit of steam. Did it sadden me that he was cycling alone? Well, yes, to some extent. But I was content in the knowledge that, though he found it difficult to make friends, he always had me. (We used to dance to 'With a Little Help From My Friends' by Joe Cocker for hours, my Dom Dom laughing and lighting me up with all the love in the world. Oh, how we danced...)

Then, all of a sudden, there was an army of children in the street, so many bicycles it was like some kind of demonstration. My Dom Dom came to a stop and began having a conversation with a rather large boy who had a mop of black hair and, well, this isn't very nice to say, but a nasty look about him. I know! I know! All children are innocent, or so we say... But let's be honest, ladies, when your cherub tells you about some little so-and-so who has put chewing gum in their hair for the fourth time in a row, or has made fun of their shoes, or has caused the whole class to laugh at them, do we not have negative thoughts sometimes? This is a safe space.

The mop-haired boy began doing what are referred to as "wheelies" up and down the street. The others joined in, competing to see who could go the furthest. And then my boy took his turn. At first, he wasn't very good. But he's a trier, my son, and he did his best twice more... It was amazing, how he flew. It was like watching an angel spread his wings. Of course, I was scared he would fall. But I resisted the urge to open the window and beg him to stop. I had to let him have his moment!

The other boy didn't like it. He began to cycle next to my son. And then – oh, it angers me even now – he rammed his bike into him. Dom Dom fell. That's when I lost it. The mother bear came out. Before I knew it, I was on the street, my finger wagging, my voice high. I told that nasty boy, 'How dare you touch my son. Haven't you been taught any manners? What's wrong with you?'

He turned white as a sheet! He and his gang cycled away. I picked my son off the ground, and he gifted me with the sweetest hug. I can still remember the warmth of his little body pushed against mine. I can still remember his arms pressing firmly against me. 'I love you, Mummy.' Are there any sweeter words? Then he said, 'Thank you. They were so nasty.'

Sometimes, my dear readers, I have to admit, I fear I made the wrong choice. Should I have allowed him to challenge the bully himself? Was what I did fairly describable as *coddling*? Ah, the questions, hindsight, the torture we put ourselves through!

There you have it: a confession, an insight into my not-always-secure psyche. Please feel free to share your stories below.

On another note, we have recently reached seven hundred and fifty thousand *regular readers*. For what started as a silly blog on a very ugly website – I'm no technophile! – I think this is amazing. Thank you all so, so much!

CHAPTER FOUR

ELOISE

'You are a powerful person,' the soothing narrator of the self-affirmation podcast said as Eloise drove Pixie towards Bristol Royal Infirmary. She felt as if she'd slipped into a nightmare. Dominic sometimes teased her about these podcasts, jokingly calling them repetitive, but Eloise felt no shame about trying to be the best version of herself. She needed that version; she could hardly believe what had happened. She wouldn't think about where the teasing would sometimes lead.

'You rise to every challenge. You have the confidence to choose the right path and act on it.'

She was shuddering, gripping the steering wheel so hard it hurt. She had been pacing around the house, doing nothing except thinking about her husband, when her mobile rang. She'd answered it without even looking at the caller. It had to be Dominic, she'd reasoned, letting anxiety bleed into hope. Perhaps it had been deluded considering his drinking and the missing Volvo, but she hadn't even considered a crash: hadn't considered that her husband might, oh, God, it hurt to think about...

Her husband *might be dying*. All without learning the truth — learning that Eloise had done what she'd done for them.

The paramedic had said, *'Hello, is this Mrs Hawthorne?'*

Eloise's breath had caught. *'Yes, why? What's happened?'*

'I'm calling regarding your husband, Dominic Hawthorne. He was involved in a serious car accident and is currently on his way to our facility for treatment.'

'Where?' she'd yelled. *'Where are you taking my husband?'*

They'd told her that it was Bristol, as they would be able to provide the best care.

'Is he going to be okay?'

'At this point, I don't have all the details about his condition, but he sustained severe injuries and requires urgent medical attention. Our trauma team is prepared to assess and treat him as soon as he arrives.'

Eloise had babbled something; she wasn't sure what.

In the back of her mind, she noted this was going to be bad for his reputation. It might mean the end of his career. People would look down on Eloise, wondering what sort of woman allowed her husband to drink a bottle of whisky then get behind the wheel.

It wasn't fair. They had been building towards something. Never mind the fact Dom hadn't known about her plans to make him a father. Eloise had wanted so desperately to see Dominic holding the baby, look up at her, his eyes glistening, a rueful smile spreading across his lips. And then he'd tell her she'd made the right choice. He understood why she'd lied. He understood why she'd had to take such ugly measures. It had been for them. But she may never get that chance.

Despite all the unspeakable things, the corners in her mind at which she stubbornly refused to look, she ached at the thought of her husband dying.

'You are the master of your emotions. You choose how to

feel, and how those feelings direct your actions. You are capable of controlling your mind. You are capable of guiding your heart. You are stronger than you give yourself credit for.'

Eloise was in the waiting room, the bright lights making her feel as if they were trying to sterilise her panic. They weren't telling her much except that his injuries were being treated; she couldn't see him. The place smelled vaguely of death, of urine, of despair. Her head pulsed. She thought about the stress this could cause the tiny life inside of her.

'Hello, miss?'

Eloise flinched, looked up, praying it was the doctor: praying it wasn't. Every long minute which ticked by was another her husband was still alive. The man who stood over her was wearing an overall. He was lean, with a night worker's hollow eye-pits. He had a kind smile.

'Yes?'

'Sorry, didn't mean to startle you, love.'

'It's fine.'

'Are you...' He hesitated. 'Are you here for your husband? Your boyfriend? Was he in a crash?'

'You know Dominic? He's my husband.'

'I rang 999. I was coming home from a long shift and saw the wreckage just sitting there. The car looked...' He sucked his teeth. 'Well...'

'Please – sit.'

He sat beside her.

'What's your name?' Eloise asked.

'Patrick. And yours? I saw you come in and I thought, maybe she's here for that man.'

'He's my husband. Dominic. And my name is Eloise.' She sniffled. 'Eloise and Dominic Hawthorne. The Hawthornes.'

'I wish I could say it was nice to meet you, Eloise.'

'Tell me what you saw. Every detail. I hate not knowing.'

'Are you sure?'

'Please. Anything. I'm torturing myself.'

'I'd just got off work. I'm a forklift driver in a warehouse. Anyway, I was driving, thinking about a cheeky cuppa before I turned in. And then I saw it. The car was totalled. In a real bad way. He must've slid into that tree fast. I pulled over and climbed out of my car, and your husband...'

'Please. Tell me.'

Patrick swallowed. 'He was barely breathing. Covered in blood. I think the car door had, sort of, stabbed into him.' When Eloise shuddered, the man touched her arm. 'I'm sorry, love. I don't have to go on.'

'Please,' she begged. She could see her man trapped in the vehicle, wearing a mask of red, lifelessly screaming for his wife, for the woman who would always be there, for better or for worse. Marriage was the most complicated human relationship. Despite what an invisible observer might've concluded, she and Dominic loved each other.

'I tried to talk to him. He made a moaning noise. I think he understood I was getting him help.'

'Could you understand anything he said?'

'Just that moaning noise. Then the ambulance was there. The police too; I think the police are still there.'

She closed her eyes for a moment, hating the fact this would surely have criminal implications. 'But nobody else? He hadn't hit anybody?'

'No, nothing like that.'

She gave the thoughtful stranger's hand a squeeze. 'I'm so

glad you were there, Patrick. God knows what would've happened if he'd been left any longer.'

'Have you got someone coming?' he asked.

Eloise felt like a fool. 'Oh, Christ. I haven't rung anybody. Not even Victoria! What's wrong with me? I should do that now.' She stood, taking out her phone, fumbled, dropped it. Patrick caught it with a fluid motion and handed it to her. 'Thank you.'

'Take a breath,' he advised. 'One step at a time. That's all you can do.'

'Thank you. You're right.' She did some box breathing for perhaps a minute: four seconds of inhaling, holding her breath for four seconds, exhaling for four seconds, and then refusing herself breath for another four. After a few cycles, she felt more clear-headed.

She rang Victoria. 'Eloise, it's late. Is everything all right, dear?'

'Have the hospital rang you?' Eloise asked stupidly. Of course they hadn't. Her mother-in-law would've been there otherwise. 'Sorry – I can't even think straight.'

'Slow down,' Victoria said. 'Explain.'

'Dom was in a car crash. He's in the hospital. Bristol. I'm here now. I don't know if he's going to...' Eloise croaked. 'Oh, God. I just don't know. Can you get here?'

'Yes, I'm on my way. Oh, God. God.' Victoria's voice shuddered, as if a dam was breaking, as if she was slowly realising what Eloise had just said. 'An accident? And he survived... and he might not... I can't go there.'

'I can't even think it,' Eloise agreed. 'Not Dominic.'

'Not our Dom Dom.'

'I'm sorry. I should've rung you sooner.'

'You've got nothing to apologise for. I'll be there as soon as I can. You're not in this alone. You never have to go through anything alone, Eloise. Are you with anybody now, you poor, poor thing?'

'Patrick,' she said. 'He was the one who found Dom. Oh, Victoria... if he hadn't found him, I think he would've—' She couldn't say it. 'He was on the road all alone in the middle of the night. It's a miracle somebody found him.'

'God bless his soul,' Victoria said passionately. Eloise had often wished her mother was more like Victoria: her heart on her sleeve, never feeling the need to hold back her affection.

'I just want...' Eloise shuddered, her throat getting tight, attempting to fight off another onslaught of tears. She failed. *'For him to be okay.'*

'I'll be right there. Stay strong. I'm coming! Mama Bear is coming!'

That was fitting phrasing. Since Victoria had moved to Weston to be closer to her son – she knew some people would find that strange, but Eloise thought it was a wonderful and proactive thing to do – Eloise and Victoria had become close. It was Victoria she most frequently met for coffee; it was Victoria with whom she discussed ideas for her book when her mind decided to stall. It was Victoria who'd rushed to her side when the flu had left her bedbound for almost a week.

'Thank you,' she said. 'See you soon.' She turned to Patrick. 'I should probably ring my parents and my sister, let them know what's happening. And maybe Garry, Dominic's friend.'

'If you think you're up to it, love,' Patrick said.

Eloise took a breath. *I am strong. I am brave. I am capable. I rise to challenges. I don't let the world beat me down.* She remembered waiting in the staging area before walking out for her Met Gala debut. The theme had leant towards the futuristic. Eloise had felt faintly ridiculous with the 3D-printed attachments on her Renaissance-style gown, a metallic choker at her throat, military-style boots on her feet. But then she'd breathed slow. She'd reminded herself this was a moment that, when she looked back on it, she'd want to appreciate. Not corrupt with negativity.

She could do the same in the hospital. When she looked back, did she want to be the positive, protective wife? Or did she want to be a woman consumed by pessimism?

'My husband's going to be okay,' she told Patrick.

He looked at her like she was mad. 'I'm... uh, sure he is, love.'

'The doctor's going to walk out any moment and tell us he's a bit worse for wear, but he's fine. Just fine.'

She rang her mother. It wasn't as if she would come flying to the West Country. She lived in London, as did her sister. They had never been especially close; neither had there been any neglect or abuse as far as Eloise was concerned. Charlotte, her sister, had often claimed they were emotionally neglected as children. It was the reason, apparently, Eloise found it so difficult to build authentic intimacy with people. With Dom, she'd got closer than ever before. Now twisted fate was threatening to take it all away, a superstitious part of her wondered if this was punishment for her darker days.

CHAPTER FIVE

DOMINIC

Haven's Close was the name of their cul-de-sac, and Mother would often kiss his head and say, 'My haven's never far away, Dom Dom. You're right here – my warmth, my soul.' Mother was watching him from the window. Dominic didn't mind. At least he was outside.

'What're you doing, Dom? It is Dom, right?'

Dom brought his bike to a screeching stop. It was Anthony from school, the big kid with all the friends. Dom had known he lived nearby – he'd seen him several times – but they'd never talked to each other. There was a whole group of kids, all of them on bikes. Dom felt suddenly self-conscious for getting so visibly enthusiastic.

'Just having a ride,' he said, conscious that his bike was a cheap model. They weren't poor; Mother just preferred Dom to stay inside, so he didn't get to ride his bike very much. It was like she'd bought him a cheap, flimsy model so that Dom would be less likely to use it.

'I'm not teasing you. Damn,' Anthony said, laughing. 'Just asking. You're a funny kid.'

'I don't tell jokes ever.'

All of them laughed. There was a girl with freckles across her cheeks and her hair in pigtails and, for some reason, Dom found he liked looking at her. His belly swirled and he wondered if this was what other kids felt like. 'See?' Anthony said. 'What'd I say? *Funny*. You know what a wheelie is?'

'I – uh – *wheelie* want to know.'

The girl giggled; it felt like a prize. He'd told a joke on purpose, and somebody had laughed!

'Let me show you,' Anthony said, casually drumming his fingers against the handlebars of his shiny, expensive-looking mountain bike. 'It takes some skill. Some bravery, too. Think you've got it in you?'

He shrugged. 'I don't know.'

'Look.' Anthony, the tall kid with the cool military-style jacket and the haircut with the shaved sides and long on top – Mother cut Dom's hair – cycled over on his impressive bike and clapped Dom on the arm.

It felt like the beginning of something. He imagined walking into school the following day, winking at Anthony, maybe even saying hello to the girl with the freckles, maybe even sitting with them at lunch rather than in the library alone pretending to read a book so people would leave him be.

'You pull, like this.' Anthony tugged on his handlebar. 'Then you have to pay attention to your weight. Not too far forward. Not too far back. Then you pedal and...'

'Voila,' the girl said, still looking at Dom.

'What does that mean?' he asked.

'You're funny,' she said.

'Come on,' Anthony called, already cycling away, pulling his wheel off the ground like magic.

Dom could feel the girl looking at him. He felt the very strong urge to turn and look at his mother for permission, but he fought it. He knew, on some level, it would lessen him in the girl's eyes. He didn't want to be small to her. He wanted to be big and funny and capable and have a cool haircut and be confident on his bike. He began peddling. He overcame about a hundred voices in his head telling him it would end in disaster, then he pulled back, and, oh wow, he was doing it. He was really doing it.

'That's it, Dom!' Anthony yelled.

'See, I told you he wasn't weird,' he overheard the girl saying to somebody.

His cheeks were glowing fiercely. His heart swelled. The wind rushed past him. He felt like he was flying. He did a few more circuits until they started to clap. He almost thought he'd fallen off his bike and this was all in his imagination and soon he'd wake in bed with Mother putting a warm compress on his head saying, 'Oh, poor dear, what did you do...'

But it was real. He was soaring across the concrete.

'Wheelie twins.' Anthony laughed, riding up next to him. 'That's it, Dom, that's – oh, crap.'

Dom let out a very embarrassing yelp. It was the same sound he made when his hand met the hot stove. Anthony veered into him, then Dom fumbled his handlebar and turned sharply, causing his wheel to violently stop. He went flying – not in a good way this time – and landed with a thump on the ground. Anthony and the other kids ran over.

'That was my bad,' Anthony said.

Dom realised he was smiling. 'That was nuts.'

The girl laughed and walked over, offering Dom her hand. She was wearing a necklace that settled between the straps of her denim dungarees. It had a small jewel on it, purple, and her eyes were almost the same shade, he realised, a blue so interesting they looked purple when she tilted her head and her face caught the sunlight just so. He was about to take her hand when Mother's voice tore through the group.

'Don't you hurt my baby!' she screamed.

Dom jumped to his feet. Mother had her knitting needles in her hand like some kind of weapon. She waved the needles at Anthony. 'Who do you think you are?'

'Mother, it's not what y—'

She shushed him and walked right up to Anthony like she was going to hit him. Anthony took a step back, trying to laugh it off, but even Dom could see he was worried. Grown-ups weren't supposed to behave like this. 'Do you think you're tough? Is that it? Are you the big man? Are you the big bad wolf? Are you something special? Well, are you? Don't smirk at me. You're a pathetic lowlife. You're nothing, and you never will be.'

Dom began to cry. The world blurred. Nobody knew what to do. Mother snatched Dom up and he clutched onto her desperately, even if he didn't want to touch her, even if he blamed her. He was sad and she was offering comfort, and he didn't know what else to do.

She carried him inside, whispering that everything would be okay, whispering that she would never let anybody hurt him. Dom didn't know how to explain the feeling this produced in him; it was a mixture of so many things. He closed his eyes; opened them and he was staring at his bedroom ceiling, Mother rushing around the room, aggressively tidying.

'What was I supposed to do? Tell me, my love, my angel, my perfect boy. Oh, Dom Dom, I couldn't just let him bully you. Could I? What sort of mother would I be if I did that?'

'It's okay,' Dom said, though it wasn't.

She knelt beside his bed, glaring at him, her expression changing to something hateful. 'We have a sedative and paralytic ready. Do you want to start with Propofol, doctor?'

'Wuh-what?' Dom said.

'Applying cricoid pressure... tube is in,' she went on.

'Mother...'

'With the TBI, we don't want him regaining consciousness – keep him fully sedated.'

Dom was about to ask another question, then a *beep-beep-beep* noise pulsed through his skull, tugging his eyelids shut, causing darkness to close in around him. He tried to scream, but he was unable to make a noise.

CHAPTER SIX

ELOISE

'Is your mother-in-law going to be here soon?' Patrick asked. Eloise detected the slight awkwardness in his voice. He'd sat with her for almost an hour since she'd made the phone calls. Garry was going to do his best to visit as soon as possible, but with his wife on a night shift and children to take care of, it was difficult. Eloise's mother had forced a concerned tone on the phone and told Eloise to ring her if she needed anything. She'd hoped her mother might insist on driving to Weston to be with her daughter, but she hadn't.

'You don't have to stay, Patrick. You've done more than enough.'

'I wanted to stay until the police arrived. For moral support. But honestly, love, I'm knackered.'

Eloise's head was fuzzy. It had been overfull since she'd learnt about the pregnancy, the secret she was keeping hidden in her womb, the secret which would soon swell her belly as if inflating with the evidence of her betrayal. 'The police?'

'They took a report from me at the scene. I think they'll probably want to speak to you too. Standard procedure with a crash, I suppose.'

There was the whisky too; the doctors surely knew about that. They'd do tests, see that Dominic's veins had been surging with alcohol when he'd skidded off the road and almost taken his own life. But he hadn't put anybody else at risk. Eloise knew she was diminishing her husband's failings. What was marriage if not seeing the best in somebody? God knew Dominic had seen the best in her, and she'd always tried to return the favour.

Patrick looked at her sympathetically. 'I know we don't know each other. But I feel a...'

'Connection?' Eloise prompted.

'Feels silly to say, but yeah, that's it. I saw him in such a bad way. And sitting here with you, I feel like I've got a stake in it, almost. Not like it's a game – I'm not phrasing this very well...'

She touched his arm. 'Patrick, I understand. Thank you.'

He left, yawning and stretching his arms over his head.

'Eloise.'

She jumped, turning sharply, causing several people in the brightly lit waiting area to glance at her and then swiftly look away. Nobody wanted to get involved in anybody else's business. They were all aware that each person could be suffering their own tragedy, or they were afraid of imposing upon another's devastation when theirs was a comparatively minor complaint.

Victoria stood over her, looking well put together as always, wearing an oversized black cashmere sweater that draped perfectly over her frame, paired with high-waisted skinny jeans that accentuated her silhouette. Her silver hair was styled in a sleek topknot. She was sixty-eight, but she was incredibly fit for her age, going to the gym five times a week, sometimes swimming after. Online, people commented on how physically impressive she was. She was a role model.

'Who was that, dear?' Victoria asked, sitting and hugging Eloise.

Eloise felt her sinewy strength in the embrace and clutched onto the other woman, desperate for the warmth. She smelled like she'd freshly showered. She smelled of perfume. Was that normal, to shower and perfume oneself before driving to check if her son was alive? Was Eloise being too judgemental?

'Patrick,' she said. 'He found Dom.'

'*Found* him? Where?'

'On the country road. Where Dom was driving.'

'And where was he going?' Victoria asked.

'I don't know. I think he'd spoken to somebody on the phone. He...' Eloise hesitated, but if she couldn't tell Victoria, she couldn't tell anybody. 'He either stumbled into the hallway mirror, or punched it, before he left. The landline was off the hook. But the caller had withheld the number. I don't know who it was. I don't know who it even could be.' Her belly tightened into a fist of tension. She was upsetting her baby. 'He'd been drinking.'

'Oh, Lord,' she whispered, squeezing Eloise's hand supportively. 'What was he thinking? I've never known him to do something like that.'

'I know,' Eloise said. 'It's so unlike him.'

'Did he say anything before he left?'

'I don't know. I was...' She couldn't tell the truth. 'Writing. You know what I'm like: headphones in, blocking out the rest of the world. I assumed he'd still be asleep when I returned to bed. It's awful to say... but he... our Dom is a drunk driver.'

'Hush,' Victoria murmured when Eloise began to cry.

She hugged her tightly, and Eloise was just so, so grateful she was there. Victoria often had a self-deprecating, witty tone when she called herself "Mama Bear", but it wasn't a joke to Eloise. She truly felt like Victoria was a big, warm, ferocious bear, ready to face whatever life threw at them. 'We're in this together. We should have more information soon. In fact, why don't I go and check? And then maybe I'll get you a nice cup of coffee, or hot chocolate, or tea?'

'Tea sounds nice,' Eloise said. 'Thank you.'

Eloise was getting sick of sitting there and waiting and thinking about all the things that could go wrong. Finally, after what felt like a thousand years, a short man with a prominent moustache appeared. Eloise could tell instantly that it wasn't good news. His jaw clenched; he gritted his teeth.

Eloise bolted to her feet. Her heart was hammering. This couldn't be happening, not to her husband, her man, her possession. Marriage was a project, a brick-by-brick construction, and even if he or she sometimes knocked some of the bricks down, they were always going to keep stacking them, until, one day when they were wrinkled and their heads were brimming with warm memories, they'd look back and say, *It was a bumpy road, and we lied more than we should have, even to ourselves sometimes, but we made it. And we love each other. That's what counts.*

'Is he dead?' Eloise almost yelled.

'Shall we talk somewhere more private?'

'Answer the question, Doctor,' Victoria said. 'My boy is a fighter. He always has been. We need to know.'

'He's alive, but I have news. Please.' He gestured towards the hallway. 'I have a room.'

Eloise felt as if her legs might give out as they followed the doctor down the hallway. She leaned heavily against Victoria until they came to a small office.

'What's going to happen to my husband?'

'Please – sit.'

'I don't want to sit.'

'Eloise, dear,' Victoria whispered. 'He's just trying to do his job.'

She sat beside Victoria, facing the doctor across his small desk.

'Mrs Hawthorne, your husband has sustained severe injuries, including a traumatic brain injury. We've placed him in a medically induced coma to help reduce intracranial pressure – the swelling inside his skull – and to give us control over his vital signs while his body stabilises. The coma allows his brain to rest and heal with reduced metabolic demand.'

Eloise shuddered, thinking of her husband broken and battered, machines keeping him alive. 'When will he wake up?'

The doctor hesitated. 'It's difficult to give a specific timeline. Recovery from a TBI, especially with cerebral oedema – brain swelling – and internal bleeding, can be lengthy. We're monitoring closely, using CT scans and MRI imaging to assess progress and watch for any complications.'

She blinked, bothered by her tears, by how badly she wanted to slap this man. It wasn't his fault her husband had left their marital bed, had a mysterious phone call, punched a mirror, then left. 'What happens next?'

'Our priority is his stability,' Doctor Reyes said. 'We'll conduct regular neurological assessments and blood work to track his response. Over the coming days and weeks—'

She gasped. *'Weeks?'* By then, she might already be showing. She had planned on explaining herself before that happened; she had planned on building a beautiful picture in her husband's mind, painting a scene which would make him enthusiastic for their future. She was certain she could bend his mind to her desired shape.

'Right now, maintaining this state is our best course for giving him the greatest chance of recovery.'

Eloise licked her lips. She didn't want to ask the next

question, but she felt as if she had to. 'Is there a chance he never wakes up?'

'There is a chance, yes. With traumatic brain injuries like this, outcomes can be very unpredictable. Some patients do regain consciousness as their brain heals, while others may take much longer or may not recover fully. However, we're monitoring him closely and using every tool at our disposal to support his recovery.' He offered a well-constructed smile. 'These are early days yet, Mrs Hawthorne.'

Eloise was strong. She could handle any challenges life threw at her. She wouldn't let it beat her down, blah blah blah. She couldn't speak. She wanted the floor to open beneath her, the world to swallow her.

She struggled to find some final words before the tears took her. 'When can I see him?'

'I'd estimate a few hours, and then only for a short while. He needs peace and quiet while he stabilises.'

'Thank you, Doctor,' Victoria said. 'Can you give us a moment?'

'Of course.'

Doctor Reyes left them, then Eloise and Victoria both broke down. Victoria was trying her best to stay strong; Eloise could see that she wanted to be the mama bear Eloise needed. But Dom Dom was her baby boy. He was her muse, inspiring her wildly popular blog. He was her everything.

'We'll get through this together,' Victoria said between desperate, hopeless sobs. 'I promise.'

Eloise moaned. 'This can't happen. Not now.' Victoria looked at her oddly. 'Not ever,' Eloise quickly added, not wanting to hint at her unborn baby. 'What if he never wakes up?'

'Shush. He's a fighter. He always has been.'

The cavern of secrets in Eloise's soul split to allow room for misery and tragedy, warrens and hideaways boring holes inside her previously sunny self. She knew that she would need to affirm, to lie, to do whatever it took to get through this, to stubbornly shape the landscape of her thoughts so the bleakness of the situation didn't engulf her. But that was for later. In that small office which smelled of disinfectant, all she could do was weep.

Victoria gathered herself. 'And – it hardly bears thinking about – but if the worst happens, I'll be here for you.'

'You'd stay even if...' Eloise couldn't say it; her shiny life was slipping away. 'Just for me?'

'Yes, my sweet angel. Mama Bear isn't going anywhere. I'll be at your side. Always.'

A MOTHER'S MUSINGS: SAD NEWS
24/09/24

Victoria Hawthorne

My son was involved in a car crash in the early hours of this morning. The doctors have put him into a medically induced coma for his own safety. It's unclear whether he will wake up. I am heartbroken. But I have to push on for my daughter-in-law's sake. Eloise needs me. I will be there for her!

Please, send your prayers, your warm wishes, your love. Please, let my baby boy be okay. I'm trying to be the mother bear we all strive to find within ourselves in times of crisis, but upon returning home for an overnight bag, I have collapsed in a heap of emotional agony. All I can hope is that I find my strength. Not for myself, but for those who need me in this difficult time.

Comments (678)

MommaLovesBooks
Oh my gawd! Lord Jesus Christ Our Saviour, send her your blessings!!!!!

SimplySarah
I cannot believe this. Poor Dom Dom!

LifeWithLittles
Sending prayers, hon.

WorkingMama365
This is absolutely horrible. I cannot express how sorry I am. I went through something similar with my godson several years ago, and even though he was able to recover, I never forgot the pain. I will think of you and your boy during my meditation time later.

ParentingProTips
Life is so unfair! I'm so sorry, Victoria. Bad things happen to good people and it SUCKS.

Click here to read more comments –

CHAPTER SEVEN
JANINE

It was difficult to know how much time had passed. She had drifted in and out of consciousness several times, once attempting to strain at her bindings. Her bladder ached with how badly she needed to use the toilet.

She wished she had her regular strength, her powerful grip, the ability to wring this psycho's neck, whoever she was. She wished she could let out a scream like when she hit a personal record on a lift, the veins bulging in her neck, making her feel like a Viking shield-maiden ready to tear the world to pieces for not accepting her.

A door opened, footsteps. She twisted, but that light was still glaring, making it impossible to pick out any details of her kidnapper, though the woman sounded on the older side and her silhouette seemed fit.

'You might be pleased to know that Dominic somehow survived the crash.'

Janine gasped. 'Really?'

'Miraculously, he's alive but he's in a coma. It seems he is a fighter, after all. Are you happy?'

'Yes,' Janine said defiantly.

'It doesn't address the question of what we're doing with you, though.'

'You can let me go. I don't know who you are. I don't know where we are. I don't know anything about you.' Talking hurt her throat, but at least she was able to produce words. 'You've got no reason to keep me here.'

'I told you – I want to know what you know.'

Janine had a vivid fantasy of rising from the bed and sprinting across the room, rugby-tackling the smaller woman, hurting her. Bone-cracking violence flashed in her mind. 'About what?'

'I'm going to share something with you,' the woman said. 'It will give you more understanding into my psychology. It will allow you to see why I had to take you. But first, let me ask you, did you love Dominic Hawthorne? Try not to break down this time.'

As Janine attempted to calculate the correct answer, the woman added, 'Don't think – don't lie. Just speak.'

'I did. I know it's wrong. I know he was married. But he was going to leave his wife. That's what he told me. He couldn't be his true self with her. She was always putting him on a pedestal, forcing him to live up to whatever her idea of him was. But with me, he was just himself.'

'How romantic. Well, that seals it. I would like to know if Dominic has changed. My name is Cassandra Simmons. See, Janine? I'm being truthful with you. A few years ago, Dominic and I engaged in a very strange affair. I'm several years his senior. I was flattered by the attention of this younger silver fox. He said all the right things, did all the right things. But then he turned vicious. He turned so abusive, I can't even describe the things he did. He put a mark on me, a stain, that I feared I'd never wipe free.'

Janine stared, her limbs feeling cold. 'I'm sorry to hear that, Cassandra.'

'Do you believe me?'

'If we're going to keep talking, can I use the toilet, please?'

'I said do you believe me?'

'What did he do?'

'Nah-uh. If you thought there was no chance I was telling the truth, you wouldn't ask me for specifics. You wouldn't need them. You would simply say, *My Dominic would never hurt a fly*. Why aren't you capable of saying that?'

'Everybody has a dark side. I don't know what you think "abuse" is.'

'That's a curious emphasis you put on the word abuse there, Janine.'

'This world is full of people who claim they've experienced things they haven't.'

'Pfft. So you're one of those women, are you? You think I'd make up something like this?'

'I find it difficult to relate to somebody like you.'

'Somebody like me?'

A sadist. A freak.

Janine's head hurt. She was getting angry. She should have been playing along, not provoking this woman. 'Cassandra,' she went on, trying to speak in a calmer tone. 'I'm sorry. I don't mean to offend you. This is just a lot to take in.'

'He picked me up, filled my head with silly ideas, used me in every sick way you can think of. Then he dropped me. Called me an old hag. Called me many, many other things too. I decided to follow him. I've been doing it for almost a year. I know, it's a silly thing to do. I watched you and he, Janine. I saw the love in your eyes. And I asked myself, *Does she really believe in the lies he's feeding her?* That's why you're here; I'm being upfront. I'm telling you the truth. You're here because you're going to tell me every detail about your affair with Dominic Hawthorne.'

'And then what?' Janine asked.

'I don't know,' Cassandra replied. 'I suppose that depends on you.'

'It would be easier if you told me specifically what you want to know,' Janine said, trying to keep her voice level. But her bladder was hurting. The after-effects of the drugs had numbed her somewhat, but that somehow made the terror worse, shivering beneath the surface. Janine was afraid she'd fall into a panic attack if her captor ever allowed the drugs to wear off.

'I just told you, silly girl,' Cassandra said. 'Every detail of your affair.'

'Please, can I go to the toilet first?'

'Feel free to go where you lie. I'll clean you up.'

'No.' Janine's eyes filled with tears. 'Let me have some dignity – Ah!' She yelped when something solid bounced off her shoulder, like a bee sting. It happened again, again. Tears slid down her cheeks. With each sting, there was a sharp *whack* noise.

'An air rifle.' Cassandra's voice was casual. 'I forgot I had this old thing lying around. It's a wonder the clutter one accumulates. Are you going to tell me how you met my ex-lover, Janine, or am I going to exhaust my supply of pellets? I don't have any desire to be cruel to you.'

Janine glared, wishing she could make out Cassandra's features. She stood there like some demonic angel with the harsh light silhouetting her.

'I'm not going to wee myself. Do what you have to do.'

Cassandra hefted the long air rifle from one hand to the other. 'This can get much worse.'

'This is psychotic. Okay, so Dominic maybe led you on, maybe he hurt you. Maybe you don't like how things ended. But to follow him? And then bring me here to... to interrogate me? You have to realise this isn't normal. You have to understand that.'

'I've never been overly concerned with normal.'

Suddenly, Janine felt her real self puncture the seal the drugs had made. The numbness faded for a few moments. She strained against her bindings, screaming, *'You'll have to kill me!'*

'Shut up,' Cassandra hissed. 'Be quiet!'

But Janine wouldn't stop. This was ridiculous. Dominic wasn't perfect. In fact, Dominic was far from perfect. He was the most complicated man Janine had ever met. He had shades of darkness and light within his heart that were constantly clashing, a never-ending war that had made Janine feel drunk, that had made her feel important just by knowing him.

She'd never been the kind of woman who would steal another's man, but with Dominic, it had somehow seemed like an adventure. As she screamed, she remembered the first time Dominic had looked at her romantically, the first non-professional touch, the first kiss, the first time he'd laid her down and took control and she'd felt so womanly, so not herself.

'You stupid little trollop,' Cassandra said, marching over with a rag in her hand.

Janine tried to wriggle away. Her vision blistered bright yellow with the harshness of the light. But for a moment, just before Cassandra shoved the rag against her mouth and her senses were consumed with harsh chemicals, Janine caught a glimpse of her face. She looked vicious, her eyes murderous, her lips curved into an insane grimace. Then Janine's voice failed, her eyes becoming heavy.

As consciousness left her, Cassandra whispered in her ear, 'You need to start thinking about your future, silly girl. If I wanted to kill you, I would simply slit your throat. If I was planning on it, would I take the effort to shine this light on you, hiding myself? Hmm? You need to think. What I want is very reasonable: to crack open your skull and devour all the secrets of my ex-lover. And then, once you have exhausted your supply, you will be free to leave. I will drop you someplace far from here, and we will never see each other again. I am not a bad person...'

Janine stubbornly clung to the last remnants of consciousness. She breathed like she did during weightlifting. Controlled. Steady. Choosing each breath. She saw flashes of her mum and dad and her little brother.

'...but if you force me to, I'll do bad things. Next time I visit you, you're going to behave for me. Believe me, I don't want to hurt you. I've never wanted to hurt anybody. But sometimes, pain is only language people understand...'

Janine didn't hear the rest. She faded into nothingness. At the final moment, she felt the urine leaving her body, warm and unwelcome. She was suddenly reduced to being a child again, weeing in her own bed, too afraid to call out because she was worried her parents would be angry at her.

When she woke, the air reeked. Her body felt stale with sweat and urine. There was a gag in her mouth. Thankfully, it didn't taste of chemicals. But it made breathing difficult. One of her nostrils had closed from all the irritation; she'd had issues with it ever since a rugby injury as a teenager.

She managed to lean up slightly, looking around the dark room. She tried to be patient as she waited for her eyes to adjust. She had no idea where Cassandra was. Why hadn't Janine just told her about the beginnings of the affair? It seemed gross, somehow, sharing that part of her life, the secret she'd held on to for over a year, the moments they'd shared which had seemed so grand and important to them, but might seem clichéd and pathetic to somebody else.

Finally, her eyes adjusted. The room was simple: a staircase at the back leading to the house, the large light – it looked like something a photographer might use – the air rifle resting against the wall. The walls were brick, cold, damp. The air was stale. At the foot of the stairs, there was a small first-aid-style bag, no doubt carrying Cassandra's "medicines".

Janine strained against her bindings, but with more purpose this time. They felt like zip ties, the thin harsh plastic cutting into her wrists and ankles. Her head wasn't tied down. The gag in her mouth was held in place with duct tape. Janine felt light-headed from the drugs and the effort of breathing through one nostril.

She had to think. The drugs made it difficult, but at least they numbed the aches and pains from the crash. Her body throbbed dully, but, miraculously, she didn't think she had sustained any serious injuries. Dominic, her sweet, complicated man... he had taken the brunt for her.

If she could get even one hand free, then get Cassandra to come close, she could throttle her. Janine would grab her as if she was a deadlift bar or a fifty-kilogram gripper, and then just squeeze and squeeze and... and then what? Stay trapped down there with a corpse?

Okay, so she needed both hands free. Could she do that?

She began twisting and pulling on the zip ties, cutting into her own wrists. She was almost certain she felt blood. She kept going.

CHAPTER EIGHT

ELOISE

Eloise and Victoria sat at Dominic's bedside in the ICU. Eloise was struggling to keep calm as she looked at her husband wired up to all those machines, their beeping noises an ever-present reminder that her husband wasn't with her anymore; he was someplace else, and he might never return. And even if he did, he might never be the same, a shadow of his former self, a husk and...

And *no*, she told herself. *Screw that*. Whatever state he was in when he returned, Eloise would face it, would dedicate herself to his rehab, and one day, he and she and the baby would share countless memories together: would share the stuff dreams were made of. Perhaps they'd even forget about the unacknowledged and unacknowledgeable episodes in the hidden heart of their marriage.

'He doesn't look like himself, does he?' Victoria whispered, a croak in her voice.

Eloise looked at her mother-in-law through a film of tears. Victoria had been strong so far, driving back to Weston to collect an overnight bag for Eloise, returning like the capable mama bear she was. But when she'd seen her only child lying in the bed like some half-robot thing, she'd broken down. Her eyes were red. Her usually well-tamed hair was messy from where she'd been running her hands through it.

Eloise took Victoria's hand. 'He's in there. I know he is. He can hear us.'

'Do you think so?' Victoria asked.

'When I was waiting for you, I googled comas. Apparently, some people think coma patients can be aware of what's happening around them. Others think they have hyper-vivid dreams... or maybe they regress into their past, experiencing different chapters of their lives. There are a lot of theories. But whichever is true, it means he's not gone.'

Victoria looked at her son, her expression faltering. She was trying to be strong, but Eloise could see the cracks appearing. She gently touched Dominic's hand and let out a sob. 'Oh, God, I hope so.'

'He's not going to leave us,' Eloise said.

A few minutes later, two uniformed police officers appeared at the door, one of them knocking lightly. When the male officer asked if Eloise and Victoria would be more comfortable speaking inside or outside Dominic's room, Eloise sensed something was wrong.

Eloise gave her mother-in-law a look. They both knew what this was about. Their Dom Dom had consumed an ungodly amount of whisky and then climbed into the driver's seat of a car, had driven while drunker than sin. He had crossed a line that could never be uncrossed. If he wasn't half dead – no, half *alive* – then she would slap him.

They went into the corridor.

Sergeant Jenkins was a tall man with sharp cheekbones and an apologetic, almost boyish look in his eyes. PC Fawcett was a broad, tough-looking woman whose expression was far more severe. As they introduced themselves, Eloise conjured up back stories; perhaps one of PC Fawcett's family members had been killed or injured in a drink-driving collision, hence the evil eyes.

'We understand this isn't going to be easy for you,' the sergeant began, drawing a brief, withering look from his colleague, 'but we need to inform you that your husband's blood alcohol level was far over the legal limit during the time of his crash.'

Eloise was momentarily stumped, wondering if she should feign shock. Playing a role was something she was good at, but she needed preparation: the time before Dominic got home to fix her hair, fix her heart, fix her lies. The minutes before an acquaintance arrived at a café so that she could pretend that she was the version of herself they expected to see.

Sergeant Jenkins took out a notebook and a pen. 'Can you explain what happened that night?'

'Are you launching an investigation into my son?' Victoria said. Eloise was tempted to tell her to calm down, but honestly, she was relieved somebody had the energy to fight in Dominic's corner against the police. He was wrong for drink-driving, but he'd only injured himself, and every minute they spent in this awful conversation was a minute Eloise could've been reflecting on the good times with her husband, hardening them in her memories, making them permanent, removing space for anything else.

'No, Miss Hawthorne,' the sergeant said. 'Not an investigation as such. We merely want to ascertain the facts surrounding the accident.'

'There is something,' Eloise said.

'Yes?'

'I was writing, as I often do late at night.' Eloise obviously wouldn't mention the vomiting or her secret pregnancy or her betrayal of her husband. 'When I returned to bed, I noticed he was missing, so I went searching for him. At the front door, I saw that the landline was off the hook. He'd dropped his mobile phone. And the mirror was shattered and had blood on it. It looked to me like he'd received a phone call which had made him angry and then punched the mirror before storming out.'

'What time was this, roughly?'

'Around midnight.'

Sergeant Jenkins nodded. 'Why did you assume your husband had punched the mirror?'

'I'm sorry?'

'Perhaps he could've fallen into it. Or maybe he dropped it, the glass shattered, and then he tried to replace it... there are any number of ways it could've been broken.'

She felt like the police officer was peeling away layers of her skin with dirty fingernails, as if he was scraping at her make-up, her psychological shields, grotesquely invading her. She'd never had cause to resent the police, but this irked her. 'I'm a writer. At least, I'm trying to be. Connecting dots has always been natural to me. I saw the phone, saw the mirror, and put two and two together.'

'Would that be in character for your husband?' Sergeant Jenkins asked.

'What does this have to do with the drink-driving charge?' Victoria cut in.

'We're just trying to—'

Victoria cut the officer off. 'Ascertain the facts, yes, you've said that. But you can clearly see that my daughter-in-law is distraught. She may lose her husband. I may lose my baby boy. And you're asking if he was violent.'

'I was shocked.' Eloise finally found her voice. 'Yes, of course I was. This entire sick night has been shocking. But I saw the phone – saw the mirror – saw he'd dropped his mobile...'

'Do you have any idea who he'd spoken to on the landline?'

'I tried ringing them back, but they'd withheld their number. You could get that information, couldn't you?'

The officers just stared. The silence became louder by the second, and Eloise was relieved when he finally spoke. But it wasn't to answer her question. 'I believe we have everything we need. Thank you. You've been very helpful.'

'Thank you, Sergeant,' Eloise said. Victoria did not thank them.

'We shouldn't have spoken to them without legal representation,' Victoria said, clenching her fists. She had a wiry, sinewy, tough look to her when she got angry, which was quite rare... but understandable in the current circumstances. 'Their insinuation is revolting. As if my baby boy routinely got drunk and got behind the wheel.'

'They didn't say that.'

'It was written all over their faces!'

'I just wish I knew where he was going,' Eloise said.

'Maybe he just wanted to go for a drive.'

'In the middle of the night, drunk?'

'I'm just trying to make sense of this. But I suppose that's a fool's errand in a situation like this. I'm sorry if I snapped. I don't mean to—'

Eloise grabbed her mother-in-law and pulled her into a fierce hug. 'Don't apologise. I don't know what I'd do without you. Whatever happens, we're in this together.'

CHAPTER NINE

DOMINIC

Dominic was standing behind a pane of glass, screaming. He knew it because the veins in his neck were pressing against his skin like they were going to rupture, his throat hurt, his head was pulsing. But there was no sound. He was beginning to realise that nothing made sense anymore.

On the other side of the glass, there was a well-to-do living room, not so upper class as to be posh or outlandish, but not lower class either. If it had been a hotel room, he would've expected it in a four-star hotel.

It must've been around 1989. Mother was spinning around with Dom Dom in her arms as 'With a Little Help From My Friends' by Joe Cocker crackled on the record player. Dominic could hear the music, could hear his mother's giggles, but he couldn't hear his own screaming.

He kept going, as if he could make any difference, but on some level, he knew this had all happened before. He knew he couldn't change anything. Distantly, he heard something beeping, as if a car was backing up. But there was no going back. There never had been. His life had always been a slow, relentless push against the weight of the world, his head down so he didn't have to look left or right, where the memories were waiting for him.

The glass shattered, cut his face, dropped him into a pit. And then, suddenly, he was in Mother's arms. She was stroking her hand through his hair. Her touch was cold and he felt corpse-like in her embrace, too stiff to move, as if it would be tempting fate if he'd asked her to release him.

She was smoking a cigarette. The smoke made Dom feel sick, but he wasn't going to say anything about that. Mother was in one of those moods where saying anything made him nervous. She was on the edge, but the edge of what, Dom never knew. He felt like he was creeping around her, like any noise would be offensive, like he was a bad son if he even thought to ask her to blow the smoke somewhere else.

'Are you happy, Dom Dom?' she said after around thirty minutes of lying like that.

'Yes, Mother.'

'But really happy?' She snuffed the cigarette out on the bedside table. Not an ashtray, just straight on the table. Dom stared at the ash smearing across the wood. The black smear had the vague shape of a smiley face.

'Yes, very happy.'

'That's good.' She stroked her hand over his head, threading her fingers through his hair. 'I was never happy when I was your age.'

'Why, Mother?'

'Why don't you call me Mummy sometimes?'

Was this a trick? 'You told me to call you Mother. You said Mummy made you feel silly.'

'Did I say that? That was very foolish. There's nothing silly about being a Mummy. It's the greatest blessing in the world. The love I felt for you the moment I met you, even before I met you... It was staggering, Dom Dom. It *is* staggering.'

'I love you, Mummy.'

'See? Was that so hard? Being a mother is the greatest thing in the world, my darling, sweet boy. We have an umbilical connection, and that doesn't stop when the cord is cut. No matter what happens, even when you're all grown up, we're going to be together. Nothing will ever separate us. You'll never abandon me. You'd never do that to Mummy, would you?'

Something felt dangerously wrong in Dom's young mind. This sensation often gripped him with Mother, especially when she was in one of these moods, but he couldn't identify exactly what it was. He loved her deeply. So much. Too much, he sometimes felt. 'No, Mummy.'

Leave her? He'd never even think about it. He looked up, past the cigarette-stained bedside table, and he saw something very strange. There was an old, scared man behind a pane of glass, his mouth open like he was screaming. He started to hammer on the glass, and then, *poof* – it was like magic – he was gone. Dom Dom rubbed his eyes.

'I didn't have this connection with my mummy,' Mother said. 'My mummy used to do nasty things to me. Do you want to know what she did?'

Dom Dom very much did not want to know. But Mother had a way of asking questions that weren't really questions. 'Um...' For some reason, he felt like he was going to cry.

'You have to be tougher than this.' She lit another cigarette. The *tsk* of the lighter felt like nails scratching down the back of his neck. How could a sound feel like something? But it did. 'My own mother, the woman who carried me and birthed me, she'd take me into the cellar and tie me to a mattress. Then she and my father—'

'What the hell are you doing?' His father stood at the end of the bed, wearing his suit from work, his sleeves rolled up. His face was pale. 'Smoking in bed? And what were you saying to the poor lad?'

Mother suddenly sat up. 'You're home early.'

'Yes, I am. And I heard what you were saying. About your mum tying you to the bed or some such nonsense. He doesn't need to hear that.'

'I'm not allowed to speak to my own son now, is that it?'

Father was a tall and strong man. His name was Joseph Langdale and he had broad shoulders and a head full of thick black hair. He wasn't chubby like some other dads Dom Dom often saw waiting outside school. He had an important job in the city, where he told other men what to do. He laughed easily and his smile lit Dom up with happiness. He was everything a boy could've wanted in a dad, and yet, when he looked at Mother like that, Dom sometimes disliked him. Maybe even hated him. It was all so confusing.

'Have you been drinking?' He strode to the bed and grabbed the cigarette from her hand, then pushed the window open so hard Dom thought the glass might shatter. He tossed the cigarette outside. 'This place reeks. Jesus Christ, Vicky. What's wrong with you?'

'Stop shouting in front of him!'

'Stop shouting? What about what you were saying? Do you think he needs to hear that filth?'

'I'm not allowed to suffer?'

'Go to your room, Dom.'

When Dom moved, Mother tightened her grip on him. 'He doesn't need to go anywhere.'

'Vicky, this is sick. He should be outside with his friends. He should be in his room reading. Or in the garden, collecting ants, or something.'

'Collecting *ants*?'

'Something, anything except this. It's not his fault you had a bad childhood, and it's definitely not an excuse to give him a bad childhood. Let the lad go. Now.'

'Fine. Fly away, Dominic. Abandon me.'

'He's not abandoning you.' Daddy ruffled Dom's hair, offering a tight smile. 'Go on, Dom. Ride your bike or something. Maybe read a book. Whatever you want. Get yourself some sweets. See what your friends are up to.'

There was something off with the way Daddy spoke. It was all too generic, as if he was tossing a bunch of child-shaped phrases out there in the hopes that one would apply to his stranger son. Dom left the room, then went into his bedroom and pushed his ear against the wall.

The *thwack* noise was very, very loud. He quickly ran to his bed, pushed his face against the pillows, and wept. The worst part, somehow, was not knowing who'd hit who.

And then he disappeared, and he remembered. Suddenly, he understood that he wasn't a boy anymore. He remembered snippets of a rainy night, ranting down the phone to... his mother, yes, and then he'd met with a woman... A name came to him.

Janine. A simple name. A beautiful name. A name that fit her, with her kind eyes and understanding, kissable lips and her embrace which was always so warm, with no pressure, no judgement.

He remembered rain – pulling up outside her house – ringing her over and over. Because he needed her. She was the one who made it better, for what felt like the first time. Not Mother. Not even... Eloise. It was Janine, their unique and non-judgemental romance.

He heard voices, his head aching, voices clashing.

'You're in no state to drive. Just come in for a cup of tea.'

'I'm going there. I need to do this.'

'You can't—'

'Get in the car or don't. I'm going anyway. I need you, Janine.'

She hesitated.

'Remember those questions you asked? About Mum and what happened when I was a kid? You were bang on the money. *She* has to know she can't keep getting away with this.'

Janine had risked her life by getting into that car with a foolish, drunken, broken man, and it had all been for him.

Dom Dom screamed into the pillow, the night melting away like rain slipping down his vision.

CHAPTER TEN

JANINE

Janine was light-headed, probably a combination of the drugs and the effort to free one of her hands. She'd managed to do it though. Her current job was to save what little energy she had left for when psycho Cassandra returned. With one hand free, she had tried to free her other hand so that she could lean up and free her legs too, but her kidnapper must've tied one tighter than the other. After pulling on the tie for what felt like hours, she'd begun to bleed. A lot. She'd had to stop.

She closed her eyes and breathed slowly. The cellar was damp. Her lungs ached.

She had no reference for time. She wasn't sure how long Cassandra had been gone. No sunlight. No clock. Just the stale air and the hollow feeling in her heart. Cassandra had said Dominic abused her. That was why Janine was there: to recount all of Dominic's so-called bad points. But Janine knew that life was far more complicated than that. Life was partly hating Dominic for begging her to get in the car that night; life was hating herself for doing it; life was being proud too, because she'd stood by him when he needed her most. It was pathetic –

it was worthy of pride. She just wished it was simple. She needed to focus on the practical things.

In fact, Cassandra hadn't said Dominic hit her. She'd said, what was it...? *He turned so abusive, I can't even describe the things he did.* The situation was so surreal, Janine wondered if she was back at the crash site.

She forced herself to lean over again, grab the zip tie of one hand with the other, pull, work her hand free. But her wrists were already stinging with an almost unbelievable level of agony. Hot fire bit up her arm.

She fell back, gasping, her eyes flooding with tears. Getting one hand free had been a miracle. Somehow, it would have to be enough. Perhaps she could get a strong arm around Cassandra's throat, force her to cut her other hand loose. From there, she could free her legs, climb out of the bed, ignore the pain, ignore the panic, and get out of there. She wouldn't die in a cellar, prisoner to a madwoman.

Her eyes fell shut.

Sometime later – who knew how long? – she woke to the sound of the cellar door opening. She was annoyed with herself for letting sleep take her, but at least she'd woken in time. She quickly put her hand at her side, where it would've been if she hadn't managed to free it from the zip tie.

'Somebody's gone to the toilet,' the woman said in her posh voice, walking down the stairs. With the light from the top of the staircase, it was difficult to make out Cassandra's features clearly. When she reached the bottom, she turned on the powerful torchlight – or whatever it bloody was – causing Janine to wince and her eyes to snap shut. 'Haven't they, dear? But the scent is...' She loudly sniffed the air. It would've been comical if Janine wasn't terrified for her life. 'Number one, if I'm not mistaken.'

'Do you get off on humiliating me, Cassandra?'

'Please, call me Cass. It's what my friends and even acquaintances call me. We used to joke, when such jokes were relevant: *Cass makes more noise than a cassette tape.* But I'm sure you're too young for such references.'

'I remember them. Just about.'

'How fascinating Dominic is, hmm? To love in such a wide range of age and appearance? You, me, his wife. I can't think of three more different women. Men are of endless curiosity to me.'

'You're going to have to change my sheets at least,' Janine said. 'I can't lie here in my own urine forever.'

'Yes, it is rather nasty.'

There was an ugly *scrape* noise as Cassandra pulled a chair across the floor. 'But first, I must confess something to you, Janine. You see, for a short time I had a dog. It didn't last long... not for the reasons you might imagine. I'm one of those people who can read fiction where the ghastliest thing happens to people, but hurt the animal? No, that is unacceptable to me. Doubly so in real life, with real lives, obviously. No. It had your problem. A urination issue. So, unfortunately, I had to put the poor barker up for adoption. But when I had it, I bought a camera. A dog camera.'

Janine swallowed. She really hated the terror this woman triggered in her. Janine had done a charity white-collar boxing fight once. She sometimes hit the heavy bag for a workout. She could've snapped Cassandra in half if she hadn't preyed on her when she was weak and vulnerable.

'You have nothing to say?' Cassandra said. After a pause, she went on. 'It seems to me you've seriously hurt yourself, probably not feeling the full effect of your self-inflicted injuries because of the drugs with which I have mercifully gifted you. The camera I bought, it's in the corner of the room. I watched you. Broken your own hand, child, and for what? To have one hand free?'

Janine despised the whining noise she made when the air rifle made a *whack* noise and a pellet bounced off the side of her face. She shut her eyes tighter. The lunatic was going to blind her. 'I asked you a question,' Cassandra said.

'Why do you think?'

'I want you to tell me.'

It was only when the second pellet hit her wrist that Janine realised just how badly she'd hurt herself trying to get free. The agony was like nothing she'd ever experienced.

'Don't scream,' Cassandra said coldly. 'I mean it.' Then she giggled.

Janine's eyes hurt, tears pouring from them. 'What's funny?'

'You, silly girl.' She tittered again, becoming every teacher who had ever talked down to Janine, every woman who'd ever sneered at her. 'Don't you get it? You really are addled in the head, possibly concussed. Don't you understand why I might be laughing? We're *talking*, Janine. Me and you, we're *talking*. We've been *talking* since I arrived home. Chitter-chatter, chitter-chatter.'

Janine's brain sluggishly caught up with her. That was right; after freeing her hand, she'd removed the gag because it was making it difficult to breathe. She had planned to replace it when she heard Cassandra returning.

'You silly, stupid, fat pig.' Cassandra sounded pleased with the situation. 'Your mind isn't working properly. Fine. You're concussed, drugged. Fine. I'll allow you all that. But didn't you think I'd notice? Or – what – did you forget?'

Janine realised she was crying, and she hated herself for it. Finally, she did what she should've been doing all along. She opened her mouth and screamed.

'Oh, silly girl.' Cassandra rushed across the room. This was

Janine's chance. She tried to swipe at the older woman, but she moved pitifully slowly. It was like she was trapped far back in her own head, watching events unfold, powerless to change them.

A rag over her mouth. Her vision wavered. The scream died on her lips. She closed her eyes and saw Dominic smiling at her, shirtless, sitting up in bed. 'Come here, beautiful. You don't have to be strong all the time.' She laughed like a lovestruck idiot, climbed into his arms, not caring he had a wife. She just wanted to be held.

When she woke – she honestly could not say if it had been an hour or a day or longer or shorter – she felt weirdly happy, relieved almost, that she didn't have to get up and go to work or do any life stuff at all. She was grateful to Cassandra for tying her to this bed, for filling her with this warm sensation. All she had to do was lie there, eyes closed, drift, not even fully awake, not fully asleep either.

'Somebody's feeling better,' Cassandra said.

'Hmm,' Janine replied.

'You can get any drug these days if you know where to look. The regular person would be shocked at the selection. You are currently experiencing the perspective-shifting joy of ecstasy. Really, you should be grateful. I have also changed your clothes and tended to your hand as best as I can, though, of course, you will need to remain restrained. I am going to gag you again soon – more effectively this time – but first, tell me how you and Dominic met.'

'Wuh-why?' Janine whispered with an infuriating amount of effort.

'I need to learn about your little fling. All the ins and outs.

Tell me. Speak as slowly as you need to. But tell me. Now. Janine. Don't make me hurt you. Please. I am not a sadistic person, nor have I ever been.'

'Puh–'

'Do not say anything else, Janine. Just how you met. It's simple. Really.'

Janine just wanted to sleep, to let this stupid smile spread across her face. She had never been into drugs. In her younger years, she'd experimented… a tiny bit, not much, just the usual amount, probably. She wasn't exceptional. She rarely even drank because it interfered with her workout recovery.

'He was one of my clients,' she murmured, each word taking a long time. Too long. 'He wanted to get fit, so he'd swing by after work. It was… easy. It had never felt that easy before. He always had a way of making me laugh, always knew how to be on the line, but not go over it. Then he started to bring me little presents. Protein bars. An expensive brand of shake I'd mentioned. Then, after one session, he said, *shall we get some steaks?* He winked at me. Just like that. *Shall-we-get-some-steaks.*' She was beginning to slur. 'With a wink. It made me feel special. It made me feel…' She was being too honest. 'Like I belonged. Like I was a regular person. Like I was all the things I'd missed out on in school and after and my whole life. He made me feel normal.'

'Silly girl. You are normal. That's the misery of people like you. You think you're special. You think you're different. But you're not, and you never have been. Now – sleep. Forget.'

Janine willed herself to fight. A silent plea in her mind. But it was far too easy to sink into the mattress and let the blackness take her.

A MOTHER'S MUSINGS: FOUR WEEKS OF HELL
21/10/24

Victoria Hawthorne

As you all now know, my son has been in a coma for the past month. It has been the most difficult month of my life. I have spent every single moment I can at his bedside, or with my daughter-in-law, Eloise. I have struggled and fought to keep myself sane, but it has been difficult. I have to say, however, that I couldn't do this without your support. The love you all have sent me has been overwhelming in the absolute best sense. Every day, I wake up and check my notifications, and I shed a tear of joy to know that so many of you out there are thinking of me and my baby boy.

The matter is growing complicated. The doctors and nurses perform routine neurological assessments. They are searching for signs that my son may one day wake up, or that his consciousness is even remotely close to the surface. One helpful doctor told me to think of it like a buoy which has gone under the waves, and which they are attempting to coax back to the top. But so far, there has been no luck. It's as if we're stuck in limbo. I fear, very soon, that they will present us with a choice. I don't want to think about it, but my mind is in a dark place. And I know my wonderful, loyal readers will understand.

We try to be brave and strong, don't we? We try not to let the world see the cracks appearing beneath the surface of our carefully applied make-up. We attempt to mask the horrors which howl in our hearts. But why do we do this, exactly? Why? For our babies… And my baby is asleep, and may never wake up, and each day, I struggle for a reason to keep going.

Soon, Eloise and I are meeting with the medical consultation team to discuss the outlook for Dom Dom. This is going to be one of the hardest things I've ever done.

This blog was never supposed to be morose, but of late, it has become that way. So, please, I'd like to change the tone. In the comments below, share a photo or a few sentences with me: something from yours and your children's lives, something to brighten the bleak spot in my soul. I love you all, always. Thank you.

CHAPTER ELEVEN

ELOISE

She guided Pixie from the upscale hills of her and Dominic's home towards the country lanes which led to Victoria's magnificent house. Victoria, after her husband disappeared – leaving a note which made it clear the vanishing was intentional: a note Victoria had torn apart in a fit of rage – had become a successful art dealer. After her husband's abandonment, she'd risen to the challenge, pursuing a childhood dream and becoming independently wealthy.

As Eloise drove, she tried to tell herself that Victoria was clearly capable. She was obviously loving. What they were about to do, it had a purpose. It wasn't merely selfish.

But pessimism tried to grip her. She'd spent the last month doing her best to cling onto some semblance of sanity, though it was difficult as she visited her husband's bedside, as she waited for news of the neurological tests to give them something, anything, a sign that he was still in there. With each passing day, she felt the hidden corners of their marriage closing up. With Dominic asleep, she was free to simply be the loving, caring wife, nothing more; she didn't have to think about or remember anything else.

Her belly had produced a very small bump. If her plan had gone to – well, plan – this would have been cause for a celebration. She and Dominic would've cherished the growing life inside of her.

Her agent had come back and told her that, while her book had received some positive feedback from several publishers, nobody wanted to put it out into the world. Eloise had barely heard her on the phone. Like any of that mattered anymore. She was becoming a recluse, ignoring phone calls from friends, going from home to hospital and from hospital to home.

Soon, she arrived at Victoria's large house on the outskirts of Weston-super-Mare. It was as though she'd picked this location because it was far enough away from Dominic to not be invasive, but close enough for her to see him often.

As Eloise came to a stop, she gripped the wheel and took several slow breaths. A month, four long weeks, and no sign of life inside her husband. The police hadn't contacted Eloise; nobody else seemed to know that he'd been drink-driving. There had been no scandal. It was like life was on standstill. This morning, Victoria had rung, left a message. Eloise had missed the call; she was sleeping in far too late.

'As you know, the doctor wants to meet with us this afternoon. I'm terrified it's not going to be good news. I know you've never been involved in my blog, but I was wondering if you'd possibly mind if we took a photo together? I know it might seem callous. I promise, Eloise, it's not. It's my way of dealing with things. If you say no, I'll never bring it up again.'

Eloise's instinct had been to say no. The last thing they should've been doing when Dominic was lying half alive, half dead, in between both and neither, was playing social media games. But Victoria had always been so kind and selfless.

Victoria's home was beautiful, creepers growing up the walls, a double garage covered in vegetation. Victoria opened the large door and rushed out. She was even skinnier than she'd been a month ago. Eloise was wearing baggy clothes; she was starkly aware of the contrast.

Victoria clutched Eloise's hands as if it had been months since they'd seen each other; it had been a day. Eloise held her tightly. 'Thank you for coming. I know this might seem odd to you.'

'I'm doing my best to understand it.'

'My blog means everything. My readers, they're like family. I want us to take a snapshot of this time in our lives. I want there to be an image of us before...'

'Before what?' Eloise said tightly.

Victoria rubbed her eyes. 'Nothing. I don't know.'

'Control yourself, Victoria.' Eloise's tone was far harsher than it had ever been with her mother-in-law. 'Dominic is going to wake up. He's going to be perfectly fine. Everything is going to return to normal.'

He'd once again tease her about putting kisses in her texts. He'd once again, with tears in his eyes, call her his precious petal, his precious prize. He'd jokingly call the self-help podcasts she listened to *repetitive*. But this time, it would be different. It would end there; joy wouldn't cascade into hate.

And then they all lived happily ever after... She was not naïve, she told herself. She merely wouldn't allow herself to sink into a pit of depression.

'I'm sure you're right,' Victoria said. 'Forget I said anything. And thank you for agreeing to this.'

'It's just a photo,' Eloise said uncomfortably as they walked into Victoria's large entranceway. Prints of her artists' work hung on the walls. All of it had a touch of the Gothic, a contrast to how bright and welcoming the rest of the décor was. 'You want your readers to see us, so they'll see us. I want to do anything I can to help you handle this. Just like you do with me.'

Victoria took her hand. 'Thank you. My set-up is in the cellar. It's easier to control the light down there.'

They walked down the steps. There was a low humming noise from an industrial-sized freezer in the corner of the room. Otherwise, it was mostly empty except for a large light, the likes of which professional photographers used. Eloise had seen the images which resulted from its use before; Victoria's blog was popular because of her words and relatability, but she also had a unique photographer style. Stark, unflinching. One of her most viral blogs had been titled *My Wrinkles and Me* and had shown her face in high-definition detail under this light.

'It won't take long,' Victoria said.

It felt as if they were exploiting Dominic's condition. Eloise was worried what people would think. But just as Eloise had obsessively listened to podcasts and self-help books to get her through the past month, Victoria had written extensively on her blog, using words to explore all the avenues of her heartache. Eloise had no right to resent or blame her for that. Everybody had different ways of coping with the miseries of life. She and Dominic knew that better than anybody, not that they'd ever talk about it with anybody else.

'Are you sure you're all right with this, dear?' Victoria said. 'We don't have to do anything you feel uneasy about. I want to make that clear. I'm aware how it might seem, as if I'm abusing my son's condition for a bitter bid at fame.'

'No,' Eloise said fiercely. Something about Victoria bringing her thoughts out into the open made them seem perverse. 'I understand, this is your way of coping.'

Victoria smiled tightly. 'We must find our ways, mustn't we?'

Eloise waited as Victoria set up the large light, bringing Eloise back to her modelling days. She felt the old tickle of self-consciousness, experienced the same desire to be beautiful. This felt far more cynical.

Eloise looked at the floor. There was a large crimson stain that spread from the rear of the room in a petal formation.

'That cost me a thousand pounds,' Victoria said as she saw Eloise looking. 'A case of wine – fine stuff – and what do I do? Drop the entire thing as I attempt to move it.'

Soon, it was time for the shot. Eloise did her duty. Neither of them smiled. Their expressions were tragic, perhaps even ones of resignation, as if they knew that the meeting with the medical consultation team was going to bring heartache with it.

Eloise couldn't sit still as they waited for the meeting to begin. Her foot was tapping frantically on the floor. She wanted to lay her hand upon her belly, let the little life inside know that everything was going to work out. Everything she had done, all she had sacrificed, had been worth it.

But of course, she couldn't give Victoria any indication; Victoria and Dominic were close, often meeting for coffee and long walks after Victoria had moved to Somerset, and so, Eloise had no doubt her mother-in-law knew that Dominic had never wanted children. She sometimes wondered if her mother-in-law knew why, because Dominic certainly never told her.

Finally, they were ushered into a small consultation room. The attending neurologist, Dr Sophia Hoang, a kind-looking woman with an American accent, was there, along with Rachel Thompson, a representative from the nursing staff.

'I would like to start by saying it's still early days,' Sophia said. Something about her American accent made Eloise feel like she was in some medical drama, as if none of this was real, like she'd return from her vomiting bout to find Dominic face down in a whisky-induced stupor.

'But?'

Eloise glared at her mother-in-law. Was there any need for that tone? In public, too.

'I'm sorry.' Victoria softened. 'But there is a *but*, isn't there?'

Dr Hoang swallowed. 'In an ideal world, we would have observed some signs of cognitive recovery by this point. A month is far, far too early to make a definitive prognosis. Any real decisions will come at the three-to-six-month stage—'

'Real decisions?' Eloise cut in. She hadn't shaped her mind, her memories, her marriage, formed her reality with stubborn determination, just to talk about *real decisions*.

'I agree with my daughter-in-law,' Victoria said. 'Let's get right down to it, shall we? What are you trying to say?'

'Let me be clear,' the doctor went on. 'I am not stating anything one way or the other, except... It is my strong opinion that you both attempt to return to whatever normalcy you can find in your day-to-day lives. You, Mrs Hawthorne...' The doctor turned her kind eyes to Eloise. 'You've been here every day, sometimes sleeping here, and everybody can see the emotional toll it's taken on you. This is going to be a lengthy process. I want to encourage you to attempt to take the long view.'

'What did you mean?' Eloise whispered, feeling the tears coming, doing her best to push them down. She was a precious prize – a precious petal. Oh, how he'd teased her... 'Three to six months, for what?'

'I'll say it if they won't,' Victoria said. 'They're talking about switching off his life support.'

Eloise gripped the table, pushed back in her chair, shook her head. 'I won't even listen to that. If you've made any plans like that, you can get rid of them. Get them out of your heads. I won't let that happen. Dominic and I, we've been through too much.'

Nobody knew how much. Nobody could ever know. Eloise, for long portions of her life, didn't even let *herself* know, a concept most people wouldn't be able to understand. She would blind herself to his mistakes, to her adaptations, to the conflagrations which turned to embers and then were forgotten.

'Like I said,' Dr Hoang murmured, 'we're not even close to discussing that. My goal here was more to address your short-term well-being, Mrs Hawthorne.'

'You don't understand. Short-term, long-term, it doesn't make any difference. People have woken from comas after five, ten, fifteen years. I've read stories about it online. The most seemingly hopeless cases have woken up. You can forget about it. Full stop. Understand?'

She noted the worried look Dr Hoang exchanged with Nurse Thompson. Perhaps they were thinking about bed spaces. Who knew what ulterior motives they could have for raising this possibility?

'I'm sorry, Eloise, but this is why Dominic did it,' Victoria said quietly.

'Did what?'

'Dominic knew, if anything were to ever happen to him, you wouldn't be able to let him go. Your love is too deep, too pure. Your soul is too tender. He made a choice. One of the most difficult of his life.'

'Speak some sense, Victoria. Please!'

'Dominic gave me legal power of attorney,' Victoria said. 'When that choice comes – if it does – I'm sorry, but it won't be yours to make.'

CHAPTER TWELVE

DOMINIC

Dom was getting very good at sneaking around the house when Mother and Father were having one of their talks. That was what Mother called them whenever Father asked Dom to leave the room. She'd roll her eyes at Dom like they shared a secret, and Dom both loved and hated it, then she'd say, 'Yes, run along, we must have one of our *talks*.' Dom crouched at the top of the stairs; they were in the kitchen, Father's voice low and urgent. 'It's a fantastic opportunity for my career.'

'I haven't told you not to take it. I haven't even hinted at it.'

'I know.' He sighed, a chair squeaking, a *thump* as he maybe rested his elbows on the table. 'But you obviously know why I'd be apprehensive about this.'

'Why don't you enlighten me?'

'Don't play games. I'll be working away for two days out of every week. Sometimes longer. That's two days for you to...'

'Don't lose your nerve now, Joseph.'

'Christ, Vicky. You know what I'm getting at. I'm not saying you're a bad person, but you love that boy too much. You stifle him. I've had to act like a prison warden to make sure he can start having a normal life. Leaving work early to basically force him to go to birthday parties, pushing him out the door so he'll ride his bike and mix with other children. I don't want you to undermine me while I'm away.'

'It's as if you think I want my son to be unhappy. Has it ever occurred to you that he doesn't like being forced to pretend to be normal?'

'He is normal.'

'Dom Dom is a very sensitive boy.'

'Even that. *Dom Dom*. It infantilises him. He's not a baby anymore. He's not a toddler. He's a young lad; soon, he'll be a young man. I'm worried you'll never be able to let go. I'm worried you'll spend your life trying to turn him into the second baby we never had.'

Mother's voice trembled in that horrible way. Dom had to cross his feet to stop from running down there and hugging her. 'Don't,' she said.

'Vicky...' Father's tone became softer than usual. 'It's not your fault we can't have another baby. And just because we can't, it doesn't mean we have to smother the poor lad. The fact he's an only child is even more of a reason to make sure he has friends, hobbies, a vibrant, active life. It's even more reason to make sure that we give him every opportunity to form social connections. You have to be able to see that.'

'I'm thinking about *him*,' Mother said. 'His well-being. He gets so nervous going to those parties you force him to. He doesn't enjoy riding his bike. He adores sitting by the fire with me, reading. What's so wrong with that? This has nothing to do with – with – my broken body.'

'Don't talk about yourself like that.'

'I've been broken since I was a little girl.'

Dom knew he shouldn't have been hearing any of this. But he remained where he was and listened. It hurt.

'Ever since what they did to me. For their sick pleasure.

They bruised my soul. Cursed me. Am I really wrong for loving my only son? Does that really make me a demon?'

'Of course not. And I'm not saying you can't read with him or spend time with him. But, please, if I've put a social event in his diary, encourage him to stick to it. Try to see the good in it. We want him to grow up to be happy and healthy, don't we?'

'Yes,' Mother said. 'Of course we do.'

They didn't say anything else for a long time. Dom smiled as he thought about them holding hands. Sometimes, they showed each other love. It was the best thing. It made Dom feel warm, like everything might work out okay. It was a nice change from this other feeling he often had, a wrenching in his gut, like something deep inside was telling him everything was going to go very, very wrong somehow.

Soon, it was time for Father to leave for work. Father gave him one of his rough hugs, squeezing him tight and then clapping him on the back. It almost hurt, but it also made Dom want to seem older and bigger in his father's eyes. 'Be good, lad.'

That night, when Dom was trying to sleep, his door creaked open and Mother stumbled in. She smelled of wine. Red wine; that was always her favourite. She didn't just smell of it. It was like it had seeped into her skin. She climbed into bed with Dom. They often lay together, though Dom was getting older and, once, at school, he'd mentioned his mother lying in his bed and the other children had looked at him like he was an alien.

The wine stunk really bad, but he couldn't tell Mother that. She wrapped her arms around him. Dom pretended to be asleep.

'My sweet Dom Dom. You're so perfect when you're sleeping. Nothing's ever harmed you, has it? Nobody has ever done anything inappropriate or evil to you. Your soul hasn't been scarred. I know what people are like. Your father would send you to parties, would let the other parents have free rein,

That would give them every chance to – well, God, well...' She shuddered. 'I know what to do.' She swallowed. A vomit stink joined the red-wine reek. 'It's simple, really. That doesn't mean it's easy, but it's simple. Your father thinks he can force you to be something, to be somebody you're not. But I know better than that. I know you better than anyone.'

She stroked her hand through his hair. It was longer than most of his classmates'. Father kept saying he should get it cut, but Mother liked it long. Finally, Father had taken Dom to the barber. But for some reason Dom still didn't understand, he'd begun to wail like a baby. Father had looked at him with disgust; it was the closest he'd ever come to hitting him, Dom was sure. Why had he cried? What was wrong with him?

'I know what we have to do, sweet boy. We have to get rid of your father. For good.'

CHAPTER THIRTEEN

ELOISE

Dominic had given Victoria legal power of attorney – when? Why? He'd done it without telling her. Was that even legal? Shouldn't she have been informed?

'Eloise?' Victoria touched her hand. Her mother-in-law was cold. She felt her baby recoil inside of her as though he or she never wanted to greet the old woman.

'I don't understand,' Eloise said. 'Why would he do that?'

'In any case,' Dr Hoang cut in with her suddenly obnoxiously assertive voice, 'it's far too early to be making decisions like that.'

'So why even bother calling us in here?' Eloise demanded. 'I'm sorry,' she said a moment later, registering the shock on their faces, silently scolding herself for slipping. 'I know it's not your fault. This whole thing – this entire situation... it's just wrong. It wasn't supposed to be part of the life I was building for us.'

The life *she* had been building, not *they*. Nobody at this table knew about the secret baby in her womb, nor about the lengths she'd gone to. Nobody knew about the future she'd dreamt of.

'I want to see my husband.' She stood. 'Are we done here?'

She barely waited for them to nod before she fled the room. Victoria said her name, but she didn't listen. She walked towards Dominic's bed, the path familiar.

She sat at his bedside, looking at her man, his eyes closed, his silver hair sometimes seeming to shine – she remembered joking about him choosing this shade rather than him going prematurely grey – his lips sometimes seeming to twitch as though he might break into a smile. Touching his hand, she felt his warmth, but he was too thin. It was like his skeleton was pressing through, like she might start picking pieces of him away, finally reach his brain, his thoughts, his secrets. Why had he done this?

'Eloise.' Victoria walked into the room. 'I'm sorry. I didn't mean to break the news to you like that.' The regret and sympathy on her mother-in-law's face made the situation worse. It would've been easier if Victoria was a simple enemy, somebody Eloise could've just hated.

'I've been trying to tell you since this began,' Victoria went on, pulling up a chair next to Eloise. She had every right to sit there with her, of course, but suddenly, Eloise wanted to scream at her to leave; this bedside had nothing to do with her. He was *her* husband, her responsibility. Victoria didn't even know him, not who he was behind closed doors. 'I hoped he'd get better. I hoped that by now, he'd be out of it.'

'I don't understand why he would do this.'

'It's exactly what I said, sweetheart. He knew, if something happened to him, you'd never let go.'

'Why would it even occur to him to think of it?'

She shrugged. 'He never said. He came to me about three years ago, asked if he could give me legal power of attorney. I don't know why. Perhaps he saw a television programme or read a book that reminded him of his mortality. Perhaps one of his friends had a health scare.'

'Look at him, Victoria. Really look at him, your son, your baby, look at him and tell me you'd pull the plug if it came down to it. Tell me you'd kill him if you had to.'

'Oh, Eloise.' Victoria blinked back tears, making Eloise feel cruel. 'I'd really prefer if you didn't phrase it like that. I never wanted this to happen. He's my baby, my Dom Dom.'

'He's not your *Dom Dom*. He's my husband. He's the...' *Father of my child*, she almost said, but it wouldn't make sense to Victoria. She would judge Eloise. Very few people would be able to understand Eloise's unique relationship to the truth. They wouldn't be able to relate to her ability to shape it, to will it into existence. 'He's everything to me.' She didn't have to fake the sob which escaped her. 'I've given him everything... and you'll take all of that away.'

'All I can do is try and fulfil my son's wishes,' Victoria said. 'I'm sorry.'

'How do I know that's even what he wanted?'

'Oh, Eloise.'

'*Stop saying that.*'

A passing nurse stopped, stared into the room. Eloise was allowing too many shadows to spill out of her. She mouthed 'Sorry' to the glaring nurse.

'I know this isn't easy,' Victoria said. 'I've been stressing, trying to figure out how to tell you. I shouldn't have blurted it out. But don't you see? This can be a good thing. You don't have to make this decision. Do you think I want to? Dom Dom is my everything. After Joseph abandoned us, we were two peas in a pod. It was us against the world. And then you came along, Eloise, and we were like the three musketeers. Don't you get it? We're on the same side.'

Her words disarmed Eloise. She was confused and angry,

but she knew one thing for sure: Victoria had always been there for her. It wasn't as if Eloise's mother had been abusive, but she'd been distant, detached, seeming borderline Puritanical in how she behaved at times. But Victoria was full-hearted and always gave everything to the relationship. She was always there, ready with a hug, a consolation, with bucketfuls of unselfconscious love.

'I know,' Eloise whispered. 'But you can't give up on him.'

'It was what—'

'Even if he told you to, even if he made you promise, you can't. Please. You just can't.'

Victoria sighed. 'It's like the doctor said anyway. We don't have to make this choice yet. Why don't we cross that bridge when we come to it?'

'No, you have to promise. I can't lose him, not after everything we've built, not when we've got such a bright future ahead of us.'

Was any marriage perfect? There were seams and cracks even in the most seemingly flawless unions. Eloise's talent was smoothing over those cracks, filling them with putty and letting it harden in her soul, in her mind, in every word she spoke to her husband, in every gesture, in every touch, even if those touches were sometimes tinged with terror.

Dominic sometimes slipped, but she always pulled him back to the path. This meant he was abandoning her. It wasn't fair.

'You have to promise,' Eloise said. 'Just say it. Say you promise. Say you won't let him die.'

'I'm sorry, but I just can't. It was what he wanted. If I made you a promise, I'd be breaking one to him.'

Later, Eloise spoke with her sister, Charlotte, on FaceTime. She was sitting in her library, the place which had brought her so much peace in the days leading up to Dominic's accident. Life had been going as good as she could reasonably expect: a novel on submission, words coursing from her fingertips in the form of a memoir, a baby in her belly. Her main concern had been breaking the news to Dominic that he was going to be a father.

Charlotte was pale and had a stylish black bob haircut. As a solicitor who worked long, hard hours in London, Eloise knew she would be able to offer advice about this. 'If what your mother-in-law is saying is true,' Charlotte said, 'Dominic most likely would have made a living will outlining his wishes. Did she mention anything about that?'

'No. She said that he'd made her promise, if anything like this ever happened, she'd switch off his – his...' Eloise took a breath. 'His life support.'

'You don't have to be strong all the time.'

'I know that.'

'Do you? That's the first time I've seen how distraught you really are.'

'I'm fine, Charlotte. Really.'

'Mum did a number on us, E. No affection, no love, no hugs.'

Eloise rolled her eyes. 'Not this again.'

'There have been studies on it. Why do you think we've always found relationships so difficult?'

'Speak for yourself.'

'This isn't coming out right. What I'm trying to say, in my classically annoying Charlotte way, is I'm going to visit Weston this weekend.'

'You don't have to d—'

'I know I don't have to. But I think you've been pretending to handle this far better than you are. I feel like a total bitch for not being there for my baby sister. No arguments. We might not have been close as kids, but we can be close now.'

Eloise smiled. 'Okay.'

'So, speaking of the power of attorney. How did you handle the insurance companies? They typically make things as difficult as possible. Haven't they reached the investigation or paperwork stage yet? I mention this because, if the car was in Dominic's name, you would have encountered this issue already.' When Eloise didn't say anything, Charlotte said, 'You haven't contacted them, have you?'

'No,' Eloise admitted.

'That was why Victoria has been able to hide this for so long.'

'She wasn't hiding anything. She was nervous about telling me.'

'That's a distinction without a difference. We need to sort this insurance.'

'I've got bigger things to worry about than insurance payouts.'

'Do you realise how privileged we are to be able to say things like that?'

Charlotte was the type with pins on her handbag and lofty declarations in the bios of her social media accounts. She'd marched for countless causes, and Eloise had often felt that their distance, partly, was caused by the fact Eloise had worked as a model for so many years, willingly subjugating herself, and, worse, enjoying it, profiting from it not just monetarily. She had relished the boost to her self-esteem; she had savoured the sense of power. She had liked feeling like she mattered, which would've made most feminists cringe. Did she need to be objectified to matter? No, but it hadn't hurt.

'You need to learn how to live in limbo,' Charlotte said. 'You have to keep going. Otherwise, you'll be frozen until something happens with Dominic.'

'Until he wakes up – until he recovers.'

Charlotte frowned. 'I hope so.'

'What can I do?' Eloise asked.

'Find out if Dominic has a living will.'

'I don't get it. Wouldn't they have to tell me?'

'Not unless you'd already acquired power of attorney. As his next of kin, if he hadn't already designated an LPA, acquiring one now would've been relatively easy. But if he already has one, it's going to be difficult.'

'But it can be done?'

'It would mean calling your mother-in-law's motives into question.'

Eloise shook her head. 'Victoria loves Dominic more than anything. She's wrong for wanting to do this, but it's coming from a good place.'

'Are you sure?'

'Yes, Charlotte. I'm sure.'

'Ask about the living will. And remember , sometimes people aren't what you've made them in your head.'

After the FaceTime call, Eloise texted Victoria. Charlotte's words wouldn't leave her alone as she went around the house, mindlessly cleaning. She paused when she was in the kitchen, staring at the island, a scene from the past playing as if she was a ghost observing the living world. She saw Dominic sneering at her, his eyes glassy, his lips moist.

'Stop it. You're drunk.'

He'd swaggered around the kitchen island, waving his phone. *'Kiss, kiss, bloody kiss, like we're little kids, on every text. Like you think we're special for being married. Like you think our life is a film or something. We're regular, boring, pathetic people, Eloise.'*

'No, you're wrong. We mean something.'
'Kiss, kiss, kiss.'

He'd leaned in, kissing her three times. She could still remember the feel of his slobber on her cheek, the callousness of his hands. She closed her eyes, forced steady breathing. What sort of wife was she, standing there when her husband was barely clinging to life, wilfully reliving his worst moments?

Her phone vibrated. A text from Victoria. *I'm so sorry. He didn't make a living will. He asked me to fulfil his wishes and I told him I would. That was enough for him xxx.*

Kiss, kiss, kiss.

A MOTHER'S MUSINGS: ON TIME
22/10/24

Victoria Hawthorne

For probably understandable reasons, I have been thinking a lot about time recently. It's a funny thing. I remember entire afternoons when I was a girl, lasting, subjectively, what would feel like weeks now. I'm sure I lay in bed with a book and entire months went by. Now, I leave the house for the weekly shop, return, then realise, in fact, three weekly shops have gone by. The interim has been a blink.

When it comes to our babies, time is our most precious commodity. Some people often say they didn't realise how valuable the time was when they were spending it, but I was blessed with the awareness to understand how special it was. Each moment I was with my Dom Dom, each minute, I savoured. I held tightly onto our love, for I knew it would pass. I knew I would never have another child.

It's a shame, however, to know that time will always play its tricks. A day spent in the world of my imagination with my

Dom Dom will pass like *that*. (Be so kind as to imagine an old, heartbroken woman snapping her fingers.) And then the time apart will stretch as if it's never going to end.

I remember when I was doing my volunteer work at one of the many rehab centres we have here on the coast, I asked one of the poor souls who had found themselves there, what was it that brought them back to their drug of choice over and over? Their answer? 'Time. I feel like my life is slipping away. But when I'm on that stuff, a minute passes like an hour. An hour is a day. A day is an entire life. I'm only twenty-four, but I feel like I've lived one hundred years.' There was something about the way the young lady said it that rang true to me, though I don't know anything about drugs.

On a more positive note, I was very flattered to see that a national newspaper published an article about my little blog. To know that my humble corner of the internet is sparking discussion around comas, grief, and motherhood brings me some small joy in this tough time.

Below, why don't you tell me about your relationship with time and your children? You can be funny, i.e. you wish you had more time because they're always rushing you off your feet! Or you can, like me, be a touch more serious. As usual, I look forward to hearing from you.

Out of respect for my Dom Dom, I have veered away from including my sponsorship code during this difficult month, but I also need to respect my business associates. I hope you will not judge me if I suggest for you to please remember to use promo code *MMusingsVictoria* to receive 10% off baby products at my sponsored shop, *All Care Wear.*

As always, thank you for reading.

CHAPTER FOURTEEN

JANINE

She had been floating all her life, ever since she was a girl and had put on a dress that didn't fit and brushed her hair in a way that felt unnatural and stood in front of the mirror and told herself, *I am just like the other girls.* Then she had gone to a party she hadn't truly been invited to, and they'd all laughed and called her names. She'd run home crying. Her dad had grabbed her by the dress and given her a shake. 'You're better than those idiots. If people enjoy making you feel lonely, make loneliness your superpower.'

The present moment came painfully into resolution when Cassandra slapped a cold towel across her belly. Since Janine's escape attempt (how long ago was that?), Cassandra had upped her efforts when it came to drugs and restraint. Janine was tied naked to the bed with coarse rope, spread out like some medieval torture victim; she was on the rack.

Cassandra slapped her again. Janine groggily opened her eyes.

'Oh, there you are. You've been moaning and groaning for God knows how long. I suppose it's my fault. I've dosed you with a true medley, uppers, downers, in-betweeners. You feel nice and pliable, don't you? Your Play-Doh body has encouraged a Play-Doh mind.'

'Please,' Janine whispered.

'Enough of that. I'd like to know how you and Dominic progressed in your little affair. What did you talk about? Where did you go?'

'It was... nothing special.' Each word was an effort. 'Nothing unusual. It *was* special.'

'How sweet.'

'He would take me to a restaurant near the gym. We'd eat steak and I'd tease him about how he had to cut his into little pieces before he started eating. Once, a group of drunk women made a comment about me. I'm not sure if they wanted me to hear it.'

'What did they say?'

'That Dominic was too attractive for me.'

'You can hardly blame them for that, dear, can you?' Cassandra said. 'I'm ancient, and even I suit him better.'

The words stung, but like everything, it was distant. Janine wished she could be sober. 'Dominic stood up for me. It was scary. But I liked it.'

'Scary?'

'He was drunk too. He got up, marched right over to them. He didn't care that everybody was looking. He raised his voice and said— He was angry...'

'Don't make excuses for him.'

'He said he'd find the women's social media accounts and show the world what callous sluts they were. When they tried to argue, he grabbed their table, shook it. All their drinks fell off. I can still remember their oh-so civilised gasps when their glasses shattered.'

'Oh, Jesus. What a man!'

'They were being cruel,' Janine said. At the time, she'd stared in shock. The manager had asked them to leave, then they'd walked along the River Avon, Dominic angrily smoking cigarettes.

'Care to share with the class?'

'After, we went for a walk. He apologised for snapping. He said that, sometimes, it was difficult for him to pretend to be a human being.'

'Those were his actual words? It seems a touch dramatic.'

'It didn't seem dramatic to me. It seemed romantic. I knew exactly what he meant. I'd always found it difficult to pretend to be human too. I felt like we were both outsiders.'

'Ah, yes, the fitness instructor and the university professor. Complete outsiders.'

'You don't understand.'

'What did you do after the restaurant visits?'

'Hotels.'

'Now we're getting spicy.'

'It wasn't... what you think.' Janine shivered. 'Please. Can I have a drink of—'

'There's your water.' The cold towel slapped off Janine's face. 'Keep going.'

'He didn't want to have sex, not at first. He said he was intimidated by sex. He always had been. He just wanted me to hold him, to lie in our clothes on the covers and for me to wrap my arms around him. That's what I did for the first few times. It was sweet. It was the most intimate thing I'd ever done.'

'You're making me feel sick.'

'We don't have to talk about this.'

'You have to do whatever I tell you to, silly,' she said. 'Are you seriously claiming that Dominic was some kind-hearted, emotional figure whose worst crime was shouting at some idiots in a restaurant?'

'I don't know what you want me to say. He was a complicated man.'

'How long did these little episodes in the hotel rooms last?'

Janine struggled to think. Everything was a slow effort. 'A few months. It became a routine. Workout, a meal, then lie together. I'd hold him. Sometimes, he'd cry.'

'In silence?'

'No, we'd talk. He'd ask about my dreams for the future. I talked about opening my own gym. He was the first person who didn't immediately tell me how difficult that would be. He said he knew I could do it. I had the skills. I had the experience. He even said he'd help me.'

'What else?'

'I don't know... nothing, everything. Our childhoods.'

'What did the poor lost lamb have to say about that?'

'He didn't have a good upbringing,' Janine said.

'That's the first I'm hearing of this.' Cassandra scoffed. 'This man, who seduced me, used me, hit me – yes, you heard that correctly, this weeping self-pitying freak laid his hands on me – had a tough upbringing, did he? He stank of upper-middle-class averageness to me.'

'I think his childhood was why he sometimes wanted me to hold him like he was a baby.'

'Excuse me?'

'If I tell you everything, will you let me go?'

'I've already said I'll let you go. Are you simple in the head? Explain what you just said.'

'He sometimes wanted me to cradle him, rock him. He'd weep. He'd close his eyes and, and sometimes...'

'Go on.'

Janine didn't want to. At the time, with this silver-haired man in her arms, it had felt normal somehow. They had bonded with touch as much as words. She hadn't needed to question him. She'd wanted to save him, to help him save her.

'Sometimes he'd call me "Mummy".'

'You are joking,' Cassandra said.

'He'd call me "Mummy" and ask me to tell him I'd never hurt him.'

'Because of this so-called bad childhood he had?'

'Yes, I think so.'

'Explain that then.'

'It was his mother,' Janine said. 'Look, if Dominic hurt you, if he was different with you than he was with m—'

The cold wet towel slapped off Janine's face.

'Explain.'

'She was overbearing and stole his childhood from him. She made it difficult for him to make friends, because he was her only son; she wanted him all to herself. She'd wanted another baby, but she couldn't have one. All his life, he's lived in the shadow of what his mother did to him. It affected every relationship he ever had. He was terrified of letting people get too close. When they did, he acted out, because it was like he was living his childhood all over again. It was like they were suffocating him.'

'Like his mummy apparently did.'

'That's what he said.'

'What did she do that was so abusive?' Cassandra asked.

'Stopped him making friends, like I said. She would sleep in his bed long after it was appropriate. She would threaten to hurt herself if he wanted to go out and do what normal boys did. And she would tell him things about her own childhood: things no boy should hear.'

'I can't believe this. He's painted himself to be the perfect victim.'

'It's just what he told me.'

'While weeping. In your arms. Pretending to be a baby and calling you "Mummy".' She tutted in disgust. 'What did his mother say then, that was so unappealing to his little vulnerable ears?'

'It's... I can't...'

'Oh, please. It's that bad, is it?'

'She said her parents tied her to a bed... and they did things. She told this to a child. Except, she actually said what they did to her. I don't know if it was true.'

'You believe an abusive man, swallow up anything he tells you, but when it comes to a woman who was most likely just trying to do her best, you immediately brand her a liar?'

'I don't know.'

'I can see that. You don't know a single thing. I have to go, but when I return, you're going to tell me what else dear Dominic told you about his hellish upbringing in an upscale neighbourhood ninety-nine per cent of people in this country, in the world, in fact, would die to have experienced a childhood in. God, he's pathetic.'

'I need the toilet,' Janine said.

'Don't worry. I'll give you something so you won't care about the stickiness in your knickers.'

'Wait.'

Cassandra sighed. 'For what, may I ask?'

'At least tell me how long I've been here.' Her family would be getting worried.

'Do you have any notion? Hazard a guess.'

'A... week? A month?'

Cassandra tittered. 'Your head truly is a monstrous mess. You've been here for two days.'

Two days? The drugs had distorted her mind more than she realised.

'I don't believe you.'

'I don't need you to.'

Cassandra shoved a pill into Janine's mouth, smothered her lips until she swallowed, and left her tied to the bed.

CHAPTER FIFTEEN

ELOISE

There was something surreal about Charlotte standing at Eloise's door. Eloise's family had never been close, evidenced by the fact it had been a month since the accident, four long hellish weeks, and this was the first time any of them had visited. Their father worked as a senior copywriter in advertisements, and their mother ran a successful bakery. Charlotte had been busy with friends and a life of her own when Eloise was little, leaving her to entertain herself in her bedroom, playing dress-up, playing make-believe. These days, Charlotte was on a journey of self-discovery and called Eloise's childhood behaviour "avoidance".

Charlotte, as usual, was dressed for business even if there was no business to be done: sleek pencil skirt, shirt with ruffled texture, a heavy dose of make-up to emphasise her sharp features.

'Sisters hug when they greet each other, don't they?' she said in her usual sarcastic tone.

'I think they might,' Eloise said, then clung to her far more fiercely than she'd planned. 'Please, come in. I'm sorry the place is such a mess.'

Charlotte paused in the entranceway, looking first at the pile of letters on the welcome mat, then at the shattered, blood-spattered mirror.

'Jesus, E. What the hell's all this?'

'I've been busy,' Eloise said defensively.

'Too busy to get rid of this eyesore?'

'Don't,' Eloise said, when Charlotte motioned towards the mirror.

'Why not?'

'This is how it was the night Dominic left. It's... it's just as it was, all right?'

Charlotte looked at her like she was insane. 'All right, E. Fair enough. Why don't we have a coffee and a chat?'

Charlotte took her hand and led her through the dust-covered house. Eloise had spent as much time at the hospital as she possibly could. It was only through her sister's eyes she realised she'd been neglecting everything, including herself. Eloise made coffee, and they sat in the back garden, which was showing signs of overgrowth. Eloise had cancelled their bi-weekly gardening contract; she couldn't face seeing anybody.

'The medical team called you for a meeting to say there was no news?' Charlotte said.

'I think they wanted to tell me to get on with my life. Every time I visit, they get this sad, pitying look on their faces. They don't want me to waste away when it could be months before there's any developments... if there ever are any.'

'Have you thought they might have a point?'

'No,' Eloise said, not sure to whom she was lying: her sister or herself. 'I need to be there for him. It's my duty.'

Charlotte just about resisted rolling her eyes. Any talk of "duty" when it came to the opposite sex made her twitch as though she was resisting the urge to burn her bra. She changed the subject. 'Have you managed to get some work done? How are your books doing?'

'My agent has asked for chapters from the memoir, but I haven't touched it since the accident. It needs work that I can't bring myself to do.'

'Have you been going to your book club?'

'Of course not. I've been busy.'

'What about those unopened letters?'

'Charlotte, please.'

Her sister sighed. 'I'm sorry. We've always been opposites when it comes to a crisis, haven't we? Do you remember when Dad had that cancer scare? I was making lists of everything we had to do in the worst-case scenario. You were upstairs writing a story about a family going on a road trip.'

'I don't know how you remember so much. I never think about that stuff.'

Charlotte smiled tightly; she had the same pitying look as the hospital staff. 'I'm here now. I've taken two weeks' break from work.'

'What? Why?'

'Because you need me. I was never there for you growing u—'

'Not everything is about childhood.'

'My therapist says it takes effort to build the connections other people formed when they were kids. I know you don't want to hear it, but this is our chance to build those connections. I'm going to help you with everything. We're going to make a list. The car. The LPA. Getting you back to some semblance of living in the meantime. Understand? This isn't a request. I'm telling you what's happening. If you had your way, you'd sit at his bedside and pretend the rest of the world didn't exist until you were forced to acknowledge it.'

Eloise felt small under her sister's supportive onslaught. But she had to admit, it was nice to have backup. 'Thank you,' she said. 'Really. I...'

A sudden bout of sickness hit her. Eloise covered her mouth and ran for the downstairs toilet. Charlotte followed as Eloise knelt over the basin and vomited up watery coffee.

'What was that about?' Charlotte asked as Eloise got herself a glass of water. 'Are you ill?'

'No.'

Charlotte laughed dryly. 'You're not pregnant, are you?' Eloise must've made a face; Charlotte seized on it. 'You *are*? Wow, Eloise, that's great news.'

'No, it's not. Dominic doesn't know about it.'

'You had an affair?'

Eloise slammed the glass down. Her hands were shaking; everything was. 'I would never have an affair. I know in this *Eat, Pray, Love* world, nobody takes their vows seriously, but I do. I meant what I said. In sickness and in health. For better and for worse. *Forsaking all others*. I dedicated myself to my man... and he dedicated himself to me.'

Charlotte touched her arm. 'Easy there, Miss Antiquity. You're not making any sense. You didn't have an affair... but Dominic doesn't know you're pregnant? Did you find out after his accident then?'

'No, I knew before the crash.'

'You're not making things any clearer, E.'

Eloise didn't realise how badly she wanted to tell somebody until Charlotte stared at her expectantly. Charlotte was correct about their childhood, though she dwelled on it far more than Eloise did; Eloise had been disconnected, and loneliness had touched each of them in its own special fashion. Could she be right about their adulthood too? Could they build the bonds they had ignored?

That was where the nickname came in, *E*. It was emblematic of their shaky ties. Nothing more specific could be dreamt up, because there was no foundation for it.

'E...' Charlotte touched her arm. 'What is it? You look like you're about to cry.'

Eloise was sick of crying. 'If I tell you, you'll judge me.'

'Screw. That.'

That drew an unexpected laugh.

'I'm serious,' Charlotte went on. 'The only person I'm going to judge is myself for not being here when I should have.'

Eloise interlaced her fingers. She wasn't religious, but it was like she was praying. 'Dominic never wanted a baby. I always did. He was upfront about it. He didn't mislead me. We had some... discussions about it.'

'Arguments, you mean.'

Eloise couldn't confirm this. It was like there was a physical block preventing any negative light distorting her marriage... or revealing it. 'We talked about it often. He was clear; he'd never misled me. He always said he was happy with it just being us. I knew he'd make a great father though. He's so loving.' Most of the time. 'I've seen him with kids too. His friend from university has children, and whenever we visit them, he's great with them. He makes them laugh. He plays games with them. I think he was getting in his own way. Stopping himself from experiencing the happiness he deserved.'

Charlotte waited patiently.

'I treated it as a game. I didn't overthink it. It was simple. A needle. A few holes.'

'You pricked his condoms, E?'

'It was the only way it would ever happen. Condoms fail all the time. He'd never know our baby was conceived by a lie. When the baby came, he would've been... he *will* be happy,' she corrected. 'I know he will. All that talk about not wanting a family will fade. The baby will make everything better. What's the point of this big house and all these cars and all this money if we can't bring a happy, smiling little life into the world?'

'This is a lot to process.'

'It doesn't have to be a big deal.'

'It's not normal. You understand that, don't you?'

'You don't need to speak to me like I'm a child.'

'You know it's not normal, right, E?' Charlotte pressed.

'I know I crossed a line. But I don't care about normal. I don't see why I should have to go without a family just because...'

'Just because your husband doesn't want one. You need to finish that sentence. If your husband doesn't want kids, you leave him, find a man who does.'

'Didn't you hear me before? I took our marriage vows seriously.'

'Why?'

'I don't understand the question.'

Charlotte glared at her. 'Why are you so obsessed with marriage vows? People get divorced all the time.'

'I want my life to be... to be something.'

'To be perfect. That was what you were going to say. You want a perfect life just like you were a perfect model, just like you've been perfect ever since we were kids.'

'Not everything is about our childhood,' Eloise said, angrier this time.

Charlotte folded her arms. 'There's nothing perfect about tricking your husband into impregnating you.'

'I never should've said anything.'

'You're probably right, but it's too late now. Let me tell you this, E. Nobody else learns the truth, not Victoria, not your friends, nobody. We're family. I'm still going to help you. But I can't condone what you did. It's sick. I need to make that clear. It's sick and wrong.'

'We'll have to agree to disagree.'

Charlotte groaned, massaging her forehead, then changed the subject.

'Have you gone through his things? His laptop? His emails? Tried to figure out who he was on the phone to or why he broke the hallway mirror?'

'I've been at his bedside almost all day every single day. I haven't had time for any of that.'

'Don't get defensive,' Charlotte said. 'I'm here to help, remember? Even after what you told me, I'm not leaving you, E. That has to mean something.'

Charlotte spoke desperately as if she was trying to convince herself they could form a meaningful sisterly connection this late in their lives.

'I want to see a copy of this LPA. Can you ring Victoria and look into that? We'll ring the insurance company today.'

'Why do you seem so keen about this?' Eloise said.

'It's the right thing to do.' Charlotte looked away.

'Now you're hiding something.'

'Insurance companies are notoriously reluctant to pay out.'

'Wow,' Eloise said sarcastically. 'That is a shocking statement.'

'Don't give me that. I'm not the one stealing men's sperm.'

They locked eyes. Charlotte smiled first. Then Eloise grinned, and soon, they were both laughing. It had an illicit edge to it, like they knew it was wrong, but it felt good to release some tension. But any mirth faded almost instantly.

'Police resources are stretched thin,' Charlotte said. 'They may not have had the time or inclination to thoroughly examine the vehicle, especially in a simple drink-driving case. But an insurance agent will. It might lead to more information.'

'What sort of information?'

'Hopefully, I'm wrong. I just have to make sure.'

'Wrong about what?'

'About whether or not this was really an accident.'

Eloise didn't understand. 'Why would you even say that?'

'Do my job long enough, you learn things are never as simple as they seem.'

CHAPTER SIXTEEN

DOMINIC

After that scary night where Mother had said that awful thing about Father, about getting rid of him, she went back to her usual self. For six months, she didn't climb into Dom's bed stinking of wine, and she even let him go around his friend's house after school. He'd met Seb in the library; they would sit in his bedroom and read books and sometimes they'd go outside and ride their bikes. It felt nice to have somebody, especially since Father's job ended up taking him away from home more often than he'd anticipated.

When Father returned from work, sometimes he'd stay for days at a time. These were always the happiest points in Dom's life. He'd wait eagerly at the front window, giddy with excitement, knowing his father's car would arrive any minute. The world actually looked brighter. Even if it was a grey day, the sun seemed to press through the sky with more stubbornness.

'Anybody would think you don't love me,' Mother said, sitting in her armchair, knitting.

Dom wasn't sure how to reply, so he said nothing.

'Anybody would think, if you walked in on me choking to

death, my eyes bulging, froth coming from my mouth, you'd just look at me coldly and ask, "Mummy, when is Daddy coming home"? Except you don't call me "Mummy". You call me "Mother" to try and make me feel like an old woman.'

Dom blinked, annoyed by the tears. She could make him cry just by speaking, which was very wrong. He also felt bad for her. A few months previously, he probably would have left his perch on the window and gone to her. But being around Seb's house, he'd had a glimpse into what regular family dynamics were like. They were nothing like his.

There was no use pointing out the fact that Mother had told him not to call her "Mummy" several times.

Soon, Father was home. Mother sprung from her chair and threw her arms around him. 'I've been waiting desperately to see you...' She kissed him in that gross way, all tongues, making smooching, fleshy noises that made Dom uncomfortable. He wanted to say hello to his father, but Mother kept kissing like she was never going to stop.

'Easy,' he said, laughing. 'Don't forget about the little one.'

Mother rolled her eyes.

'Come here, lad.'

Dom ran into his father's arms and hugged him tightly.

'I've got you a present.' Father reached into the bag he'd dropped when he entered. He brought out a set of boxing gloves and some big pads; they looked like they were made for hitting. 'What say we have a go with them?'

'Boxing?' Mother said. 'Since when did our Dom Dom become a fighter?'

'It's never too late to find out you're stronger than you thought.'

'How profound.'

'Let's have a go, Dom,' Father said. 'It's warm out there. We'll do it in the garden. Do you want to?' Dom wasn't particularly interested in hitting anybody or anything, but he would've agreed to walk across hot coals to keep that smile on his father's face.

'That sounds really cool, Dad.'

Mother flinched at the D-word like Dom had just sworn. 'I suppose I'll get dinner started then. Let the brutes beat each other to a pulp in the garden.'

Father shook his head, clenched his jaw. Then his smile returned. 'Come on.' He playfully ruffled Dom's hair.

They went into the garden. Father helped Dom to get the boxing gloves on, then he put the focus mitts on his hands. Father's new job had made him an even better dad, Dom felt, because he gave Dom so much attention every time he came home. It was like Dom was his entire world; that was why his return always meant so much. Before, he'd worked as a manager in an office. He always said "manager" with a tired expression, as though he was boring himself. He said "PRODUCT CONSULTANT" with capital letters, smiling as he said it, inviting question. All Dom knew was before, he sat in grey rooms all day. Now, he travelled around, spoke to people. It brought out the best in him.

'We'll start with your stance. You want your feet to be like this.' Father demonstrated. 'That's it, that's perfect.'

Dom stood as his father instructed, savouring the word "perfect".

'Now we'll start with the jab. Flick your left hand out like this.' Dom pushed his hand out. Father frowned. 'More like this. Yeah... that'll do. Let's work on that for a bit.'

They moved around the garden, Dom flicking his hand at Father's pad. Every time Dom punched, Father would move the pad forward, slapping it against Dom's gloves. It hurt Dom's knuckles. Almost immediately, he wanted to stop, but he couldn't let Father down. He kept hitting.

'That's it.' *Whack.* 'Again.' *Whack.* It was like Father was the one hitting Dom's gloves, not the other way around.

'Add a right hand into it.'

Dom tried; Father laughed with a mocking edge, sounding like the kids at school who made fun of him and Seb for sitting in the library every chance they got. 'Not like that.' Father laughed again. 'Don't throw it like a ball. Like this, look. Turn your body. The power comes from your legs and core. No, turn, rotate.'

'But I'm facing the wrong way now.'

'Rotate without facing the wrong way then, Dom. Come on. Get your head in the game.'

His father's grin was wide, his eyes manic. Was he bullying his own son? Was he as bad as Mother had implied so many times? He much preferred when Father came home and sat on the porch and watched Dom ride his bike, or when they went to the cinema, or even just for a walk. This was different; Father suddenly expected things of him.

'Better,' Father said. 'But keep your hands up.'

Father hit him in the face.

Dom stumbled back, gasping, tears springing to his eyes. 'Duh-Daddy,' he whimpered. 'You hut-hit me...'

'It was a tap,' Father said, sounding confused. 'You need to keep your hands up when you're boxing, Dom. It's the whole point.'

'Please don't hit me.'

'I didn't *hit* you. What are you talking about? You think I'd hit my own son? I literally just tapped you on the chin. Like this.' Father gently prodded himself with the focus mitt. 'This is supposed to be fun. Let's get back to it.'

Dom did his best, but Father kept thwacking the gloves with the focus mitt. Dom's knuckles ached. His vision blurred with tears, but Father either didn't realise or didn't care.

'What did I say about those hands?' Father laughed, slapping Dom across the face.

Dom stumbled back, slumping down on the grass and bursting into tears. His cheek stung. His hands throbbed. 'Stop hitting me.'

Father tore off the focus mitts. 'I wasn't hitting you, lad. Christ. Are you crying? Chin up. I was trying to teach you proper boxing form, that's all.'

'You kept hitting me.'

'Will you stop bloody whining?'

This just made it even worse. Dom's tears came in horrible waves, his belly cramping with each sob. Father grabbed Dom's arm and tried to haul him to his feet. Dom's arm ached like Father was trying to pull it from the socket.

'Ow, Daddy!' Dom yelled.

'Joseph!' Mother stormed into the garden. 'What are you doing to our boy?'

'I was teaching him boxing and then he started to cry like I'm some sort of monster. Now he won't get up. Look at him.'

'Maybe he doesn't want to be a fighter.'

'I'm not saying he has to be a fighter, but Christ, all I did was tap him in the face a couple of times.'

'You hit him,' Mother said coldly.

'No, I didn't hit him. In boxing, you need to keep your hands up, cover your chin, so when he dropped his hands, I gave him a tap... like this.' Father touched his own face again, but it seemed far lighter than when the focus mitt had slapped off Dom's cheek.

'You assaulted your own child,' Mother said.

'How dare you say that, Vicky. We're supposed to be a team. You know I'd never hit my own son.'

Mother knelt in front of Dom, gently putting her hand on his shoulder. 'Dom, I need you to be honest with me now. Did your father strike you in the face, or did he lightly tap you, to teach you boxing, like he claims?'

'Vicky, stop messing with his head.'

'I am not messing with his head!' Mother exclaimed. 'I'm trying to understand exactly what happened here. Frankly, your desire to stop me from getting the full facts of the situation is suspicious.'

'The "full facts of the situation"?' Father's voice got louder. 'Don't start speaking in those terms. Don't make this into something it's not.'

'You assaulted your son.'

Dom couldn't take it anymore. He ducked past his mother and ran for the house, tears streaming down his face. He always felt like he was being pulled apart whenever they got like this. There were two boys inside of him: the tough one, the one who wanted to rise to his father's idea of who he should be. And then there was the comfortable one, the boy who sought the warmth of his mother's embrace, who enjoyed the way her breath tickled down his neck when she held him at night and told him he didn't have to go to school the next day if he didn't want to.

On some level, he knew there was some wrongness in both – perhaps one more than the other – but he was in no way equipped to parse this. He retreated into his bedroom and climbed under the covers, pressing his face against the pillow and letting the sadness take him.

The door flew open a moment later. 'Oh, my baby, my sweet boy.' Mother clawed at the sheets. 'You have to tell me. Did he do it? Did he hit you? Did he go too far?'

She stripped the sheets away, gripped his face. Her hands felt like talons. Her voice was low and borderline hysterical.

'This is it,' she said. 'Dom Dom, my angel. This is our chance to do what we should've done a long time ago: get rid of the evil man. Why would he do this to you? What else is he going to do if we let him stay? We can finally take action... together. All you have to say is, "Yes, Mummy. Daddy hit me". That's all you have to say.'

She wouldn't let him turn away, forcing his gaze to stay on hers. Downstairs, Father was going berserk. Plates were smashing. A loud wooden *crack* sounded like he'd torn one of the cupboards from the wall and was beating it into shrapnel.

'You have to be strong now,' she said. 'You have to say it. Just say it, Dom Dom. Please. Just say, "He hit me". Just say, "He's hit me before". You can do it.'

'Please.' Dom whimpered. 'I just want to sleep, Mummy. Please.'

Slowly, she let him go. Her eyes refocused as though she was waking from a dream. She stumbled away from him. 'Fine. Sleep. I'm sorry. You...' She made a croaking noise that instantly filled Dom with guilt. 'You deserve so much better than us.'

A MOTHER'S MUSINGS: HOW FAR WILL A MOTHER GO?

23/10/24

Victoria Hawthorne

When I was a younger woman, I had a friend who was a philosophy student. I was studying art. We'd often sit in her attic flat, cigarette smoke swirling in the air (if you need help quitting smoking, click this link; I mention the smoke for colour, not to glamorise). She once asked me, 'If you ever become a mother, how far would you go for your child?' Even then, when motherhood seemed like a distant dream, the answer was clear to me.

'I would do anything,' I told her. She smiled in this slightly patronising way. She argued that I couldn't possibly know that. There were plenty of cases, according to her, of mothers becoming crippled with fear and inaction when the time to rise to the challenge came. 'For example, if your baby fell into a pool of shark-infested waters...' I told her what you all would, my dear readers. I would jump into the pool. I wouldn't care if they bit me, tore at me. In fact, I'd prefer it, because it would mean they'd be distracted from my child. She sneered. 'You can't know that until the time comes.' (As you have probably guessed, this insufferable lady and I have not remained friends.)

I share these morbid thoughts because I am reaching the point where my maternal drive to do the right thing will be put to the test. I pray I will not be forced to make the decision I fear I might (and I apologise for the vagueness), but life often doesn't give us mama bears a choice. My posts have become rambling of late, so I'm so grateful to you all for sticking with me. I'm so grateful to know that, out there, you're rooting for me and my Dom Dom.

Please, give me your luck, your prayers, your goodwill. Give me everything you can spare. I'm going to need it.

Please remember to use promo code *MMusingsVictoria* to receive 10% off baby products at my sponsored shop, <u>All Care Wear.</u>

As always, thank you for reading.

CHAPTER SEVENTEEN

JANINE

'You can do it,' Dad said, grinning at her from across the garage, the air thick with summer and sweat and the smell of metal from the weight plates. *'Just a few more reps. Then I'll take you to that all-you-can-eat buffet. I don't want to hear any nonsense about feeling bad for enjoying the meal, all right? But just in case, I'll make sure to eat like a proper pig to make you feel better.'*

Janine rose to her feet, her body aching. With her dad's support, she knew she'd be able to complete the last set. His eyes were bright and alert with pride. She loved when he looked at her like that—

A wet towel slapped off her face. 'Wakey, wakey. You sure do enjoy your sleep, don't you, dear?'

A moan of animal pain escaped Janine. The agony in her wrist had returned. Or perhaps it had never gone anywhere, simply slipped under the haze of drugs. It had only been... *days* since this lunatic had dragged her down there.

'Enough of that,' Cassandra said. Something sharp punctured Janine's arm, then warmth flooded into her.

Suddenly, the pain was... not gone, but distant, a throbbing she was able to ignore. She peeled her eyes open and saw Cassandra's shadow on the ceiling from where the blinding light shone.

'We were talking about Dominic, remember? About him and his mummy... and no, Janine, I'm not talking about you. I was laughing thinking about that earlier. He made you hold him and called you "Mummy"! That's just the most ridiculous, pathetic thing I've ever heard.'

Janine whispered, 'Water, please.'

'Oh, shut up. Here's your water.'

This time, when Cassandra struck her with the wet towel, Janine was ashamed by how she sucked in sharply, trying to draw a few droplets into her dry mouth.

'I'll make a deal with you, you silly thing. Tell me everything that Dominic told you about his mother. Think hard. Don't leave anything out. If you do that, I'll find a way to let you go.'

Janine had no reason to believe this madwoman; she didn't have any other options either.

'She was determined to get rid of his dad,' Janine croaked. 'She wanted him all to herself. She often said that she wished she'd used a sperm donor instead of getting married and having a kid the "inconvenient way". Once, she tried to encourage Dominic to lie about his dad hitting him.'

'Lie?' Cassandra asked coldly.

'Dominic lived for the times when his dad would come home from his work trips. They were the most exciting parts of his childhood. His dad bought him some boxing gloves, and they were practising in the garden. He was trying to keep his guard up. If he let it drop, his dad would touch his chin to remind him.'

'"Touch his chin".' If Janine hadn't been so drugged, she might've paid more attention to the murderous shiver in

Cassandra's voice. 'That's an interesting way to phrase striking one's son.'

'It wasn't like that. I've done some boxing. A coach will often give their athlete a little nudge in the face to remind them to keep their hands up. It's better to forget in the gym and be reminded, than forget in the ring or on the street.'

'Of course, a big, butch, grotesque thing like you has done some boxing. God, you're ugly and gross.'

'I'm just telling you what you want to know,' Janine said.

'A mother saw her husband strike her son and tried to help him. What an evil woman.'

'Dominic said he didn't have the emotional maturity to make sense of it at the time, but after, he hated his mother for doing that. He hated how she kept bringing it up, trying to get him to turn against his dad. She wanted to force him to testify that his dad was abusive so that she could get full custody.'

'You only got his side of the story. You can't possibly know if any of it was true.'

'I believed him,' Janine said. 'He's a successful man. He's done so much with his life, made millions in hotels, become a professor. But when it came to his childhood, he was broken. Maybe you didn't see that side of him.'

'Or maybe dear Dominic is very skilled at only showing the side of himself he wants people to see.'

Janine wanted to beg for water again; she wanted to wring Cassandra's neck. There was so much she would've done if she wasn't spreadeagled on this bed, drugs pumping numbness through her body. She hated the slur in her own voice.

'What else did this paragon of honesty and virtue say?'

'Why do you care?' Janine whispered. 'Cassandra, if Dominic hit you... if he beat you—'

'Oh, Christ,' she interrupted. 'You truly are a dumb slut.

Cassandra. Please don't tell me you believed, even for a moment, that my name was Cassandra. Please don't tell me you haven't worked it out. I'm Victoria, you ignorant pig. I'm his mother.'

CHAPTER EIGHTEEN

VICTORIA

Victoria sat at her desk, reading the reply from Patrick Dixon, the man who'd discovered her son's body. He'd found her through her motherhood blog and reached out, asking if there was anything he could do to help.

Victoria had written him: *Patrick, that is ever so kind of you, and "thanks" seems like a paltry word for what you did. I wonder if you would care to meet for a coffee and a chat? If you'd spare an old lady a little oversharing, I don't have as many friends in the south-west as I do back home.*

This was true, but only because Victoria had so many friends and connections back home in Oxfordshire. Through her work in the local mums' groups, the rehab facilities, and her volunteering at the library, Victoria was a well-loved and well-respected figure even in Weston-super-Mare. Patrick's reply offered any time after five o'clock. Victoria wrote, *How about today?* His reply came almost instantly, *Sounds like a plan.*

She was curious to meet this saviour, this knight in shining armour, this man who had bravely plucked her son from the metallic prison of the ruined car and forced upon him some mimicry of living. Sipping her coffee, she tried to focus on her blog. Sometimes, words poured like blood from a wound that refused to stop bleeding; other times, like the present, she had to search for them like contaminants in the same wound.

Her phone rang. It was Eloise. Victoria frowned. Eloise was a glamorous, emotional, beautiful young woman. The only negative Victoria had been able to conjure about her daughter-in-law, before Dominic's coma, was her lack of a baby. Now there was tension between them where there had never been.

'Hello?'

'Yes, hello, Vicky?'

This wasn't Eloise. The voice was harsher, far more confident. She sounded like some of the artists Victoria had dealt with in her previous life as an art dealer. 'Excuse me, but who am I speaking with?'

'Right, sorry,' the woman said. 'I'm Charlotte, Eloise's sister. As you can probably understand, she's really going through it right now. I heard you had a bit of a to-do at the hospital?'

'I'm not sure what you've heard, but my daughter-in-law and I had a discussion, nothing more.'

'I heard it got a little heated.'

'That's not my perception of it.'

'In any case,' Charlotte said, 'Eloise doesn't feel up to meeting at the minute…'

That wasn't good. Victoria couldn't risk people learning about some perceived rift between her and her daughter-in-law. She put Charlotte on loudspeaker and clicked onto the analytics page on her blog. Her numbers had been soaring since Dominic's crash. Every metric was up: impressions on social media, clicks, time spent on the page, affiliate code usages, even reads on her backlist of older posts.

If people learnt that Victoria and Eloise were at odds, it would affect her reputation as the mama bear she had always been. It wasn't Victoria's fault Eloise refused to even entertain the notion of doing what was best for her husband.

'Hello?' Charlotte said.

'I'm here.'

'I thought I lost you.'

'No.'

'Right,' Charlotte said. 'I wanted to ask if I could see a copy of the legal power of attorney documents?'

Victoria ground her teeth. Eloise never would've begun poking around like this. She was far too placid, far too manageable.

'May I ask why?'

'I'm a solicitor,' Charlotte said. 'It saves Eloise the time of hiring somebody. And, if we keep it in the family, there's no need for any unpleasantness.'

'What sort of unpleasantness?'

'Making official requests – or you can call them demands.'

'Demands?'

Charlotte sounded smug. 'I'd just like to see the documents. It's a reasonable request, don't you think?'

If Victoria Hawthorne was anything, it was adaptable. She'd proved that every day since she was a young girl, when the demons called Mother and Father had done indescribably inhumane things to her for the pure thrill of causing agony.

'Of course, I have no problem providing the documents,' she said.

'Great. I could swing by now?'

'I'm busy for the rest of the day.'

'Tomorrow morning, then?'

'Yes. Fine. Shall we meet in town? There's a café on the seafront with wonderful views.'

Charlotte laughed in a belittling manner. 'The only thing

I'm interested in viewing are the LPA documents, but whatever floats your boat.'

'I'll text you the address,' Victoria said. 'Or, rather, Eloise's phone, which you seem to have commandeered.'

'Commandeered,' Charlotte said sarcastically. 'You have a wonderful vocabulary.'

'Thank you.' Victoria ignored the sarcasm. 'I'll see you tomorrow.'

After the phone call ended, Victoria switched off her computer. There was no chance she was going to produce any words after a conversation like that. Charlotte was implying – through her tone, through her little digging comments – that Victoria had obtained the LPA for nefarious means. It was a disgusting implication.

She sighed, deciding she would make herself a coffee and attempt to do some reading before the meeting with Patrick. Being in this house had once felt comfortable, serene. She'd felt like she was precisely where she belonged. Her son was close... but not too close as to make people whisper about the stifling old crone who, two decades since her son had fled the nest, couldn't let go.

Another sigh, then she decided to go down into the cellar. She couldn't keep putting this off; it had been too long already. But the truth was – and she hated admitting this even in the privacy of her thoughts – she was terrified. Not just of what was down there, but of what was inside herself. Of who she was. There had been times in her life when drastic action was required, but that was with a purpose. And yes, fine, this *had* had a purpose too... but had she enjoyed it? On some level? It was a terrifying question.

She didn't want to walk over to the industrial freezer and open it, but she couldn't keep going on like this. She had to take action. Her hand trembled as she reached for the handle.

She couldn't open it. She shivered all over as she tried to make herself do it. She stared at the accusatory wine-like stain on the floor, the implication being that blood had been shed. But no... had it? Victoria's head hurt.

She spun and fled the freezer. Her heart was pounding hard in her chest. There was just something wrong about it, the fleshiness, the cold deadness, the familiarity the corpse had with her Dom Dom. She didn't want to face it. Not yet.

Getting Janine into the cellar had been difficult enough. She had been able to stumble towards Victoria's car at the wreckage site. But then she had passed out during the drive.

Victoria had to admit it: she had got carried away. She hadn't enjoyed it, had she? She wasn't a monster... was she?

It had been necessary. Just like she always did, Victoria had summoned the mama bear in her tough sinewy heart and bared her teeth at the chaos of the world. If Victoria's beautiful but misguided son had told his mistress their secret, she needed to know.

CHAPTER NINETEEN

JANINE

'Your name's not Cassandra,' Janine said sluggishly, trying to process the news.

Cassandra – no, Victoria – nodded mockingly. 'Uh-huh.'

Janine's senses were too dulled to react properly. This woman was Dominic's mother; she had been lying this entire time. 'It doesn't matter.'

'It doesn't matter that I tricked you? That you fell for an obvious lie? Don't you see...' Victoria began to trail something cold and sharp up Janine's naked belly. 'Don't you understand? I have to know the truth. I have to understand what was going through his head. He's always been troubled, confused; he's always needed a maternal hand to guide him. You have to tell me... what else has he said about me?'

'If you're his mum, you know what happened between the two of you far better than me.'

'Life isn't about what happened; it's about what people believe happened. I learnt that the moment I told a family member about what my parents were doing and she told me I must be confused.'

Was she trying to provoke pity? They were past that.

125

'There's something,' Victoria went on. 'I can see it on your piggy face. There's something you don't want to tell me.'

She was right. It would make Victoria angrier, which was the last thing she needed when the psychotic mother bear was trailing her cold claw up Janine's midriff, between her breasts, to her neck. The icy point of the knife stroked with sick softness across her throat.

'I truly don't want to go any further with you,' Victoria said. 'I can let you go, Janine. I'll take you someplace far from here, drop you off, make sure I'm not seen. You'll have the good sense not to go to the police. Or, if you do go to the police, it will be difficult for you to prove what happened. I'm a far better actress than you, I'm certain of that. So, tell me.' When Janine hesitated, Victoria added pressure with the blade. 'Tell me.'

Janine didn't want to. She tried to think of a lie: an invented confession she could share with her lover's mum. But her mind was working too slowly.

'He...' She began to cry, hating the weakness. 'He told me what you did. When you didn't get your way... he told me the lines you crossed.'

'Be specific, dear.'

'It started with climbing into his bed, sleeping with him. But then you got drunker. Your desires got sicker. If he told you he didn't want you in his bed, you got angry. You had a crate that some heavy furniture had been delivered in. It was too small for him.'

'What on earth are you talking about?'

'You made him get inside. You hammered it shut. You kept him in there an entire day, taunting him, belittling him. *Torturing* him. Your own son.'

'No, no, no. He didn't say that. Did he? Dom didn't really say *that*?'

'I held him. He cried. He said he'd never talked about it

before. It was why he'd always felt so trapped. He said you got a twisted thrill out of it. After, you always apologised, but you couldn't keep the smile off your face. And the more you drank, the easier it was for you to find reasons to put him in the box.'

'I would never.' Victoria sounded outraged; Janine almost believed her. But Dom had sounded so genuinely convincing, and she had instantly believed him, too. 'You can't be remembering that correctly. You must be mistaken. I've always done my best for my baby boy, always. I can't believe he said that. He didn't *say* that, because I didn't *do* that...'

Victoria stumbled away, the knife clattering to the floor. She sat with a heavy thumping noise.

'Think hard, Janine. Did he really say that?'

'Yes,' Janine whispered. 'He was crying. He was drunk.'

'He was drunk?' Victoria seized on it. 'There you go then. He didn't know what he was saying. Or he was making up stories because of all the attention you were giving him. It's simple. I can't believe he would even think such a thing, let alone say it. I... I need time to think. It's time for you to sleep again.'

'No.' Janine managed to wriggle against the bindings. Small, impotent movements, but they took an absurd effort. 'Please. I need something to drink. Please.'

'Just for a little while,' Victoria said. 'Don't worry. In your dreams you won't suffer.'

The whole bed trembled. Her eyes bulged. She saw her dad in the garage, smiling at her, telling her she could do it, telling her she could do anything.

'No, Janine, no,' Victoria yelled someplace far away. 'This wasn't supposed to happen. Stay with me, girl. Let's get you on your side. That's it. You're going to be okay. Can you hear me? Stay with me. Please stay with me. I meant what I said. Oh, God. I meant it; I was going to let you go.'

CHAPTER TWENTY

VICTORIA

Victoria sat on the bottom cellar step, staring at the industrial freezer. The low hum almost sounded like Janine's groans of pain.

Time had been something Victoria had stolen from the poor woman. Janine had only been in the cellar for three days, but Victoria had drugged her so severely, the tragic figure had lost all idea of hours and minutes and days and weeks and months.

Victoria hadn't intended on killing her. She'd wanted to discover how much Janine knew: what Dominic had told her, the truth and the lies. When Janine had spewed that nonsense – and it was nonsense, warped and wicked deceit – about Victoria locking him in the box, Victoria had just wanted her to sleep. That was all.

She'd given her too many drugs. Victoria couldn't vouch for their cleanliness. She'd acquired them through one of the fallen souls who frequented the rehab meetings, hanging around outside with a hungry look in their eyes, waiting to prey on those who were attempting to drag themselves out of the pit. She'd spun a story about having a friend who was coming down from drugs and had become suicidal. This was a last resort.

Victoria had cried, begged for help. Of course, the dealer was more than happy to provide it.

'I'm truly sorry,' Victoria whispered. 'I promise, I didn't mean for that to happen. But my son lied to you. I never did anything so absurd and sadistic as *that*. I won't say I was a perfect mother. Who is? To say something like that, though... Don't you see how wrong that is? Don't you see how sick that is?'

She went upstairs and stripped naked, taking a cold shower, closing her eyes and breathing slow when a panic attack threatened. She had to keep her head; she had to work up the courage to get rid of the body. She knew she had that in her, but she was procrastinating. Guilt was a painful demotivator. She found it difficult to even think about the... the *thing* in her cellar. There was something terrifying about handling Janine's corpse.

She'd been able to handle her confused and disoriented body easily enough though. At least, spiritually, emotionally. The physicality of it had caused her muscles to burn despite her unusual and impressive fitness. She had tweaked two muscles, and her spine had protested loudly. She was almost seventy. Fit for her age, yes, but time was a monster whose teeth nobody could avoid forever. Her religious commitment to the gym, not to mention her near perfect diet, had made it just about possible.

Victoria had told herself every step of the way she was going to let the girl go. She'd meant it. When she learned how much Janine knew, she would release her. Hence the lie about Cassandra: a lie which she'd given up because... because she'd enjoyed the look on Janine's piggish face? No – she didn't want to think like that.

She had some fire in her, it was true, but to touch the cold dead flesh of the woman who had given her son hope, the woman he'd made love to and lied to was wrong somehow.

Facing it meant facing herself. She could ignore it down there; nobody was looking for or cared about it. *It*. That's what it was, what it had to be.

If she was going to make it through the next few months intact, she had to be strong. That was what a mama bear did.

After her shower, she decided it was time to watch the footage from the pet camera. If she couldn't face *it*, she could at least do this. She'd set up the camera in the cellar while Janine had been alive. Victoria hadn't got rid of it yet. She needed to smash it into tiny pieces, eradicate it completely, just like the memory of what she'd done.

She grabbed it from the corner of the cellar, wiping away dust. She took the webcam to her computer, plugged in the USB, and double-clicked the file. The memory of the wine stain was irking her.

Janine had overdosed, hadn't she? A bloodless accident. Victoria's mind was blurry. She stared wide-eyed at the video, terrified of turning up the audio, but also terrified of not knowing the truth.

'You have nothing to say?' Victoria sounded psychotic... it was like watching somebody else. 'It seems to me you've seriously hurt yourself, probably not feeling the full effect of your self-inflicted injuries because of the drugs with which I have mercifully gifted you...

'It's time for you to sleep again,' she said, holding a knife up, the *knife*, like she was admiring it as it gleamed in the light. 'Just for a little while. Don't worry. In your dreams you won't suffer.'

Victoria stabbed Janine in the side. 'No, Janine, no,' she went on in a calm voice, stabbing her again. 'This wasn't supposed to happen. Stay with me, girl. Let's get you on your side. That's it.' She stabbed her again. 'You're going to be okay. Can you hear me?' Again. 'Please stay with me...'

Victoria quickly clicked off the video, deleted it, then took the camera into the garage and obliterated it with a hammer. At the same time, she obliterated the memory from her mind. She couldn't dwell on these– what to call them? – slips, blips, hiccoughs. She had work to do. But when she began to get dressed for her meeting with Patrick, she collapsed onto her bed and broke down in tears of guilt and confusion.

See? She wasn't evil. A monster wouldn't cry; a monster wouldn't care. This was proof she was a good person who had been forced, through no fault of her own, into a bad situation.

She met Patrick in a pub just off the seafront. It was a depressing place; it fit his physical appearance. He was lean, hollow-eyed, with that *woe is me* demeanour that was so common to her countrymen. When she entered, he rushed to his feet, approached her. He had shaving foam clinging to the spot just under his ear. It seemed somehow offensive.

'Victoria?' he said.

'You can call me Vicky.'

'I'm so sorry,' he replied. 'About your son. About everything. Would you like a drink?'

'I wouldn't say no to a white wine.'

They sat in the corner near a piano that had seen better days. As Victoria sipped the cheap wine, Patrick began to tear apart a paper coaster, apparently without realising what he was doing.

'I can't stop thinking about it,' he said. 'How he looked in the car. All mangled up. I've never seen anything like that. It's not what you expect to find on your drive home. I thought I was dreaming at first.'

'Dreaming?'

'Fourteen-hour shifts will do that.'

'What do you do, Patrick?'

'I work in a warehouse.'

He said this with a degree of pride that seemed odd to Victoria.

'Excellent,' Victoria said.

'I'm going to be made manager soon,' he replied.

'Fantastic.'

'Anyway.' His mood darkened. 'The lights cut across the road, then I saw him. It was awful. It looked like he was part of the car, know what I mean? Like he'd grown out of it. I'm sorry. You don't need to hear this.'

'You don't have to apologise. In fact, it's a relief to hear somebody speak so frankly. Everybody tiptoes around the issue. So, you've read my blog?'

He smiled with an air of embarrassment. 'Yeah, I've read pretty much every entry. It seems you and Dominic had a great relationship.'

'The best a mother could ask for.'

'I'm jealous, I've got to admit.' He had a hangdog expression. 'Me and my mum weren't close.'

Cogs began to turn in Victoria's mind. She slid her hand across the table and touched Patrick's hand. 'That sounds awful. Would you like to tell me why?'

He looked down at her wrinkled hand upon his. She wasn't *old* old; she took care of herself, exercised, dieted, wore stylish clothes and shielded herself in well-applied layers of make-up. But some men Patrick's age would've sneered at the contact. Not him. He looked grateful for it. She sensed that he was a very lonely person.

'Careful... you might give me ideas.'

She tutted. 'Patrick, how old are you?'

'Thirty-three. Why?'

'I won't tell you how old I am.'

'I don't care how old you are.'

'You will when I drop the bombshell. Brace yourself. I'm sixty-eight.'

He shook his head. 'Nope, still don't care.' Neither of them remarked upon how utterly bizarre this was; perhaps this natural intimacy was what true relationships were made of.

'Don't change the subject,' she said, giving his hand a squeeze. 'You were going to tell me about your mum.'

'Are you sure you want to hear this?'

'Certain,' she said, meaning it.

As he spoke to her about his alcoholic mother, Victoria thought about how useful it was to have a desperate, resentful man looking at her as if waiting for his chance to claim a kiss. She wasn't sure what his purpose would be – or if he would even have one – but she knew better than to turn down an asset. Perhaps she might weaponize him against Charlotte in some inventive manner. Or perhaps – Victoria allowed herself to think this only guiltily and quietly – a kiss from a young, desperate man would have value all on its own.

With so much pain in her life, would it make her a bad person to seek some pleasure?

CHAPTER TWENTY-ONE

CHARLOTTE

'Please don't argue with her,' Eloise said.
Charlotte had to suppress a lot when Eloise spoke in that tone. Her sister had always been more submissive, less forthright, and her husband's accident had highlighted these traits: perhaps even made them worse.

'I'm not going to argue with her, E. I just want to make sure everything is on the up and up with the LPA. Our first job is to make sure she actually has legal power of attorney.'

Eloise frowned. 'Are you saying you think she lied?'

'I'm not saying anything yet. That's why I want to see the document. Relax, E. I've got this.'

Charlotte left their large, frankly gorgeous home, pausing in the hallway to study herself in the shattered mirror. She hoped the rest of the world didn't see the desperation she was certain clung to her every expression. She'd spent her entire adult life living for herself: work, cheap encounters with men, parties when she had the time, and far, far too much alcohol.

Eloise had categorised her new-found desire for family connection as an *Eat, Pray, Love* journey. She'd intended it as an insult, but Charlotte had devoured the bestseller. She didn't find anything insulting about the idea of reinventing oneself. In fact, she thought it was brave to try and form a sisterly connection where, previously, they'd had none.

Fine, it may have felt forced, but nothing worth doing was easy. The brutal fact was, Mum and Dad were narcissists who stubbornly fixated on their own worlds and refused to look at anything else. Self-reflection had led Charlotte to the depressing conclusion that she had developed narcissistic traits too. But it was never too late to change.

The café sat on a small pier and had big windows that showed the beach and the horizon. The day was clear, giving views of the Viking islands of Steep Holm and Flat Holm, with Cardiff beyond. Victoria was a stylish woman. When she rose from her seat, Charlotte had the feeling that she was happy to see her despite the circumstances. It was disarming.

'Charlotte, I presume?' the older woman said. Older, yes, but lean and fit. Charlotte struggled to believe she was almost seventy; she could've passed for fifty.

'Victoria?'

'I knew it was you. You look ever so much like Eloise.'

'Nobody's ever said that before.' Charlotte realised she was smiling. She enjoyed the compliment; being compared to her model sister was flattering. 'Would you like a drink?'

'I've already got one, but can I get you something?'

'It's fine. I'll get my own then meet you at the table.'

'I just hope you can forgive my impatience.'

This woman spoke posh. Eloise had the same way of speaking, to some degree. When asked, Charlotte described herself as middle-upper class to take some of the sting out of it, but the somewhat embarrassing fact was they'd been raised in an upper-class home. Charlotte had lost some of that through the down-and-dirty dealings as a solicitor, the quick liaisons with rough men, the political protests and the marches. Eloise had lost none of it, and Victoria was the same.

Charlotte took her flat white to the corner table where Victoria sat.

'Can I say something before we get started?' Victoria said.

'Sure.'

'I love my son more than life itself. I've only ever wanted the best for him.'

'I'm not questioning that, Victoria.'

'One might be forgiven in thinking you are, in fact, questioning it. Otherwise, you wouldn't need to make sure the LPA documents are valid.'

'I wouldn't be doing my due diligence as a sister if I didn't make sure,' Charlotte said, suddenly uncomfortable. 'Eloise is a wonderful, passionate person, but I think we can both agree, she sometimes lives with her head in the clouds.'

'I think that's one of her most admirable traits... and the quality that is going to make her an excellent writer.'

'I agree,' Charlotte said. 'So, shall we get down to it?'

'Did we speak at the wedding?' Victoria asked, ignoring Charlotte's question.

'One would be forgiven for thinking you're changing the subject.'

'I was thinking I would've remembered you, that's all,' Victoria said. 'A woman as capable and confident as you.'

She was going to make her say it. 'I wasn't at the wedding.'

Victoria stared with disbelieving disgust. 'You weren't at your sister's wedding.'

Charlotte wasn't going to give Victoria the whole – as Eloise might put it – *Eat, Pray, Love* speech. Charlotte had been going through a messy break-up at the time, had put her own sadness in front of her sister's happiness.

'I'm not proud of it, but that's not why we're here.'

'You weren't at her wedding, but now you see fit to glide down from London like some angel of law to champion your sister's cause, even if it means disregarding what her beloved husband specifically asked for.'

'Without a living will, I can't make any assumptions about what Dominic wants.'

'I'm a liar then.'

'Without a living will—'

'And you're a parrot, apparently.'

'Victoria,' Charlotte said, somehow keeping her voice calm. Instinct had slammed into Charlotte like a fist: this woman was hiding something. 'Do you have the document or not? You're not exactly allaying any suspicions by behaving in this manner.'

'Ah, there it is: solicitor speak.'

Charlotte took a purposefully long sip of her coffee, wondering what it would be like to throw it in the other woman's face.

Victoria tittered. 'I'm just having a little fun with you, dear. I have it right here.'

Charlotte didn't state the obvious: having fun while her son was in a coma, his future unsure, was the last thing she should've been doing.

'Were you working during your sister's wedding then?' Victoria reached into her bag and slid a folder across the table. 'Or were you otherwise engaged?'

Charlotte had selfishly been locked inside a hotel room, booze bottles scattered everywhere, a man whose name she didn't even remember snoring beside her. She'd lied and said she was ill, but in hindsight, she could've made it. A cold shower, some painkillers, some willpower.

Charlotte ignored the question and studied the document for several minutes. At first glance, everything seemed to be in order. It was the correct format, all sections completed, with the signature and dates Charlotte had expected to see. There were two witnesses listed.

'Who are they?' Charlotte asked, tapping the paper.

'Garry Cheshire is one of Dominic's friends and colleagues from the university. We hired the other witness from some service...' She waved a hand. 'I can get you the name if you like.'

'Presumably, if I were to contact the Office of the Public Guardian, this would all check out.'

'No, Charlotte,' Victoria said with heavy sarcasm. 'I've forged a serious legal document in the unforeseen event that my son uncharacteristically got behind the wheel of the car while drunk and ended up in a coma.'

'Would you mind if I make a copy of this?'

Victoria snapped her fingers. 'I knew you would ask that. There's another in the folder.'

This was true. Charlotte took it out and slipped it into her handbag.

'I understand your concern about the living will, or lack thereof,' Victoria said. 'But I've always been very close with my Dom Dom.'

That was creepy, and Charlotte didn't care if Eloise didn't see it. Calling a fully grown man by a nickname that made him seem like a little kid... it was weird. Or perhaps Charlotte's family, with their lack of terms of endearment, were the strange ones? That was the issue with being raised in the cold; warmth was forever suspicious.

'Your Dom Dom,' Charlotte repeated. 'The man who caused you to move across the country to be closer to him. When he was in his forties.'

'I've heard this many times. You can mock me if you like. Remaining close to one's family was the norm for most people once upon a time. It's only in recent years the family unit has decided to scatter. For reasons which will always escape me. In many countries, even today, family units live as one.'

Charlotte took another sip of her coffee.

'It seems like you're trying to drink that as quickly as humanly possible,' Victoria commented, sounding hurt.

Charlotte studied her. It was possible Charlotte was imposing her own prejudices, her own lack of affection, the dearth in her own family's cohesion. It was like when she saw a father and a daughter hugging on television, sharing a bond that Charlotte had never known. It automatically made the hairs on the back of her neck stand up. Her gut feeling was always to think, *What a couple of freaks.*

'I don't mean to give that impression,' Charlotte said.

'I'm sorry if I've seemed a little... abrupt.' Victoria chewed her lip. 'This entire thing has been heartbreaking. If I were to lose Dominic, it would kill me. But to lose my daughter-in-law too... Please, try to make Eloise see I only want the best for Dom Dom.'

Charlotte would do no such thing, namely because – and she didn't know why, precisely – she didn't believe her.

When Charlotte returned to Eloise's big, beautiful house, her sister was sitting in the front room, cross-legged on the floor just like she'd done as a kid when watching television. She had a laptop balanced on her knees. She had a folder open.

'It's Dominic's,' she said, sounding guilty.

'Any luck?' Charlotte asked.

'Not yet. I'm going to keep looking. So far, there's nothing out of the ordinary. You're right. I've been sitting around waiting for life to happen *to* me. How did the meeting go?'

'The document seems legitimate,' Charlotte said. 'I'm going

to run some more thorough checks just to be sure. Do you ever get peculiar vibes from Victoria?'

'Vibes?' Eloise chewed her fingernail. Even with her hair messy, wearing baggy joggers and a vest that swallowed her, with no make-up, Eloise was magazine-cover worthy. Charlotte was jealous and proud.

Charlotte shrugged. 'Does it ever seem like it's too much? "Dom Dom" this and "mama bear" that. It's like she's trying to hide something.'

Eloise looked at Charlotte like she was insane. 'Victoria and I disagree about Dominic's future, and that hurts. When it comes to her as a mother, though, I've never had any reason to doubt she was the most wonderful, most caring woman a little boy could've wished for. When Dominic spoke about her, it was always in glowing terms. When she moved to the south-west to be closer to him, he was ecstatic.'

Charlotte knew her sister was telling the truth: *her* truth. That was the thing with Eloise, however. Her truth wasn't always *the* truth. She had always lived in the world she wanted to, like when they were teenagers enduring another forced Christmas dinner, Eloise chirping and smiling as if anybody cared, as if they weren't sitting there pretending to be a family.

'Isn't this fun? Isn't this just the best day?' With tears glistening in her eyes as she looked at Mum and Dad and Charlotte, and none of them could summon the same effort, the same feat of self-deceit.

CHAPTER TWENTY-TWO

DOMINIC

'I'm sorry, Mother, I can't,' Dom whispered the day after the boxing incident. He couldn't lie. He couldn't say that Daddy abused him. He'd spent the rest of the day and the following morning and afternoon in his room, hiding from the world. His parents had argued, Father sleeping downstairs. Dom kept thinking about the boxing session in the garden, trying to be the tough son his dad obviously wanted.

Then Mother had come to him, swaying, holding onto the door frame to stop herself from falling. A wine stink followed her like a bad omen. Dom cuddled the sheets closer around himself hoping she wouldn't climb into bed with him. He was too old for that; he was probably too old to be lying in bed all day on a Sunday, even alone.

He was relieved when she knelt beside the bed, touched his hand. She'd said, 'You have to tell them he hits you.'

When he told her no, she squeezed his hand harder. 'What do you mean, no?' she said. 'He *did* hit you.'

'It was boxing, Mother—'

'Mummy,' she hissed.

He never knew where he stood when it came to what she wanted to be called. It made his head spin.

'Mummy,' he went on. 'It was boxing and he was trying to help me. I don't think he wanted to hurt me. I think he wanted us to be like a dad and his son on one of those TV programmes, you know, where they play catch or whatever.' He felt sick when his voice cracked. Was he really about to cry? What was wrong with him?

'You know Mummy wants the best for you, don't you?'

'Yes,' Dom said, unsure if it was true.

'You know Mummy would never hurt you, not like Daddy.'

'He didn't.' Dom swallowed a sob. 'It was *boxing*.'

'You're whining. You need a Mummy cuddle.'

When she tried to peel back the sheet, Dom clutched it tightly. He turned his hands into vices. He squeezed so hard his fingernails bit through the fabric and into his own palms. Mother leaned back, tilting her head, looking at him as if he had become somebody else.

'Is there something you want to say to me?'

'Where's Daddy?' Dom asked.

'It's a depressing thing, Dom Dom. You call him "Daddy" without needing me to remind you, but when it comes to me, it's "Mother", as if I'm some old, unwanted crone. As if I'm some ugly old bitch.'

The swearing made him flinch.

'Why don't you want Mummy cuddles?'

'I'm not a baby anymore.'

'You're lying in bed all day, you're almost crying, and you're too scared to do what's right when it comes to Daddy. Don't you think that makes you a baby?'

He sniffled, but he contained the sob. 'I'm sorry, Mummy. I don't want to cuddle. You smell…'

'I smell?'

'Of wine,' he said. 'You stink of wine.'

'Oh, I stink?' She stood, almost fell, then turned and put her hand to her chest as if there was an imaginary audience. 'Do you hear that? Apparently, I stink of wine. What a terrible mother I must be, having a glass of wine on a Sunday afternoon while my husband is out doing God knows what with God knows who.'

She sighed. 'Right, up, out of bed. This is getting ridiculous. If you don't want to cuddle, you shouldn't need to lie there feeling sorry for yourself. We need to cheer you up! We'll dance to our favourite song. Just like old times.'

It was far more preferable than her filling his room with her stale stink. He climbed from the bed.

Mother sneered. 'You're wearing all your clothes in bed?'

Dom said nothing, stunned at her change in mood. Then she smiled, and it was so sudden, he wondered if he'd imagined the sneer. She took his hand. 'Let's go. I love dancing with you. It makes me the happiest woman alive. Don't worry about Daddy and the boxing. Don't stress your little head about it.'

She took him downstairs and put on the old record player, then picked him up, spinning around as 'With a Little Help From My Friends' by Joe Cocker played. When the song ended, Mother played it again, picked Dom up, kept spinning... and again, and again. Seven times later, Dom put his hands on his belly, slumping on the sofa.

'That's enough, Mummy.' He was dizzy.

'Don't be silly.' She had a manic glint in her eye. 'This is *our* song. These are *our* memories.'

She picked him up and spun and spun. Dom pushed his hands against her chest, squirming. She was sweating and moaning with the effort of carrying him; he was far too heavy for this.

'What are you doing?' she said. 'Sing the song. You know the lyrics. Stop ruining it.'

'Mummy, plea—'

'For God's sake!'

She stumbled – or did she move with intention? – towards the mantelpiece. Dom's head bounced off a hard corner. He slumped on the floor, shuddering, a goose egg sprouting on his skull as his vision blurred and he stared up at his mother.

'Look what you did. You silly boy. *Look what you did.*'

He closed his eyes.

'Mr Hawthorne, can you hear me? Can you open your eyes?'

'If you can hear me, squeeze my hand.'

'I'm going to apply some pressure to check your reflexes. If you feel it, try to move your arm or leg.'

'I'm going to shine a light in your eyes to check your pupils.'

He opened his eyes, and Mother was much older. The sea raged behind her, a storm crashing, but her expression was bright and happy. She clutched one of his hands in both of hers with desperation.

'Aren't you happy, Dom Dom?' she said. 'I know it's rather unconventional, but what use is it living on opposite sides of the country? We're the only family we have left. If you and Eloise ever have babies – hint, hint – I'd love to be there for the little bundle of joy.'

'I think it's wonderful,' Dominic lied. 'But don't get your hopes up about grandkids.'

Mother pouted. 'But why?'

He wouldn't bring a life into this world as long as his mother drew breath. He laughed humourlessly. 'I'm too selfish.'

'I think you'd make an amazing father,' she said. 'I know things weren't always easy for you growing up. After your father left, I had to dedicate too much of myself to work. I couldn't give you the attention you needed. I couldn't be the mother I should have been.'

Was she serious? Dominic felt like screaming in her face, which would've meant screaming into the void. It wasn't a coincidence he'd chosen a wife who was so skilled at reshaping reality; they said you picked a partner like your parent.

'You'll be different. You've already sold your hotels. You've already taken on a job that requires less of you...'

They were sitting on the small porch of a café, nobody else out there with them, alone, like Mother had always preferred it. Two messed-up peas in a messed-up pod. 'You want this baby because your womb rotted after I was born. You're defective. You're broken. You're a bloody *mess*.'

Her reaction was devastating. There was no gasp, no civilised recoil, no self-righteous assurance that she didn't deserve to be treated this way. Instead, she simply stared down into her mug of coffee. The lack of response was the worst part. He felt like a sadist who'd dug a blade into his victim, only to receive a dead-eyed stare in return.

'I've never been a religious man, Mother,' Dominic went on, feeling sick, feeling powerful, feeling pathetic. 'But I almost believe God understood what sort of person you are. As you were pushing me out, God decided that He couldn't allow you to inflict your misery on anybody else. He wrecked your body. He did the world a favour.'

Mother sighed. 'Oh, Dom Dom. Your mind has never been settled when it comes to your childhood.'

'That's because you unsettled it. You made me too important to you.'

'You have severe mental issues,' Mother said matter-of-factly. 'Remember your breakdown in your early twenties? You've invented many things about your childhood that never happened. I'm not sure if it's because you want to believe them; perhaps they bring you some freakish comfort. They simply never happened, my sweet boy. Your father and I argued... he left. That's about as run-of-the-mill as it gets.'

It was true Dominic had endured a mental breakdown in his early twenties, a brush with psychosis that had left his concepts of true and false shaky. It was also true that this wobble had been directly related to his childhood. He'd spent a long time ruminating on what it had been like being the son of Victoria Hawthorne.

'You're wrong,' he whispered, but his voice wavered.

'You needed a villain after your father left,' Mother said sadly. 'And I fit the bill. I'm not saying I'm perfect. I sometimes drank too much. I shouldn't have worked such long hours after your father abandoned us. But are you perfect, Dominic? If you want to go there, let's go there. Are you beyond reproach?'

She stared at him, the lines in her face becoming hard.

Suddenly, he wished he'd never crossed this line. As much as he wanted to be, he *wasn't* sure he was blameless. There were prisons in his memory better left locked.

He took a sip of his tea, then smiled. 'I'm so happy we'll be able to spend more time together, Mother.'

Her face softened. She didn't need him to say anything else; under the rug this little misadventure went. 'Isn't it going to be wonderful?'

It was as easy as that in their family.

A MOTHER'S MUSINGS: PROGRESS UPDATE (NOT GOOD)
10/01/25

Victoria Hawthorne

I am constantly shocked by life's ability to keep going despite the sadness in my heart. The last time I felt anything like this was when my husband abandoned me and my son. I would walk through the park, bars, shopping centres, looking at people, their smiles, their everyday concerns, and wonder how it was possible. It was a rather self-involved point of view, I suppose, but that's what grief and tragedy does to us. It forces us to look inward.

I spend as much time as possible with my Dom Dom, but, ladies, oh, I have to confess something: it is beginning to become rather depressing. The team performs routine checks to see if there is any responsiveness in my son. Sometimes, there are small flutters of hope, inklings that my boy is in there somewhere. And sometimes – God help me – I wonder if these infrequent signals are only adding to the torture.

Eloise has been a trooper, often sleeping at the hospital. I've never seen a wife more dedicated than her. She has put her life on hold. I know she might resent me stating this publicly, but it breaks my heart to see her in this state of stasis. She was writing so much before the accident, had big plans, and now life has paused them for her.

What else is she going to do? She loves my son more than life itself. She is the best daughter-in-law a woman could possibly ask for.

You have all been so supportive, but I am beginning to lose hope. I am struggling to convince myself this is going to have a happy ending. All my life, I've been a selfless mama bear, putting my son first. As the months wear on, however, I'm starting to think I may have to put my sanity first. Visiting my baby is so painful.

Christmas was beautiful and tragic in equal measure: Eloise and I sat around Dominic's bed, talking to him, joking, loving as though he could hear us.

I'm not going to share my sponsor today. I'm sorry. I just can't.

To all those going through hardships, I won't tell you to stay strong. I won't claim there are better days. I will simply say…

I am with you.

CHAPTER TWENTY-THREE

ELOISE

Eloise stood in front of the mirror in her bedroom, adjusting the hoodie. This had never been part of the plan: the bump beginning to show before Dominic knew about the pregnancy. As she smoothed her hand over her bump, she thought about what had happened when she'd asked Garry about the LPA; Charlotte had intended to be there but work called her home early.

Garry had been shocked that Eloise didn't know about it.

'Dominic told me you agreed, Eloise. He said, if anything ever happened to him, you didn't want to be responsible. He said that you'd done the same with a family member. It seemed odd to me, I won't lie, but it wasn't my place to question it. Every marriage is unique. I wasn't about to get involved more than I needed to. I agreed I'd be a witness, but that was the extent of my involvement.'

'But how did he seem on the day?'

'I don't know. Normal? You know what Dominic's like. When he decides to clam up, there's no opening him. He seemed distracted, I guess, but not stressed or anxious. Like I said, it all

seemed very run-of-the-mill, just a chore that had to be completed, no big deal.'

Eloise sighed and went into her walk-in wardrobe, finding her largest jacket. She was dangerously close to having to reveal the pregnancy to Victoria. During the last few months, Victoria had been the rock upon which Eloise had leaned as her sadness and her hopelessness mounted. The LPA was a sore point, but they avoided the issue. Charlotte had gone back to London, promising to ring. To her credit, she'd kept that promise, though the calls were brief and Charlotte often sounded distracted or drunk, sometimes both.

In the wardrobe, she brushed her hand along Dominic's suit jackets, tears welling in her eyes. This had become something of a ritual, trailing her hands along his clothes, pretending she was close to him. Occasionally, she replayed the worst moments in their relationship, the uncivilised secrets neither of them had addressed in public or even to each other except rarely.

No marriage was perfect, certainly not theirs, but the coma had convinced her that she wouldn't be happy without her husband. If the worst happened, she'd have to live for her baby. But it would never be the storybook she'd envisioned when bringing the needlepoint to the condom wrapper, knowing it was wrong, knowing it was right.

Charlotte called her old-fashioned for wanting the picture-perfect life, as though she was a relic from the fifties, but was it so bad to aspire to higher standards? When she watched families with their children, pushing them on swings, smiling in delight as they made airplanes of their food and guided it to their mouths, she experienced an ache that went beyond reason.

Eloise was startled when the doorbell rang. She wasn't expecting a visitor.

She checked herself in the mirror again. Did she appear pregnant at first glance? She wanted to keep it a secret for as long as possible, because soon, the lying would have to begin. Oh, thank you, yes, they had been planning it for some time, and yes, it was a tragedy that her husband had suffered such a horrible accident so soon after the wonderful news...

She walked across the small inner courtyard to find a man in a suit and a uniformed police officer standing at her gate. The man had a clichéd look: hungover, stubbly beard, like a character from a detective novel who'd gone through three divorces and was now married to the job. The uniformed officer was a young woman with rosy cheeks who looked excited to be there.

'Can I help you?' Eloise said.

'Mrs Hawthorne?' the man asked.

'Yes...'

'Would you mind if we speak? I'm afraid it's serious.'

'Is it Dominic? Is he okay?'

She wondered if that was procedure. Would the hospital send the police to her house if something had happened to her husband? She felt her longed-for future slipping further away.

'It would be better if we spoke inside,' the man said. 'I'm DI Cartwright, and this is PC Skellon. PC Skellon is very soon going to be a DC and will be assisting me on this investigation. Would you prefer to speak here or inside?'

'Give me a moment.' Eloise typed in the code for the gate, and it began to whir open. She noticed them exchange a look, as visitors often did when walking onto the lavish property. 'Please, come in. Would you like a drink?'

'No, thank you,' DI Cartwright said.

In the entranceway, they exchanged another look when they saw the mirror, the dried blood seeming ancient, the cracks multiplying their reflections. 'I read about this in the report,' DI Cartwright murmured.

'I've been at the hospital endlessly,' Eloise said, conscious her accent was becoming posher as it often did when she felt put upon.

In the living room, DI Cartwright ran a hand over his salt-and-pepper stubble. 'This is going to come as quite a shock. Your husband's car, we have learnt, appears to have been tampered with before his collision.'

Eloise put her hand on her belly, felt hers and Dominic's baby rebelling against the news. Charlotte had hinted at possible tampering, but Eloise had never believed it; it all seemed too far-fetched, the musings of an under-stimulated solicitor. Or perhaps Eloise was too naïve. 'Tampered with?'

'His brake lines show signs of unnatural wear,' DI Cartwright said.

Eloise's head swam. She closed her eyes for a moment, tried to think of the last self-help podcast she'd listened to, but it just went blah blah blah. She snapped her eyes open. 'Somebody tried to kill my husband?'

'I can't comment on that.'

'Why else would somebody cut his brake lines?' Eloise asked loudly. She was shocked at herself, but when she considered apologising, she saw that they were unfazed. They must've been subject to outbursts like this countless times.

'It's a fair point, Mrs Hawthorne. What I'm trying to say is, it's better to withhold all judgements until we have evidence. In that view, I'd like you to think back to the weeks and months before your husband's accident.'

The rosy-cheeked PC had taken out a notebook, staring expectantly at Eloise.

'Like what?' Eloise said.

'We'd like to get a picture,' he replied. 'Anything that would help us understand your husband. Do you often get visitors?'

'Not often. But sometimes, his colleague, Garry, will swing by for a movie night with his wife.'

'Garry...'

'Cheshire. He works with Dominic at the university. And two months before the accident, we held a party. There were roughly thirty attendants. I can get you the guest list if you like.'

'Thank you, yes, that would be helpful.'

'I can't believe somebody would do this,' Eloise said.

'Did your husband ever mention anybody who might be out to get him? Jealous colleagues? Bitter lovers?'

'Excuse me?' Eloise hissed.

DI Cartwright looked abashed. 'I'm sorry. Ex-lovers.'

Had he been trying to catch her out, fishing for hints of an affair? The suggestion was grotesque. Eloise would never forgive her husband if he'd done something like that. And anyway, he knew better; he might misstep at times, but never so catastrophically.

'He didn't mention anything. I just don't understand. How does a person even know how to do something like that? Wouldn't I have heard the... the tools, or something?'

'Some cars are easier to tamper with than others,' DI Cartwright said. 'With the right knowhow, almost anybody could do it. There are various methods.'

'But if you told me, you'd have to kill me, right?'

It just came out, like banter at the supermarket, nonsense words.

He let the silence stretch. 'Again, Mrs Hawthorne, this is all hypothetical.' He paused. 'Do you have any idea where he was going that night?'

'None at all. But somebody rang him on the landline. I tried to ring the number back, but it had been withheld. You can find out who he was ringing, can't you? Now that this is a criminal matter?'

'Yes, we'll get right on that,' DI Cartwright said. 'Forgive me for asking, but how were things between you and your husband before his coma?'

'Perfect,' she said instinctively.

'Every marriage has its ups and downs.'

'Our downs were brief and hardly worth acknowledging.'

Were they implying she'd had something to do with this? Police often assumed that the spouse was involved. They looked at her as though this was a test. The silence stretched. They were trying to make her uncomfortable, and it worked.

'My husband is a good man,' she said. 'I know he made a mistake with the drink-driving, but he's never done that before. Something happened that night. That was why he hit the mirror. He was angry about something.'

'And you don't have any indication as to what that could be.'

'I wish I did.'

'Your marriage was perfect, but he neglected to share that with you.'

'It was late. He thought I was sleeping.'

'You weren't?'

'I was writing.'

'You're a writer.'

The rosy-cheeked girl scrawled this down as though it had a special significance. Eloise imagined her writing, *The suspect is an author. Active imagination?*

'Is there anything else?' Eloise asked. 'I was getting ready to visit my husband before you interrupted.'

DI Cartwright stood. 'That's all for now, Mrs Hawthorne.'

Once they were gone, disbelief and heartache gripped Eloise. She did something some might consider odd, but she wasn't exactly what one might call a normal person. She never had been, and so when she climbed into Dominic's section of the walk-in wardrobe and lay down amid his clothes, she didn't turn a spotlight upon herself.

Instead, she pulled his clothes over her body, inhaled deeply, trying to smell her husband past the laundry detergent. Tears streamed down her face. Terror tightened her chest.

Somebody had tried to kill her husband.

CHAPTER TWENTY-FOUR

VICTORIA

This wasn't lovemaking; what she did with Patrick, the man who'd discovered her son's body in the car wreck, was more like a service she was providing for no payment. On his end, there was intimacy and honesty. As they intertwined on the springy mattress of his old double bed, the younger man caressed her face, his eyes glimmering as though he might cry.

'You're so beautiful, Vicky,' he said. 'You're absolutely perfect.'

They had been going for perhaps two minutes. Victoria knew it was callous, but counting the seconds was simply the most effective method of passing the time. There usually weren't that many of them. She sunk her hands into his shoulders as though holding him was her sole purpose in life. The confusing thing was, though she tried to be callous, she couldn't deny the something fluttering within her each time they embraced. It was confusing matters. She still hadn't figured out a use for him, which begged the question: what was she doing? Was she flattered? Was she enjoying this? Towards the end, this question received a toe-curling answer.

'Oh, oh, Patrick,' she moaned... genuinely.

'When you moan like that...' His face bunched up into that slightly off-putting configuration of guilt and hopelessness as he struggled to hold onto his lust. 'You know what – you do – to me...'

They began to move again.

Victoria was a creature of instinct. She always had been. When she was a girl and her parents did what they did, they'd crushed the piece of her mind which might've succumbed to poetic fancy or rumination or reflection. They'd turned her into an animal whose actions came from a deep place borne of survival. That was her story, and she was sticking to it.

That was what this was: staying alive. If anybody had asked her to articulate precisely what she meant by this, she couldn't have. But she knew it. He would come in useful. If Charlotte returned, she'd persuade him to... do something. The vagueness of her non-plans hammered nails into her conflicted heart and libido. She hadn't felt like this in years. Patrick may have been a sad figure, but he was half her age, enthusiastic, and looked at her as though there wasn't a single wrinkle on her face.

He collapsed atop her, nibbling her ear as though it was a sweet. 'Did you...'

'You don't have to ask,' she replied. 'When I'm with you, it happens so fast. I'm shocked you can even get excited for me, though, I must admit.'

He rolled to the side and brought her into his arms. He didn't shower before she came over, even if he'd worked twelve hours in the warehouse. He often reeked of BO. See, how could she care when she detested him so? She would have to maintain this stubborn belief that he was revolting to her.

'Why would you say that?'

'I'm over twice your age.' It was one of the first things she'd asked him. Sixty-eight and thirty-three; it had a bad ring to it, and yet he didn't seem to care.

'You're more beautiful than any woman my age.'

They didn't say anything for a long time. After their first meeting, Victoria had asked him if he'd like to go for a drink. She wasn't shocked when he said yes; she'd read the intent in him the moment he looked at her. After all, they'd held hands after exchanging only a few sentences. That was something else which appealed to her on a level she didn't want to acknowledge; they were both abnormal. The third meeting, Victoria had laid her hand on his chest, unsure if it was for show or if she was only justifying this bizarre bond by telling herself he was a pawn.

'Am I imagining that look in your eyes...?'

The kiss had been awkward. He tasted of that little vape thing he was often suckling on like a mother's teat. The closer they grew, the more fitting that thought became; Patrick's father had left when he was only seven, and his mother had been an alcoholic who, while not explicitly abusing him, had neglected him. One birthday, Patrick had made an effort to find some joy in their family of two, waiting up for his mum to get back from the pub with a handmade bracelet wrapped in newspaper. She'd looked at him like he was a ghost. Like he didn't even exist...

People were so complicated and unique in their own estimation, but so simple when viewed critically and with a mama bear's calm. Victoria was still puzzling, thinking, wondering. She didn't know precisely how this would play out, but there was still a corpse in the freezer in her cellar – and she was still frustratingly fearful of it – and her son was still floating between life and death, and Eloise was still desperate to keep her husband alive. She wasn't sure how or if Patrick would be able to help with any of this, however. Their meetings had grown since that third date, the kiss which had led to a melting of her resolve and her cunning. Since October – it was now January – they had met at least three or four times a week... and for what? What was she thinking? What use did he have?

She kept telling herself he was a tool, nothing else, but if that was the case, what was he *for*? Or maybe she needed to accept that, though she believed she should despise him, there was something else between them.

'Are you all right, Vicky?' Patrick asked.

'Yes. It's just...'

'You can tell me. Anything.'

'I'm thinking about Dominic.'

'Course you are. I've read every blog post. I know how much you love your Dom Dom. I'm here for you... for as long as you'll have me.'

He said this with an unmistakable note of desperation. Patrick didn't have many friends. He felt disconnected from people at his workplace, and he had been passed up for the manager's job. His family all lived up north. He'd once attended a quiz night only to discover he'd misinterpreted a rejection as an invitation, and the team was full.

He kissed her forehead, then tried to kiss her cheek but somehow missed, colliding with her eye. He wriggled down the bed so that their noses were touching; she imagined him reading that this position was romantic on some sad single-males forum on the internet. 'I'll never judge you. Let me be honest, all right? I think I'm falling in love with you. I know it hasn't been long. I know it's... unusual.'

'You know I'm ancient and you're a spring chicken, you mean.'

'I don't care how old you are. You're young at heart; I'm an old soul.'

When she spoke, she inwardly claimed her words were

false: a lie, tactics. 'Oh, Patrick. I think I'm falling in love with you too...'

His eyes welled up. 'I know it's only been a few months...'

'I don't care,' she said, thinking: *I will find a use for you.* But as time went on, she was beginning to think this was a shield, a way to protect her dignity, her vision of herself. She was so much better than him, wasn't she? 'I lied, Patrick. I said I *think* I'm falling in love with you, but that's not true. I already have.'

Victoria was grateful, at least, to have spotted the police officers before they saw her. She brought her car to a stop at the end of the road, watching as the uniformed officer and the haggard detective knocked on her door.

Had somebody somehow linked Janine back to her? She needed to get rid of the body, but it wasn't as though she was some hardened criminal. She didn't know what to do, where to take it, and honestly, she found it worryingly easy to put it from her mind. Compartmentalising had always been a necessity for her. She still hadn't looked at the thing, *it*.

She breathed steadily, emptying her mind, filling it again with who she needed to be. Just as she had as a girl: out went reality and in came tolerable make-believe.

She drove to her property, stepped from the car, her voice pitched in civilised concern. 'Can I help you?'

They turned. 'Miss Hawthorne, I presume?'

'Yes. What's wrong? Is it Dominic?'

The detective looked at her appraisingly. She wanted to slap his dickhead face off his skinny shoulders. 'No, Miss Hawthorne. Would it be possible to speak inside?'

'I'm afraid I wouldn't be comfortable with that,' she replied.

'I don't know you. I haven't seen any identification. I don't know why you're here. You see all sorts of stories these days: people posing as workmen, even police officers, to gain access to homes.'

'I'm DI Cartwright. This is PC Skellon. She's soon going to become a detective constable, and, in that capacity, is assisting me in this investigation.' He reached into his pocket. 'Here's my badge.'

Victoria looked at it, nodded. 'Well, even so... I'm happy to talk out here.'

She couldn't allow them access to her home. It was her right; they didn't have a search warrant, or they'd already be in there. If they went poking around in the wrong place...

'Fair enough,' he said. 'I wanted to inform you that we have launched a criminal investigation into your son's crash. We've learnt that the brake lines on his vehicle were cut.'

Victoria gasped. 'I don't understand.'

'Somebody wanted him to crash.'

She put her hand on her chest, stumbled, almost fell. PC Skellon rushed forward and offered her an arm. Victoria gripped it tightly so that the officer would know how shocked and upset she was. 'Come here, love,' the young PC said in a kind girl's voice. As she led Victoria to the front porch seats, she was sure she detected some tightness around DI Cartwright's mouth.

Victoria dropped into her seat, her hand on her head. 'I'm sorry.'

'Take your time,' PC Skellon said.

DI Cartwright looked flustered again.

'It's just... I don't understand... somebody wanted to hurt my baby?'

'The brakes were tampered with, yes,' DI Cartwright said.

'Oh, God. How did they do it?'

A sharp look. Sometimes, rarely, Victoria wondered if she wasn't as smart as she thought she was. She had shown too much eagerness to learn the specifics.

'In an interesting manner, as a matter of fact. They used a technique which wouldn't have required much physical strength.' His eyes flitted up and down her body for a moment.

Victoria was fit for her age and had even posted a photo of herself in a bikini at age sixty-six. It had become one of her most popular posts and grabbed a few regional headlines in the newspapers.

'There's something else, Miss Hawthorne.'

'Yes?'

'The night of the crash, you rang Dominic from your landline. The phone call lasted one minute and seven seconds. It may aid in our investigation if you can recall what you discussed.'

Victoria had purposefully not been recalling it ever since the call had taken place; she had, as with so much else in her life, consciously and stubbornly erased it from her mind. 'It was... strange,' she murmured.

'Strange how?'

Her mind worked. 'I rang to check up, as I often do—'

'So late?'

'If you want the truth,' Victoria said tersely, thinking fast, 'I'd had a nightmare concerning a private moment between us. It made me think of him. I wanted to hear his voice.'

The detective looked annoyed... and interested. *So, she's a liar,* she imagined him thinking.

'What was strange then?'

'He answered... but he didn't speak. He just moaned down the phone. I kept asking him if something was wrong, but he wouldn't say a word.'

'Why do you think he would answer the phone to say nothing?'

'What do you want from me?' She sobbed convincingly. 'Maybe he stayed on the line to hear his mama bear's voice.' That drew an unmistakable cringe from the detective. 'Maybe I caught him just as he was leaving. Maybe he wanted me to talk him out of it.'

'Talk him out of what?'

'Driving while under the influence. Or maybe...' She turned away, seemingly coming to her senses.

'Maybe?' DI Cartwright prompted.

Victoria said with apparent reluctance, 'Dominic has always had a sadness about him. He was the same way as a child. During holidays, when he was supposed to be enjoying himself, he would already be talking about how it would all be over soon. It was as if he was afraid to allow himself to feel joy because he knew it would pass.'

DI Cartwright raised an eyebrow as if to say, *Right, yes, how poetic...* 'Your son suffered from depression?'

'I don't know.' There would be records of such things, and Victoria didn't know if they existed; they'd handled his first breakdown together, privately, without any medical involvement, and his second... The less said about that, the better. 'I only know what I've just told you.'

'Do you think it's possible he would cut his own brake lines?'

'Oh, God.'

Victoria broke down again.

PC Skellon glared at her colleague, and he took the hint.

'We're sorry for upsetting you, Miss Hawthorne. We didn't mean to cause you any undue distress. Please understand that our questions are intended to get to the bottom of what happened that night.'

'I understand. I'm sorry I couldn't be more help.'

'We'll get out of your hair... for the time being.'

After they left, Victoria rushed around the house, trying to think, trying to make sense of this. She ended up in the cellar, hunched over the freezer, tears streaming down her face. But she couldn't open it. She was weak. As much as it pained her to admit, she wished Patrick was with her.

CHAPTER TWENTY-FIVE

CHARLOTTE

They weren't supposed to have phones, but Charlotte hadn't been able to go without some lifeline to the outside world. Her friends had been part of the problem: the reason she was in rehab, three days off the booze, a banging headache and shame coursing through her.

The Christmas season, with both her parents abroad and Eloise determined she wanted to spend it with her comatose husband, had turned into a weeks-long binge which had turned into a spiral which had transformed somehow into her showing up at work drunk in January.

She was on suspension, and, if she didn't get her act together, was in danger of being struck off by the Solicitors Regulation Authority. When Eloise rang her, she should've ignored it, focused on herself. But though she had allowed selfishness to consume her for almost an entire month, she was still determined to be a good sister.

When she pressed the green call icon, she knew that answering had been the correct choice. Eloise sounded heartbroken. 'Charlotte?' she croaked.

'What is it? What's happened?'

'It's everything.' Eloise sounded like a little girl. 'My whole life. I'm not a real person. I've never been a real person. I'm a reflection.'

'I don't understand.'

'I'm what I think people need me to be. A pair of legs on a runway. A quick shag in the back of a limo. A laugh at an unfunny joke. A home-cooked meal after an argument. A nod when my husband tells me I'm destined to become old and lonely once he's gone, no baby, no future, no legacy.'

Charlotte bit the inside of her cheek to prevent her natural response. Eloise's old-fashioned talk bothered the feminist in her, but this wasn't the time for that. 'Has something happened to Dominic, E?'

'No, yes. The police came.'

'For what?'

'To tell me that somebody cut his brake lines.' She laughed humourlessly. 'Don't you get it, Charlotte? This isn't real life anymore; this is just another fiction.'

Her sister sounded drunk. Had she lost the baby? Charlotte knew Eloise would never drink while pregnant; that was something reckless and selfish, the kind of thing Charlotte probably would've done. No, this was shock.

'Somebody wanted to kill my husband,' she said. 'He's a good man.'

Then why did somebody want to kill him? Charlotte's solicitor brain began ticking. Apparently her binge hadn't eradicated it completely.

'Can you come and stay with me? I know I said I didn't care at Christmas. Mum and Dad did their typical Mum and Dad thing. Off they went, not a care in the world. *Kids, you don't mind, do you...* What are we supposed to say to that? It's ludicrous. But I do care; I care too much. Please, Charlotte.'

'Uh, E...'

'Never mind.' Eloise sighed. 'What am I even saying? You've got work. You've got a life. I can't expect you to abandon everything. I'm sorry.'

'Wait,' Charlotte said. 'Don't hang up.'

Her head was still pulsing from her last drink three days prior. She was ashamed to admit that the urge to drink was a powerful tug. That was why she'd checked herself into rehab, eating into her savings; she'd never noticed how much alcohol there was in England before. Everywhere she looked, bottles glinted. Each breath brought the smell of booze.

Charlotte thought of all the times Eloise had come to her as a kid with some project, some grand plan. *'Why don't we start a cooking book, Charlotte? We can think of recipes and make them together, and then we can each write about what went good and what went bad. Doesn't that sound great?'* And Charlotte had just looked at her, unable to summon any enthusiasm, shaking her head.

'I'll be there,' she said.

'Really?'

'I'm going to drive over today.'

'What about work?'

She was on suspension for a month. 'I've got loads of holiday saved up. I need to use it or lose it anyway. Don't worry about it, E. I'm coming to you. You've got me.'

Eloise sobbed. 'Thank you. So much.'

Charlotte said goodbye and then packed her bag. At the front desk, Lila, the hippie proprietor of the upscale rehab clinic, frowned severely. 'May I ask why you are holding a suitcase, Charlotte?'

'I'm leaving.'

'That would be unwise.'

'I'm not a prisoner.'

'We cannot hold you here against your will, that's true. But you are a prisoner, and leaving before the term you promised yourself will prove it; you're a prisoner to your addiction.'

'It was a Christmas binge that got out of hand.'

Lila tutted, adjusting her colourful scarf which had seemed endearing three days previously. Charlotte thought about garrotting her with it. 'Addiction will always find a way to justify itself to your mind.'

'Maybe you're right. Maybe I'll end up some toothless junkie in a doorway shaking a tin cup for spare change so I can afford just one more sip of White Lightning. Maybe I'll never get my job back. Maybe I'll eat through all my savings. But you know what, Lila? Before any of that happens, for once in my life, I'll finally be able to say I was the older sibling my sister deserved.'

Hefting her suitcase, Charlotte stormed out of rehab.

The sun was setting as she drove into Weston-super-Mare. Eloise's house, being on a hill, gave her a stunning view of the sea. Charlotte made a conscious effort to see a new beginning in the glistening yellow light bouncing off the waves.

Eloise answered the door, looking like she hadn't slept in weeks. Her clothes and lack of make-up made her look younger and more vulnerable. Beneath her hoodie, there was a very slight bump, Charlotte's niece or nephew beginning to show.

'Cha... Charlo...'

'Come here.'

Charlotte pulled her sister into her arms. As Eloise wept, she stroked her hair, whispering that it would all be okay, though she had no right to say that. Somebody had cut Dominic's brake lines, which meant, clearly, nothing was okay about any of this.

She took Eloise into the kitchen and put the kettle on. As she made the tea, she sensed that Eloise didn't want to speak straight away. She stared off into space like she was looking at somewhere else: a place in her mind. It was classic Eloise. She was probably disappearing into memories or ideals of the future instead of focusing on what the hell was going on.

'How's the baby doing?' Charlotte asked as she placed a World's Best Wife mug down; she hadn't intended to choose that one and only realised her mistake too late.

It was a relief when Eloise noticed with a shaky smile. 'Everything is going well. No gender; I'm not sure I want to know. I'm going to love the little bundle one way or another, so it doesn't matter. Though, you know me, I may change my mind.'

'That's great. I can't wait to be an aunt.'

'Are you okay?' Eloise asked as Charlotte brought a trembling hand to her mug.

'Fine,' she said, thinking of a stiff drink. Dammit. She had to stop that. Selfish Charlotte was rearing her unkillable head again.

'Have you been drinking again?'

'Why would you say something like that?'

'When you drink a lot, you get anxious. You get shaky. I've noticed it sometimes... on the rare Christmases we make an effort to pretend to be a family.'

'Don't worry about me. I'm here for you. How're things with Victoria?'

'Victoria... What about her?'

'The LPA, for one.'

Eloise got that annoyingly distracted look. 'I asked Garry about that. He said it was Dominic's idea.'

'Did you believe him?'

'I can't think of a reason he would lie.'

Charlotte wanted to slap her baby sister. She was speaking like she was on sedatives. 'How did he seem?'

Eloise turned away, looking at the garden which was steadily becoming a jungle. Charlotte wouldn't make a comment about the unchecked growth mirroring her sister's decaying mental state, but it was true. 'He sounded fine. Just like Garry.'

'Sounded? You didn't meet with him?'

'I thought a phone call would do.'

'I think we should meet with him.'

'Why, Charlotte? I've just found out somebody tried to kill my husband.'

That was exactly why. Charlotte's instincts had been piqued the moment she sat down with Victoria at the café. There was an innocence to Eloise that didn't fit into a situation like this. She'd never had a normal job; praise and attention had been lavished on her for years as a model; and then she'd come here, a princess in this castle, free to disappear into alleyways of imagination with no concern of the wider world.

'Call it a sister's intuition, E.'

'I don't thi—'

'I came here to help you. This is step one. Arrange the meeting.'

Eloise looked shocked, but then she docilely went along with it. Maybe Charlotte should've felt guilty, but her nerves were taut. It was that bloody booze monkey clambering all over her back, whispering in her ear. She shut it out. Eloise rang Garry and they arranged to meet for a coffee the following morning.

In the meantime, Charlotte unpacked her things and went for a run in an attempt to shut her nerves up. When she returned, she searched everywhere for her sister, eventually finding her in the walk-in wardrobe of the master bedroom, lying in a pile of Dominic's jackets.

'Oh, E.'

Eloise wept like she was trying to injure herself with the violent sobbing. Charlotte knelt, cradled her. 'I only ever wanted the perfect marriage,' Eloise said.

Charlotte had a lot to say about that – namely: there was no such thing – but she kept her judgemental comments to herself as her sister went on.

'When we met, it was so perfect, like something out of a novel. I wanted every moment to be like that: a series of bright and beautiful steps leading to a happily ever after. I know how that sounds, Charlotte. Don't worry. I know I'm an idiot. I know real life doesn't work that way. But it's what I wanted... no, it's what we had.'

'Shush. Let's run you a shower. I'll order some food. Then we'll get an early night. How does that sound?'

Eloise sniffled. 'Will you sleep with me?'

Charlotte was touched. Whatever else was happening, this meant something. It was progress.

That night, Charlotte held her sister in her arms, waiting for her anxious breaths to become steady with sleep. She didn't get much sleep herself, her heart pounding and her belly tight and her mouth dry. She thought about the fact this house had an extensive wine collection, because of course it did, because they were *that* couple.

Finally, she drifted off. Her dreams were a hallucinogenic mess. Eloise was standing on a balcony far above her, eyes red, a storm clashing in the background. *You think you know me. You think you understand. You stupid woman.*

She jolted when she woke and Eloise was standing over the bed. Her sister smiled, seeming more like her usual self this morning. 'Sorry. I didn't mean to scare you.'

The dream clung for a few weirdly terrifying moments. Then Charlotte shook herself fully awake. 'You seem in brighter spirits.'

'I was thinking we could maybe go shopping after the meeting with Garry, since we'll be in town anyway? Like sisters?'

Like sisters. That stung more than it had any right to considering Charlotte's track record. 'Sounds good. Let me grab a shower then we'll get going.'

They met Garry at a Costa Coffee on the high street. He was a short, wide man wearing a sweater that was a size too big. Charlotte cruelly wondered if it was to hide his paunch before remembering she wasn't exactly lacking in that department herself.

'This is Charlotte, my sister,' Eloise said after they shared a quick hug.

They all sat down, and Eloise explained what the police had told her. Garry massaged his forehead. 'Cut his brakes? It's just... unbelievable.'

'I know. But it's what the police said.' Eloise shuddered.

Garry drummed his fingers on the table, seeming awkward. Charlotte watched him closely. Sweat slid down his forehead, though it wasn't particularly warm. 'So...' He forced a smile. 'Why did you want me to make the drive? Don't get me wrong. I'm happy to do it...'

'The LPA,' Charlotte said.

There. For a second, perhaps less, Garry looked terrified. He looked like he'd never been more scared of anything in his life; he looked like he wanted to run as far and as fast as he could. Charlotte was sure of it.

He composed himself. 'Dominic's LPA?'

'Who else would we be talking about?' Charlotte felt Eloise glaring at her, but she pressed on. 'Why did you agree to be the witness?'

Another moment; his eyes narrowed, then widened. He tried to mask it with an apparently confused laugh. 'I told Eloise about this on the phone. It was Dominic's choice. He seemed fine on the day. He told me Eloise already knew about it, and I had no reason to doubt him.'

'Hmm,' Charlotte muttered.

Another forced chuckle from good-guy Garry. 'Why do I get the feeling that I'm being interrogated?'

'I'm sorr—' Eloise began.

'I just want to understand,' Charlotte cut in, 'why a devoted husband would go behind his wife's back to give his mother legal power of attorney for no apparent reason.'

'Wait.' Garry shook his head. 'Do you think his *mother* is behind this?'

'What?' Eloise said, as if the thought hadn't occurred to her. 'No, she's not saying that. Are you, Charlotte?'

That was precisely what Charlotte was saying. Her gut had warned her about Victoria Hawthorne. 'I just want to understand.'

Eloise put a hand over her mouth. 'Excuse me for a moment.'

'Are you ill, Eloise?' Garry asked with apparent concern.

'No, no. It's just... everything. I'm sorry.'

Eloise walked briskly through the café to go and deal with her morning sickness. Charlotte kept Garry pinned by her gaze as he took a delaying sip of coffee.

'I really don't understand what you want from me. I thought I was here to offer some support. As Dominic's friend.'

'How did Victoria seem on the day?' Charlotte leaned forward, noticing more tics and tells in Garry's expression.

'I don't know her,' he said, and it sounded like a lie.

'Did she seem eager to get the business done? Excited?'

'She seemed... normal. The whole thing was very normal. You need to relax, woman.' There it was: the masculine anger, the misogynistic disbelief that he was being questioned by his inferior. She felt the reek of his sexism as he jabbed his finger at the table. 'What would a loving mother have to gain if her son died? Why would she arrange it years in advance? She's not on his life insurance, I'd bet. I'm assuming Eloise is still going to receive anything and everything in the will. What's your angle here?'

'You're very angry for a man who has nothing to hide.'

'Jesus Christ. You think you're something special.'

She wanted to slap the little prick. Hard. Several times. Instead she said, 'I think you getting emotional about this is suspicious, Garry. I think there's something else going on here.'

'And I think you look like a woman who hasn't slept for a week. Your eyes are bright red. You look like shit. I don't like saying it. When I drove down this morning, this is the last thing I imagined. But I think you want to feel big and important and this is how you're going to do it.'

'Just tell me what's really going on with the LPA.'

'There's nothing,' he snapped. 'Except what I've already admitted.'

'Admitted?' Charlotte seized on it.

He laughed in disbelief. 'What are you – a detective? Look, I'm sorry about Dominic. I'm sorry about this family drama. But it has nothing to do with me. I did a favour for a mate. That's the beginning and end of it.'

Eloise returned a moment later. Garry stood. 'Listen, love. I have to get to work.' He drew Eloise into a hug, glaring at

Charlotte over her shoulder. 'Let me know if you need anything.'

'Are you happy now?' Eloise sulked once Garry had gone. 'That was just awful.'

And Eloise hadn't seen the worst of it.

'You can't think that, Charlotte. That disgusting thing he said.'

Eloise wouldn't even bloody vocalise it. In her world of make-believe and narratives, she probably thought saying it would make it real.

'I wouldn't be doing my duty as a sister if I didn't ask the questions you're too afraid to ask.'

'It's not about being afraid,' Eloise said. 'It's about living in the real world. Victoria loves her son. She's never given me any reason to think otherwise; neither has Dominic. I don't see how you, who met her a few months ago, and then only briefly, and who has only met my husband a few times, can think you know more about their relationship than me.'

That was just it though. Because Charlotte knew less, she was able to judge more critically without emotional baggage weighing her down.

'Just leave Garry alone, all right?' Eloise said. 'I have enough stress in my life. Did you hear me, Charlotte?' Eloise's lip curled. For a moment, she became just like she'd been in the nightmare. 'Or you can piss off back to London.'

CHAPTER TWENTY-SIX

DOMINIC

He didn't want to live like this anymore. Sometimes, he wondered if he wanted to live at all. Sebastian had talked about dark corners of the mind which had appealed to Dominic on a far greater level than he could accept; they'd exchanged book recommendations like *The Bell Jar* and *To The Lighthouse*, and Sebastian had eagerly whispered about ending it all just like the authors of those great works had.

Dominic shuddered, wrapped his arms around his knees. He didn't want to die, but he wasn't sure he would ever have the fortitude to live either. He felt like an old man forced into a boy's body; he felt unalterably different from those around him, and sometimes, often, he hated himself for this.

There were people in the world, in the country, on his street, probably, whose lives were far worse than his. He didn't have the right to feel the way he did. It was out of alignment with the facts of his existence.

He hated his life; he despised himself for hating his life.

The door trembled as Mother tried to open it. 'Dom Dom, baby boy...'

'Leave me alone,' he whispered.

'Let me in.'

'No.'

'Why not, my sweet, perfect child?'

'I know what you want to do,' he said.

'What is Mummy going to do?'

'You know what. You're going to drag me to the box. You're going to lock me in. For days.'

'Oh, Dom Dom. Just let Mama Bear in. Mama Bear will make it all better.'

'I don't want to.'

Suddenly, the door burst open. He was forced to scurry quickly away to stop the door from eradicating him completely, erasing his existence like he apparently wanted. He spun, and there was Mother, swaying from side to side with a glass of wine in her hand. She was wearing just her underwear; her stretch marks showed.

'Mama Bear will help you, my sweet baby.'

'No,' Dominic whispered. 'Please.'

Mother laughed, and then she was wearing clothes, and she was no longer holding a bottle of wine. Dominic's head hurt. Had he hit it when she barged the door open? Had he passed out? He didn't understand how she was suddenly dressed.

'Oh, you poor man,' she said. 'Is this what you wish happened? You want me to have done *this* to you... why? Because then it would make it all easier to manage. Hmm? You had to make sense of it somehow, had to take the facts of your existence and twist them into an acceptable shape: one that would make sense of your malformed mind. If I'd locked you inside a box and left you there to torment you, at least then you'd have an excuse to be as pathetic as you are.'

'Stop it,' he croaked.

'My poor broken boy. You truly don't understand who you are. You looked at our shared agony once or twice and it broke your little mind, and now you're here, wishing that your mother abused you so that you can live with the guilt. Do you realise how pitiful that is? Do you realise how sad that is?'

'Please. Just stop.'

'Why do you wish I did that to you? Is it because you understand that what you suffered, while tragic in its own small way, while negative, while not entirely *normal*, was manageable? Is it because you understand that other men, stronger men, could have continued their lives and never once thought about any of it ever again?'

Dominic began to cry, but she wouldn't stop.

'You've never taken a full account of who you are and what led you to where you are. You disappear into work, into flings, into nothingness. When you do look at it, *poof*, there goes your mental stability... your entire sense of self is a sandcastle built too close to the waves, ready to be washed away at a moment's notice, one mental slip.'

'Just let me be normal. Let me be free.'

'Shut up. There is no "normal". There is no "free". You were born with a mental deformity called being a fucking baby.' She screamed the final words, then giggled in a sickeningly girlish way. 'I never, nor would I ever, go to such extreme lengths to hurt you. I have never purposefully hurt you. We both know it. You've felt guilty ever since you told the lavish *Momma put me in a box* lie to Janine, but you enjoyed the attention it won you. You enjoyed the fact it meant you didn't have to reveal the true secret: the real reason for your self-indulgent mental breakdowns. You kept on spinning your little tales. You really are a sad sap.'

He buried his face in his hands, weeping child's and man's tears.

'You're incapable of living in the real world. The worst thing you've ever done is try. Look at you and Eloise, for example. You know how malevolent and deranged your marriage truly is. You know what happens when the doors are closed and the lights go out and it's just the two of you in that big empty house. You know what you are; you know what she is. You can't run from it. The past, the present, none of it.'

Mother knelt, grabbed a chunk of his hair, and slapped him across the face.

'The only thing you can run from is the future, and that's when the thoughts start, isn't it? *I don't have to be here anymore. I can end it all. Blah blah...* Except, you pussy, you wimp, you never do it. You just keep on living your lies. Keep on disappointing your wife. Keep on disappointing yourself. Why can't you just let it go?'

She slapped him again.

'I gave you my figure. I gave you my privates. I ruined my body for you. I gave you my attention and my creativity and my soul. I gave you my protection and my investment and my intellect. I gave you my time. I gave you everything, and still, you can't keep it together.'

CHAPTER TWENTY-SEVEN

VICTORIA

'I gave you everything,' she said. 'Everything a woman could be expected to give, and all you had to do was stay sane. That was it, Dom Dom. You silly misguided boy.'

Victoria choked back a sob as she looked at her son, his eyes closed, his body still, the machines beeping as they always did. The doctors seemed far less optimistic than they had once; Victoria noticed quick looks between them, anxious tightening of the mouths whenever Eloise eagerly asked about signs of life.

'All you had to do was accept that Mummy knows best.'

Victoria stood when she heard footsteps behind her.

'Oh,' Eloise muttered, pausing in the doorway. 'Hello, Victoria.'

'Sweet girl.'

Victoria rushed to her daughter-in-law, sweeping her into her arms and lavishing her with all the love she'd never received from her family. She didn't do this in a cynical manner; it was merely instinct, which was how Victoria functioned, always had, always would. She held her tightly.

'Are you all right?' Victoria asked. 'You feel cold, child.'

Eloise buried her face in Victoria's chest. 'I'm okay.'

The truth was, Eloise felt fatter than Victoria had ever known her to get. There was extra weight around the middle; her face, too, was chunkier than Victoria could remember seeing it. Was she eating away her feelings? Could Victoria blame her if she was?

'Sit,' Victoria said. 'Let me get you something. A coffee? A tea?'

'A tea would be nice. Can you get one for Charlotte too? She's seeing to the car, but I couldn't wait; I wanted to get in here, be with him, see him.' Eloise slipped into her usual chair, clasping her hand around Dominic's as she always did: desperately, hungrily, as though her touch might snap him awake. 'Hey, handsome. You'll be glad to know I've finally arranged to have the gutters cleaned.'

Victoria left them. So, Charlotte was back, the solicitor sister with the bad attitude. Was that going to complicate matters? Not that matters could conceivably become more complicated. There was a corpse in her freezer, a man half her age in her bed, a son full of secrets who may awake any moment and spill them all out.

Charlotte appeared like the proverbial devil on Victoria's shoulder as she was seeing to the hot drinks. The woman looked far worse for wear than when she was in Weston before Christmas. Her cheeks were red, her hair messy, her eyes sunken. She looked like she'd been piling as much booze, food, and drugs into her robust figure as possible.

'Hello, Charlotte,' Victoria said in a friendly tone. 'What a lovely surprise. To what do we owe the pleasure?'

'Eloise told me about the police visit. The brake cutting. I'm assuming you know?'

'Of course.' Victoria frowned; she was the put-upon mother who could never catch a break. 'Life is a cruel game.'

'Do you have any idea who could've done something like that?'

'No,' Victoria said. 'Except – well...'

'Except?' Charlotte said sharply.

'It hardly bears thinking about, but Dominic wasn't always the "Jack the Lad" he presented to the world.'

'Strange way to take his own life, if it's that.'

'You asked,' Victoria said, picking up hers and Eloise's plastic cups. 'You may want to sort your own tea. I only have so many hands.'

'I'll go without. I'd like to stick as close to Eloise as possible.'

'That makes a pleasant change for her, I'm sure.'

Victoria enjoyed the flustered look on Charlotte's unhealthy face. The piggy wrinkled up her features, then waddled beside Victoria as they returned to Dominic's room. Eloise was still speaking to her husband, as was often the case, the heartache clear in each syllable.

Victoria sat, quietly sipping her tea. Charlotte sat in the corner, tapping her foot on the floor.

'We've got so much to look forward to,' Eloise said. 'I think, when you wake up and we begin your rehab, we'll document the experience. I'll keep a diary of each session, each milestone, and then, when you're back to your usual self, we can write a book together. How does that sound?' Eloise paused. 'Yes, it sounds nice, doesn't it?'

Charlotte gave her sister a worrying look.

'She likes to imagine him replying to her,' Victoria explained. 'It helps her to imagine that her husband is still with her... Completely understandable, as I'm sure you'd agree.'

'Uh, obviously,' Charlotte said.

But it wasn't obvious at all. Charlotte was staring at her sister as though she was completely insane.

Victoria enjoyed the next few minutes. Eloise spoke to

Dominic as though he was offering replies, and Victoria watched Charlotte trying to mask her disgust. She could swallow it, pretend she felt otherwise, paper over it in her own mind even, but that was what she felt. She was sickened by Eloise's display of unhinged devotion towards her husband.

Finally, Eloise stopped, putting a hand over her mouth. It looked like she was about to be sick. She stood, went to the window, looking out at the car park.

'All I want is for him to wake up,' she said after a long pause, 'hold me, and tell me it's all okay. Everything is okay. Nothing matters. Nothing from before, nothing...'

'Nothing from before?' Charlotte said. 'Like what?'

Like, presumably, whatever marital secrets had led to Dominic having an affair. Victoria should've let Janine live longer, wrestled more secrets from her memory, but Dominic's box lie had snapped something within her.

'Like... everything.' Eloise sighed. 'You know, sometimes, often, every day really, I go into his side of the walk-in wardrobe and I move my hands over his jackets, and I lie amidst his clothes, and I imagine his body is still filling them. I imagine the warmth, the reassurance. I imagine...' Eloise spun, her face turning white. 'Excuse me.'

She ran from the room into the corridor. Victoria watched her as something dawned, pieces clattering into place, first on their own – Eloise was pregnant; it was obvious – and then as part of Victoria's greater plan. This settled it then. If she was pregnant, if Victoria was going to become a grandmother, she had to act.

'Care to share the joke?' Charlotte said.

'I'm sorry?'

'You're smiling.'

'I didn't realise.'

'You must've been thinking about something rather funny. Or heartwarming?'

'A memory of Dom Dom,' Victoria said.

'Which one?'

'Something private, Charlotte.'

Victoria was doing her best not to snap; it was like Charlotte wanted her to.

Eloise returned. 'I'm sorry about that.'

Victoria strode to her daughter-in-law, putting a hand on her shoulder. 'I'd like to make something clear, Eloise. You have nothing to apologise for. Nothing – do you understand me? If you think there's something I should know, but you've neglected to tell me for whatever reason, I won't be angry. I won't be offended. Or, if you'd prefer I never mention this again, I won't resent you for that either.'

'E...' Charlotte tried to interject, but it was too late.

Eloise fell into Victoria's arms, sobbing as she held her. Charlotte stood as a spare part, watching like the outsider she was. 'When did you guess?'

'Honestly, sweet girl, just now. It should've been obvious sooner. I've never known you to dress like this. Come – sit down.'

Charlotte glared as Victoria led her to the seat. Victoria pulled her chair close and took Eloise's hands.

'Does Dominic know?' Victoria asked.

Eloise shook her head, letting out a terrible croak. 'It was – uh – unplanned. I didn't have a chance to tell him. What if I never get one?'

'Hush,' Victoria said. 'Mama Bear is here. Everything is going to be okay. Whatever happens, this child is going to be the most cherished, valued, and special baby who's ever been born. I swear, Eloise. This is a good thing.'

Victoria wrapped her arm around Eloise, certain she could

feel the little life burning through Eloise's skin, trying to communicate with Victoria: with the pieces of Victoria which Dominic had ruined, which had made a second baby impossible, which had seen her stuck with the ungrateful man who, if he woke, would never let Victoria love her grandchild in the way she knew best.

'I'll always be here for you,' Victoria said.

'So will I, E.' Charlotte pulled up a chair, glaring over Eloise's head at Victoria.

'Thank you. Both of you. I don't know how I'd do this on my own.'

Victoria thought about the things Eloise had said, then she thought about using Patrick's phone to finally google the Janine situation. It hadn't been as bad as she'd feared. Janine had been reported missing, but as there was no body yet, no one had connected the dots. Plus, Janine hadn't been anybody's idea of photogenic, and she wasn't wealthy. There was small worry of her becoming some national sensation.

It was still possible for Victoria to get her happy ever after.

A MOTHER'S MUSINGS: THE SANDCASTLE
12/01/25

Victoria Hawthorne

I remember the first time I ever visited my current home of Weston-super-Mare. It was when Dominic was just five and things with my husband had yet to degenerate; I've often wondered if those bright, happy memories are the reason my Dom Dom chose this town as his home so many years later.

One memory will always burn with joyous light in my mind. Dominic was determined to build a sandcastle, but he was equally determined to do it close to the tideline. He liked the sound of the sea. He liked the way it tickled around his ankles. When he giggled, my husband and I would exchange a look, and I was convinced we would never be more in love.

As Dom Dom built, however, the tide crept higher, washing away his efforts. His father tried to persuade him to move his project further away, but I told my baby boy, 'You'll have to be quicker. You'll have to try harder. You can do this, angel.' How can I describe how he looked at me then? It was like I was the solution to every problem he would ever have in his life.

Alas – yes, ladies, I just used the word "alas"; deal with it – the tide was more stubborn than my son. In the end, he shrugged in a way that broke my heart. He looked so grown-up, as if a little magic in the world had drained away. Perhaps I'm being melodramatic. In fact, I know I am, but there is a special strangeness in looking upon one's child and seeing the man they will become so clearly pressing through his child's features.

'I don't really care about the sandcastle anyway, Mummy.'

We played in the shallows as the sun skipped over the water, as the whalelike hump of the island Steep Holm seemed to shift in the water as if it truly was alive, as the Grand Pier pointed towards Cardiff – visible on the stunningly clear day – like a finger giving directions. I will never forget the sound his little splashing feet made.

The point, ladies? When shall I arrive at it, you ask yourselves, I'm sure…

Well, that's the thing about today's post. I want *you* to tell *me*.

What's the significance of the sandcastle? Why does it matter that Dom Dom tried, and failed, to build it? What could the sea's relentless destruction represent? Why didn't I listen to my husband and get Dom Dom to build his castle in a safer place?

CHAPTER TWENTY-EIGHT

DOMINIC

Dom stumbled up the path towards his house, putting his hand on the wall, taking a moment, taking a breath. Booze rushed around his system. He was fourteen; getting drunk with their mates was what fourteen-year-old boys did. And yet he always felt a wrench of guilt if he returned home like this. *Mother* wouldn't approve; *Mother* would say he was better than this. He owed himself more than to constantly get drunk and, in her view, make a fool of himself.

He gritted his teeth, breathed out, his breath fogging the air. He and Sebastian were meeting a few nights a week, drinking alone in his bedroom, talking about the parties they weren't going to, the girls they weren't dating, the lives they weren't living. It was depressing, but also oddly comforting. They'd even got their hands on some weed a few times, and Sebastian was talking about getting some pills "just to try". Dominic wanted anything to take him outside his own head.

When he was drunk, he didn't have to think. He liked not thinking. It made his life easier to swallow. The few times they'd experimented with weed, it was like he'd been standing outside his own mind, able to analyse himself on what had felt like a significant level. His issue, he realised, was that even when he wasn't with Mother, she was there, watching him, judging, tutting, *being*.

Pushing the door open, he paused. Something was different. It hit him a moment later. Dad's shoes were in the entranceway, which meant he'd returned from his most recent work trip sometime between when Dom had left for his friend's house and his return. This wasn't good. Mother knew about Dom's drinking, and though she complained and criticised, she didn't stop or punish him. He had grown too large for her old punishments: the "accidental" collisions with the mantelpiece, the "unintentional" burns on his hand from when she pressed it against the hot stove.

Dad was waiting in semi-darkness, sitting in his armchair, a glass of whisky on the armrest. 'Evening, son. Or should I say morning?' He nodded at the clock; it was 2am.

Mother stood at the door, her arms folded, doing her best impression of an upper-middle-class mother draped in understandable and civilised concern, and not the manipulative freak she was.

'Hi, Dad,' Dom said, then tried to walk past his father towards the stairs.

Dad intercepted him quickly, glaring like he was getting ready for a fight. 'Don't *Hi, Dad* me. Where have you been? It's a school night. You reek of booze.'

'I could say the same to you.'

'Don't, Dom,' Dad grumbled. 'I thought you cared about your studies. Your mother tells me this is a new development. Why would you do this just a month before you need to start properly revising for your exams?'

'It's just SATs, Dad,' Dom said. 'And some coursework stuff.'

'That "coursework stuff" is GCSE prep. Do you want to be a failure? How many have you had?'

Since it was clear Dad wasn't going to let him pass, Dom sat on the sofa, resting his forearms on his knees as he stared at the floor. Dad followed him, his tone lecturing, annoying. It was the tone of a man who didn't spend more than half his life somewhere else; it was the tone of a man who had turned a blind eye to his psycho wife turning Dom into a little stunted weirdo who girls wouldn't look twice at.

'Don't you want to make something of yourself one day, Dom? Don't you want to *be someone*? I know it doesn't seem like it right now, but this is very important. This is the difference between you being happy, successful, and miserable.'

'You did well in your exams,' Dom said. 'And sure, Dad, you're successful. But happy?'

Dad knelt down and then grabbed Dom by the chin, forcing him to meet his gaze. 'Don't forget who you're talking to, lad. If I'd spoken to my old man like that, I wouldn't have seen the light of day for weeks. Don't even ask me if I would've been able to sit down; I wouldn't, because he would've belted me black and blue. You need to liste—'

'Joseph!'

Dad glared at Mother. 'No, Vicky, he needs to understand. We have to stop him before he goes down this path.'

'Dad, she lied to you,' Dom said, because even if it meant more pain for him, it'd mean more pain for Mother too. 'This isn't a one-time thing. This isn't new. I've been going out almost every time you leave for work. It's not just booze either. I've been smoking weed. I'm not sure why she told you it was just this once.'

Dad bolted to his feet, spun to Mother, glared at her like he was contemplating doing something severe. 'Is this true?'

'I...' Mother approached them, her lip trembling; she could

put on a show when she wanted. 'Oh, Dom, why would you say that? Yes, it's true, but he's a good boy, Joseph. He's going to get control of this. Aren't you?'

Dom glared at her. 'No. I'm going to get more drugs, harder stuff. We're starting to think about pills and powder actually.'

'You need to shut your mouth and think about what you're saying,' Dad said.

But Dom couldn't stop. He wanted to tear them all apart, wanted it to end, wanted Mother to stop pretending to be normal every time Dad returned home. He thought about all the times she'd forced him to dance, or crawled into his bed, or hit him then gaslighted him when he was little, all the times she'd made him feel like a rodent stuck in a trap with no way to escape except to gnaw pieces of himself away. He would gnaw then, if that's what it took.

'Mother knows about it too. I've told her that I'm drinking a lot because it's easier than thinking a lot. I've told her about the weed, and I even told her that my mate said he could get some pills. She doesn't care. Her precious boy can't do any wrong in her eyes.'

Dad leaned forward, his whisky breath moving over Dom. 'You think you're being so clever, don't you, lad? You think you can pit me and your mother against each other. You think it's as easy as that?'

'I don't care what you or that woman do with your time,' Dom said. 'I just want to be left alone: to try and be normal. You don't know what she's like anyway.'

'What's that supposed to mean?'

'She drinks all day, lounges around the house. She tries to get me to sleep in the same bed with her, Dad. Even now.'

Dad turned to Mother. 'Is this true?'

'No – well, not like he's saying.' Mother clasped her hands as though in prayer. 'I get scared at night. My mind plays tricks on me. I start thinking about what happened when I was a girl, and it's like I just can't stop it.'

'And you think that's acceptable,' Dad said.

'It's just... it doesn't matter.'

'Of course it matters,' Dad snapped, marching over to Mother. 'Don't you see? It's just like when he was little. Oh, God, Vicky, I thought you'd stopped all this.'

'All what?'

'Your mad shit,' Dad shouted. 'All the twisted stuff. I thought you were finally, *finally* being a good mother.'

'Never going to happen,' Dom muttered.

Dom heard the slap before he felt it. It was a violent cracking noise, like a whip, and his mind struggled to catch up to what had happened. Very slowly, he thought, *Dad definitely didn't hit me when I was little and we were boxing, because that felt nothing like this. I would've remembered if it felt like this.*

Then he was on the floor, staring up at the ceiling. The blow had knocked him off the sofa. Mother was screaming. Dad was yelling at her. Dom's head pulsed and, for a surreal moment, he heard a *beep-beep-beep* like he was already in hospital. He sat up, groggy, just in time to see Mother slap Dad across the face.

'You're never going to touch my boy again,' Mother shouted. 'Do you understand me? Not my baby; not my angel. *Never.*'

When Dad struck Mother in the mouth, the last few years were erased from Dom's mind. He couldn't remember his resentment or the sense of tragedy or his anger or any of it. All he could think about was the cold, coarse fact that somebody had hit his mother, this sweet, loving, angelic woman: this woman who, while she had her flaws, didn't deserve this.

Dom rushed at his dad, shoved him in the back. Dad spun on Dom, grabbed him by the throat and tossed him to the floor. The first kick thundered into Dom's belly, the second cracked him in the nose. *Stop*, Dom tried to say. *Please.*

'It's time you all remembered who's in charge of this house!' Dad roared. 'Do you understand me? Well, do you?'

Dad hauled Dom to his feet. Where was Mother? Had she run? Dom's back pulsed when Dad shoved him up against the wall. Tears were glimmering in his eyes. He looked guilty for what he'd done and what he was about to do, but not guilty enough to stop.

He pulled his fist back. 'I should've done this a long time ago. Beat some bloody sense into you bo—'

He croaked, a guttural, haunting sound, when Mother stabbed him in the back. Mother stumbled away, her hand over her mouth, shuddering as Dad turned and looked around like he was lost. He tilted his head at Mother with a look of surprise, then betrayal, and Dom didn't know which was worse. He remained like that for far too long. It was almost a relief when he fell to his knees, gasping as he tried to reach around and claw for the knife sticking out at an awkward angle.

Mother looked down at him for a moment, then sighed and leant down, tore the knife free, and stabbed him several more times. Dom stared in horror as the blade slipped in and out, in and out, almost rhythmically. It was the most grotesque, unbelievable thing he'd ever seen.

Mother dropped the knife, took a few steps back, then collapsed onto the armchair and began to sob.

Dom fell against the wall, slipped through it, then he was watching himself; he watched the gangly teenager put his hand on his mother's arm, whisper, 'We can hide him, Mummy. We can make this better. Mummy, you don't have to cry. We can hide him. I'm strong, Mummy. I can do this. I can help. Please.'

'I can't touch him. I can't look at him. At it. *It*. I just can't – don't make me. This isn't who I am.'

The teenage boy, suddenly seeming sober, nodded. 'I can do

this for you, Mummy. I'm a good boy, aren't I, Mummy? I can save you. I can save us.'

Dom watched as the teenage boy wrapped his father in an old rug. Mother had retreated upstairs, leaving him to deal with it alone. Dom grunted and panted with the effort of dragging his father's corpse towards the garden.

Then the scene shifted, crackling like an old-fashioned television trying to find its station. Instead of the body disposal, he saw himself again, but this time, he was older. He had hair on his face. He was lying in bed, moaning, as Mother sat beside him with his hand in hers.

'Hush,' she said. 'You just need to get it right in your head. That's all. Just decide what happened, my sweet Dom Dom, and force yourself to accept it. Don't overcomplicate it. Don't torture yourself.'

'I don't want to be insane,' the adult version of Dom said. 'I don't want to be like this anymore. I don't want to live with this.'

'What's the alternative?' Mother said with some fierceness in her voice. 'Would you rather tell the truth? Would you prefer it if everybody knew?'

'I'm tired of these lies.' The man began to weep. 'That's all we have, Mother. Family lies. That's all we've ever had.'

'That's not true,' Mother said, and then both versions of Dom began to weep, the teenager trapped behind the wall and the half-insane man in the bed. 'We have each other. And we always will.'

CHAPTER TWENTY-NINE

ELOISE

Eloise's main pleasure in life, lately, was standing in front of the mirror without her shirt on. She liked to arch her back to emphasise the steadily growing bump, liked to gently trail her fingers over her body, imagine herself swelling until kicks began, then, one day, her child would be in the world; all the best aspects of she and Dominic, and none of the bad would go into their baby.

This child would be special, loved, and, unlike Eloise, have a family who made an effort. If her child ever enthusiastically suggested an impromptu daytime trip to the arcade or the theatre or anywhere else, *she* wouldn't be too busy.

'Knock, knock,' Charlotte said from the other side of the door.

'It's open.'

'I've got you some decaf tea.'

Eloise turned with a smile. Her sister was overstepping her boundaries in some respects, especially when it came to the LPA stuff and her frankly absurd notions about Victoria. Charlotte was suspicious of true love and connection. Eloise had taken their lack – she hated dwelling on childhood, but it was true – as motivation to find it herself. Charlotte had branded the entire world as cold because their family had been icy for so long. Any warmth was immediately on trial.

'How are you feeling?' Charlotte said, laying the mug on the bedside table.

'I'm all right, I suppose. Just tired of living in stasis – and wondering who on earth would want to hurt my husband. A successful man. A university lecturer. I can't see any rhyme or reason to it. I can't see a motive.'

Charlotte sat on the chair near the window, folded her arms, stubbornly avoided Eloise's gaze.

'What?' Eloise said.

'It's nothing, E.'

'It's obviously something, so you might as well say.'

'She just gives me a funny feeling.'

'Is that how your profession works? You get a "funny feeling" about somebody and suddenly they're suspect number one?'

'Maybe I let my thinking run away with me,' Charlotte said. 'A hazard of my profession, I guess.'

'You're wrong about her. Anyway, there's nothing we can do until the police get more information.'

Charlotte chewed the inside of her cheek. It was the same look she'd got as a girl when she was waiting to leap away from a family function and go drinking and smoking with her mates. 'Yeah, you're right.'

'Are *you* all right?' Eloise asked.

'Me?' Charlotte laughed awkwardly. 'I'm fine, E.'

'It's probably strange being away from London, from all your friends, from work.'

'It is. A little. But I'm happy to be here.'

'What shall we do about dinner? I could be persuaded to

use this little lady or lord...' Eloise tapped her bump, 'as an excuse to get a takeaway, but only if you try very hard.'

Charlotte smiled, then slid to her knees. 'Please, Eloise. I beg you; let's get a curry so hot we'll be on the toilet for weeks.'

Eloise laughed. 'You're disgusting. I don't think I'd be able to stomach a curry now. Let me get my phone and we'll look at the apps; maybe you could have a glass of wine too. If you wanted.'

Eloise turned her back, reached for her phone.

'A glass of... I wouldn't want to put you out.'

'Don't be silly. It's not like I've got any use for it. When Dominic comes home, he won't miss a bottle or two.'

'Are you trying to get me drunk?'

Eloise sat on the bed, swiping through the takeaway apps. 'You can get drunk if you want. I don't mind.'

Charlotte drummed her foot on the floor. 'So, what are you in the mood for?'

'I'm thinking a kebab,' Eloise said.

Charlotte grinned.

'What?' Eloise asked. 'You're looking at me funny.'

'For most people, E, a kebab is a regular sort of thing. You say it like we're going tightrope walking.'

That was because she'd spent so long eating like a rabbit. Bulky, greasy food that stuffed her and put her into a food coma was like a drug. 'I'm getting a large. I don't even care. Here.'

Eloise made her selection then passed the phone to her sister.

Charlotte chose, then said, 'You know, E, I might have a glass of wine. Just one.'

One takeaway and two bottles of wine later, Charlotte was asleep on the sofa. Eloise draped a blanket over her sister then watched the end of the film. Charlotte had always enjoyed her alcohol. Eloise had enjoyed it too in a way: watching her sister take pleasure in the wine, comment on its quality. Eloise's phone buzzed. It was Victoria.

Can we speak? I could swing by if you like? It's important x

Eloise texted back, telling her yes, of course. She instinctively went to grab a hoodie that would hide her shape, then realised she didn't have to. Victoria knew, and, as usual, she had been supportive. What would happen when Dominic woke? Eloise would have to persuade him to lie for her; his mother couldn't be allowed to know how she had really got herself pregnant. Eloise would force Dominic if she had to.

Victoria rang when she was outside. Eloise opened the door, then the gate, finding Victoria looking almost shell-shocked. Her eyes were wide pits.

'Victoria. What's wrong?'

'There's something I should've told you months ago.'

'Come in, come in.'

She rushed her into the house, into the kitchen, sitting at the small table. The older woman had never seemed so vulnerable. Her hair was in disarray as though she had been running her hand through it. She was wearing no make-up.

She wrung her hands together. 'Oh, Eloise,' she whispered. 'He put me in such an awful position. He...' Victoria crumpled onto the table, choking on sobs, sounding like a woman who was drowning.

Eloise put her hand on her mother-in-law's shoulder. The emotion was so palpable, tears sprung to her eyes too. 'Whatever this is, Victoria, we can get through it.'

Victoria couldn't compose herself. She cried for several

minutes, then abruptly stood and went to the counter, grabbed some kitchen towel.

'I wish he hadn't told me.'

Eloise followed her. 'Just tell me. Please.'

'Let's sit,' Victoria said. 'I'm sorry. I didn't plan on breaking down. You deserve the truth: at least, the truth as far as I know it.'

Eloise held Victoria's hands as they took their seats again.

'The night of Dominic's crash,' Victoria said, 'I rang him.'

Eloise gasped. 'It was... you. And you're telling me *now*?'

When Eloise tried to pull her hands away, Victoria held tightly onto her. 'He made me promise. He made me swear not to say anything. I rang because I'd had a nightmare. I wanted to speak with him. I know it seems silly, but the dream was about him, and I was worried... When he answered, I knew instantly that he was drunk. Too drunk. Worryingly drunk.'

Eloise shuddered. She couldn't speak.

'He told me something,' Victoria said. 'I almost don't want to tell you, but soon, the police will visit. They'll tell you I'm the one who rang him. They might even go digging further. I can't have you finding this out from them. So, I'm breaking my promise to Dominic. I'm going to tell you his secret.'

'Just say it,' Eloise whispered, forcing the words out.

'Dominic was having an affair. That was why he was so drunk. He was drinking away his feelings. I tried to tell him he needed to sober up, get some sleep, then we could meet and talk about it. But he wouldn't hear it. He said he was going to break it off. Right then. When he was drunk. When I tried to persuade him again, he lashed out.'

Eloise's mind spun, the phone call finally making sense. But an affair? His hands on another woman, his lips, them naked together, writhing, sweating, moaning, giving each other pieces of themselves... It just didn't fit. They had issues, fine, and perhaps those issues were far worse than Eloise would even admit to herself, fine – but to think that he'd be with another woman...

'You must be mistaken,' Eloise said.

'I can't fathom it either.'

'He wouldn't cheat on me. With who? And why? We made a promise to each other. We would be loyal until the end. We took our vows seriously. We would rather die than break them. That's how seriously we took them.'

'I know, Eloise. I'm so sorry.'

'Have you told the police?'

Victoria looked down at the table shamefully. 'No. I panicked. I don't want people to think of Dominic as that sort of man. He loves you so much, Eloise. It's all he ever talked about.'

'Did he say why?' Eloise asked, her voice oddly calm, her emotions suddenly muted. Later, alone, she would process this; she would scream into pillows and slap herself across the face to force the betrayal to tattoo her mind, to make it become real.

'It was only a short conversation. He was ashamed and guilty, and he was determined to end it, but he didn't say anything else. I wish I had more to tell you. Eloise, you have to understand, he made me swear not to tell you. I was hoping he'd wake up soon, tell you himself...'

Eloise stood. 'I think you should go. I need time to make sense of this.'

Victoria swept Eloise into her arms. 'I'm here if you need me. I know I made a mistake, but please, don't let that make you think I don't care. I'll come any time, day or night.'

Eloise hugged her mother-in-law: a liar, a woman she loved. 'Thank you.'

'I'm so sorry.'

'You don't have to keep saying that.'

'But I am. I could say it a thousand times and it wouldn't be enough.'

'When Dominic wakes up, he'll explain what he meant. It will all be okay.'

Eloise said this desperately; it, like so much else, was a lie. If Dominic really had cheated on her, nothing was going to be okay. If he'd been with another woman, Eloise would tear out his life support and watch him die without shedding a single tear.

CHAPTER THIRTY

VICTORIA

As Patrick spoke about his work problems, Victoria told herself a story. She was still seeing him to make him more smitten with her. It had been almost three months of her wrapping him around her finger; three months of turning him into a possession. When Charlotte had left before Christmas, Victoria had intended to end things with him. What use would he have now? But she'd kept seeing him, kept making love, kept taking walks, kept bonding. Why? What was wrong with her?

Charlotte had returned, and so Patrick had a purpose again. Her plan was to ask Patrick to help her with Charlotte. How long would the busybody sister want to hang around in Weston if she became the target of some unknown stalker? How long would her supposed interest last? She needed Patrick to have an endpoint. Otherwise, this feeling might grow too large, claim too much of her. She couldn't afford to care.

'They should appreciate you more,' Victoria said, when he was done venting, squeezing onto his arm and leaning close to him as they walked down the beach together. And perhaps, fine, there was something romantic there, something real, something beyond the manipulation Victoria had aimed at him each time they'd met.

Victoria, in another world maybe, could let herself feel something for this unlikely man and this unlikely relationship.

'I don't want to complain,' Patrick went on, sighing. 'But I do double the work, Vicky, double, and what do I get for it?'

'Let's get a coffee. My treat.'

'I'm a lucky man. I've got the best sugar momma ever...'

She laughed when he playfully tickled her, slapping him on the arm. They often joked about their age gap, but she had never detected any sign that Patrick was truly bothered by it. He had opened up to her as they'd spent more time together. He'd become... human in her eyes. What was he before then? A tool; he was still that, though, had to be that. Victoria's instinct dictated as much, but she'd be lying to herself if she claimed she didn't enjoy sitting on the beach with him, sipping their coffees, looking out at the sea.

She took his hand. 'I love you. I know I've said it before, but I want to say it again.'

She'd hooked him; she was reeling him in. But how much did he care, really? How much would he tolerate? Would he ride with her to the destructive end? Would he sacrifice himself upon the altar of her mistakes? Would he help her with the nosy solicitor? Would he commit crimes for her?

He touched her chin warmly, turned her gaze to his. His expression was hard. At first, his eyes had seemed dull, but she was growing to perversely like their solidness. 'You've given me...'

She leaned close, brushed her lips against his, an almost kiss. These were his favourites. She sensed the hunger in him from the manner his breath changed. If she was being honest, they were her favourites too. 'What, Patrick?'

'Meaning. A purpose. Life. A life, Vicky.' His eyes glistened. 'What do you want to do today?'

'I just want to be with you,' she whispered. 'Alone, the curtains closed, the door locked, the past shut out, the future shut out. Just us.'

He pushed his lips against hers, wrapping his arm around her. She felt his heart pounding against her body. 'We'll do that,' he said. 'Always and forever.'

'Always and forever,' she repeated dreamily.

And yes, fine, all right, there was a shimmering piece of her that wanted this. But to survive, she would kill this piece, stamp on it as she'd crushed so much else, eradicate her softness and let the predator in her surface.

'Let's ditch the coffees,' she whispered, kissing him just under his ear, the spot that made him wild. 'I want you all to myself...'

After the lovemaking – and, shamefully, it *was* beginning to feel like lovemaking – they stepped into the shower together.

Again she was struck with one of those brief, unhelpful moments, letting herself imagine a world in which she allowed this warped mimicry of a romance to develop. But she couldn't give in to that girlish notion. There was too much at stake.

They shared a bottle of wine in the living room. She'd be lying if she said she didn't like the hungry glimmer in his eyes... just a little. Not enough to stop what she had planned.

He took her hand. 'Do you have any idea how beautiful you are, Vicky?'

'Only when you tell me.'

He grinned. 'You're beautiful.'

She laughed. 'Say it again.'

'Beautiful, beautiful...'

They laughed like teenaged lovers and then went on with their wine.

'I was thinking about selling my house,' Victoria said.

Patrick's eyebrows shot up. 'Woah... why?'

She rolled her eyes, trailing her hand up his arm. 'Why do you think, silly? I'm thinking about the future: *our* future. Before I met you, I was happy to live in this big empty house and just try to enjoy my simple little life. But things have changed. *You've* changed me. Now, I'm not sure it's enough. I want us to go travelling together, to experience the world... And, well, weddings aren't cheap.'

She climbed into his lap 'What am I even saying? You probably think I'm a mad old crone. Before you say no, just kiss me.'

She grabbed his face in her hands and gave him the best kiss of his life. His body responded. He made animal grunting noises. Victoria flipped a switch in her mind; from this point on, she promised herself, no more caring. She would become ice.

'Do you mean it?'

'I love you,' she told the naïve fool. 'So much.'

'I love you too,' he said, tears glimmering in his eyes.

'Would you be ashamed to be married to me? I'm so old...'

'I don't care what anybody thinks,' he said, which was most likely true because he didn't have anybody who would judge him. No friends, no connections, just a sad flat and a dead-end job.

'I want you,' he went on. 'I need you. You're my angel.'

'You're my hero,' she said.

How could he not hear how cheesy and over the top this was?

'Shall we have some more wine?'

'Yeah...' A wet smile. 'But first.'

He leaned in for another kiss. Victoria allowed it to happen. After, she poured him another glass.

'Where would you want to go?' she asked.

'Uh, I don't know. Cornwall?'

Victoria almost laughed. She was talking about selling her ridiculously large and lavish home – which would net her at least four hundred thousand – and his first thought was *Cornwall*. Feeling bad about this was evidently a waste of time and energy; life was wasted on him. He wasn't fit for it. He didn't have the imagination.

'Perhaps somewhere more exotic?'

'My mum used to take me to Cornwall, one of the only good memories I've got,' he said. 'I remember sitting in her arms, looking at the sea. It ain't much, but it's something, isn't it?' He had tears in his eyes. '*Isn't it?*'

Suddenly, Victoria decided to put off her request for another time. She had been planning to ask him to help with Charlotte, or, at the very least, lay the groundwork for it: present a sob story which would make him more pliable when it was time for the request.

'It is,' she told him, wriggling into his arms. 'Will you just hold me?'

As she laid her cheek against his chest and listened to his heartbeat, she felt her confusion drift away. She was able to simply exist in this moment.

When Patrick fell asleep, Victoria left him there and went into her study, taking a leather-bound journal from her desk drawer. She had taken examples of her son's handwriting from his home office while Eloise was using the bathroom, and matching his voice was not a difficult feat for an observant and talented mama bear. Her plan would, she hoped, give the police what they wanted: an easy explanation, an excuse to close the case. She had ordered the journal online, wearing gloves whenever handling it; covering it in her son's fingerprints would be a simple task, considering how often she was at his bedside.

Once she had worked on her project for around an hour, she returned to the living room and slipped into Patrick's embrace, falling into a surprisingly peaceful sleep.

Her peace was disturbed when she woke to a wide-eyed Patrick glaring down at her. He shook her, trembling all over, his cheeks ghostly pale. 'You need to come with me.'

'What's wrong?'

'Now, Vicky.'

'What's going on?' she asked when he led her to the cellar door.

'I was going to make us some dinner. You were sleeping. I didn't want to disturb you.' He sounded shell-shocked. 'There was nothing in the freezer in the kitchen, but I remember you told me once, when I asked what was in the cellar. *There's nothing down there except a big old freezer*. So I thought I'd take a look.'

Victoria's heart began to pound, her mind scrambling as she searched for a way out of this. It was her fault for not getting rid of the body sooner, but the truth was, she wasn't always as tough as she wished she could be.

'Patrick...'

'You need to tell me what's going on.' He was almost shouting.

'I don't need to go down there again. I don't need to see it.'

'Do you think I wanted to see it?' He stumbled against the wall, shaking his head. 'Her – do you think I wanted to see her?'

'I can explain,' she whispered.

He looked, for the first time, like a man with a backbone. 'How could you explain this?'

'It was... Dominic,' she said after a pause, her instincts

rearranging her world, putting pieces together, as she adapted to this new reality.

'What?' Patrick snapped.

'My son isn't the person I made him out to be on my blog.'

'I don't understand.'

'I developed a loving relationship with my son. But when he was a boy, he was sometimes violent. He would find animals, hurt them. He would act inappropriately with girls. When he got older, he would...' Victoria croaked. 'He would hit me, Patrick. He would make fun of me. He would abuse my love. But I could never accept that side of him, so I bottled it up. I poured love into the blog. I only wanted that side of him to exist: the angel, my Dom Dom.'

'How does that relate to this – to *her*?'

'Before Dominic ended up in hospital, he showed up on my doorstep with a woman in his car boot. Dead, Patrick... He said I had to keep her here. He threatened me. I tried to say no, but he got physical. He could be so scary sometimes. He made me promise not to tell anyone. He said he was going to come back for her, but then he crashed and it was too late...'

'And you agreed?' She could hear his tone weakening; he wanted to believe her. He wanted to believe that these three months – probably the most significant in his sorry life – had meant something.

'What choice did I have? I didn't know what else to do. If he did that to her, what would he do to me?' She clutched onto Patrick's shirt, holding him fiercely, staring into his eyes. 'I didn't want to.' When the tears came, they were real. She didn't force them. She was telling the truth; she hadn't wanted any of this to happen.

He held on to her for a moment, then gently pushed her away. 'I can't be here. I can't even look at you.'

'I love you,' she said. 'Please, Patrick. This wasn't me. It was my boy. Please, don't abandon me. *Please.*'

He walked quickly to the door, pulling his shoes on.

She erupted into sobs... some might call them theatrical; some might call them manipulative. Perhaps if she thought she could physically stop him from leaving, she would have. But she'd felt his strong hands all over her body. Victoria was more powerful than anybody would've guessed by looking at her. But she knew he would be able to overpower her. Her tears were her weapon.

'Pah-Patrick. Puh-please.'

'I need time to think.'

'Are you going to ring the police?'

He grabbed the door handle.

'Are you going to ruin my life?'

He pulled the door open.

CHAPTER THIRTY-ONE

ELOISE

Eloise hadn't been to the hospital in two days. She'd spent her time at the house struggling to come to terms with what Victoria had told her. For almost an entire day, she remained in bed, her hands clutching her belly, thinking about Dominic with another woman, his hands roaming over her, his lips claiming hers, their nakedness colliding in messy and noisy betrayals. She didn't want to think like this, didn't want to imagine or entertain it, but she had to.

And, depressingly, her mind had begun to comb over the months before the crash. She remembered the long absences, the old "working late" excuse, the way he had seemed uncharacteristically reluctant to touch her. It had never been like that before, but once Eloise looked bluntly at it, she couldn't ignore the truth.

That morning, she and Charlotte were eating breakfast in the dining room, sunlight pouring in. Charlotte's eyes were dark pits.

'You're going to drink me out of house and home,' Eloise said good-naturedly.

Charlotte winced. 'Sorry.'

'I'm only joking. Don't worry about it. You need something to keep you busy. My life must be dull to you.'

Charlotte shook her head, but Eloise knew she was right. Charlotte was used to high-stress situations, burrowing to the bottom of legal cases, used to *doing* something. Eloise slightly resented her sister, because with Charlotte there, it was obvious how useless Eloise was being. Lying around the house, dwelling on the affair, instead of taking action.

But what was she supposed to do? The last thing she wanted was for anybody to know about the affair; that would almost be as bad as there being an affair itself. Or worse, honestly. Now, at least, she was able to maintain the fiction of the perfect marriage. Even if Victoria and she knew about the affair, Charlotte didn't, the police didn't. The world didn't.

The doorbell went. Eloise sighed and went to the front gate, a stab of panic striking her when she saw the two police officers waiting for her. What were their names? DI Cartwright and PC Skellon. The woman had been in a police uniform before, but this time, she wore a dark coat, tailored but worn, over a simple crewneck and black trousers.

'Yes, hello?' Eloise said, walking across the courtyard.

The male detective, DI Cartwright, was stubbly just like last time, as though he only shaved when it was absolutely necessary.

'Mrs Hawthorne,' DI Cartwright said. 'We have some more questions regarding your husband's crash.'

Eloise was keen to give them a better impression this time. She wanted them to see her as the tragic wife, a suffering figure deserving of sympathy, not somebody to stick up on a whiteboard in their station with the word "Suspect" above it. 'Of course. I'll open the gate. Would you like a cup of coffee, tea?'

She ignored the look they exchanged; it was their job to be

suspicious, she reminded herself. Charlotte stood as they entered.

'This is my sister, Charlotte,' Eloise explained. 'Charlotte, this is DI Cartwright and PC Skellon.'

'A PC in plain clothes,' Charlotte muttered.

PC Skellon stood up straighter.

'She's going to be one of us very soon,' DI Cartwright said, a hint of warmth penetrating his gruff exterior.

'Charlotte is very protective,' Eloise said, giving her sister a look. 'But she understands you're only trying to get the best outcome for everybody. It's okay, Charlotte. I can handle this. Unless you need to speak with her too?'

Again, Eloise noticed that subtle suspicion on the faces of the officers. Why was she suddenly being so helpful? It was simple really; she didn't want to give any hint that she knew about the affair. She didn't want people to know. If Dominic woke, she would teach him the error of his ways. Before then, any drama was best kept behind closed doors.

'I need a shower anyway,' Charlotte grunted, sounding miserable like she got in the mornings after a heavy night of wine.

Eloise made the hot drinks and they sat at the table.

'We're here because there's been a development,' DI Cartwright said. 'We have obtained CCTV footage that shows somebody else in the vehicle with your husband on the night of his crash.'

Eloise gasped, her mind going to the obvious place. 'Who?' she demanded.

'The footage doesn't make that entirely clear, as it's dark and they're not completely visible,' PC Skellon went on, 'but the passenger and your husband seem physically familiar with each other.' The officer gave her a knowing woman-to-woman look. It was a challenge; it was supposed to break Eloise.

'Physically familiar?' Eloise wanted to slap her across the face.

'The footage was, unfortunately, not of very high quality. But we were able to observe them gesturing passionately and kissing.'

'Kissing,' Eloise repeated, her world imploding, her brain aching, thoughts shattering. Call her dramatic; call her old-fashioned. But she always wanted a fairy-tale picture-perfect marriage, something to be proud of, something untouchable. They weren't just touching it; they were tearing it to pieces.

'We'd like to know if you have any idea who this might be,' DI Cartwright said. 'This person obviously wasn't at the crash site.'

'You think they fled the crash?'

'Why do you say that?' DI Cartwright said.

'Well, what else would you be saying?' Eloise was letting out far too much anger: far too much of her real self.

'Do you have any idea who this person might be?' DI Cartwright asked again.

They stared expectantly. There was an issue with living so stubbornly in the world of make-believe. When she couldn't persuade the real world to take the shape she wanted, she felt lost.

'You can understand where our suspicions might take us,' DI Cartwright went on.

Eloise felt like they were attacking her. Was that fair? 'Can I?'

His lip twitched; it was as if this was the reaction he had wanted. 'A man, drunk, driving at night with a woman...'

'You said you couldn't see them properly.'

'We couldn't clearly discern her features, but from her general shape and from their relations, we are assuming that she is female. But even if we're wrong, the presence of another person raises additional questions. To answer those questions, we need to know who she is.'

Eloise felt like the room was spinning. She didn't want to answer them, didn't want to share her suspicions. It was one thing to hear about it, another for evidence to be so bluntly presented. It felt like an attack.

'This woman, whoever she is,' DI Cartwright said, his tone like he was explaining something to a child, 'might have her own reasons for not wanting her whereabouts that night to be known. Perhaps she doesn't want people to know she was in a married man's car in the middle of the night...'

Eloise ground her teeth. 'I'm not sure what you're asking me.'

They all but rolled their eyes. PC Skellon said, 'Do you have any idea who might've been with your husband that night?'

Eloise took a long sip of her coffee. It was black, hot, burnt her tongue; she didn't care. She kept sipping to buy herself some time. But when she laid the mug down, she wasn't closer to an answer. She didn't want to implicate Victoria in a lie to the police, though she was still annoyed at her mother-in-law for keeping this secret. She understood why she'd done it though. That didn't mean she approved.

'Mrs Hawthorne?' PC Skellon pressed.

Eloise stared at the woman, her rosy cheeks, her clear ambition. They were like a different species. 'I... I don't know,' she said.

Her heart pounded.

'Is there something you'd like to tell us?' DI Cartwright said.

'I don't *know* anything.' Eloise realised two things too late: she sounded defensive, therefore guilty; and she'd put the emphasis in a suspicious place.

'You don't know,' he replied. 'But perhaps you've noticed things?'

'It's difficult for a wife not to notice when her husband is behaving differently,' PC Skellon went on. 'The last thing we want is to upset you, but if we can learn who was in the car, we may be able to make some serious progress towards learning who might've wanted to hurt your husband.'

Eloise ground her teeth again, then forcibly stopped herself. This was something she couldn't ignore. An affair, a spit-in-the-face, kick-in-the-teeth affair, something other people did, not her, not Dominic. Inside, they'd had their fractures, but the damage never reached their surface, their anniversary photos, their fantastical trips. An affair was too much. An affair was almost a capital offence. Eloise's mind swarmed with all the times she'd thought she'd smelled perfume, with Dominic's excuses to avoid sex, his growing reluctance to meet her eye.

She'd thought it had something to do with... well, *her*, Eloise, the layers their hatred sometimes took, the growing difficulty of their reconciliations. Eloise wasn't innocent, fine, but obviously Dominic was twice as guilty.

Her head throbbed as they just stared and stared, waiting for an answer.

'Perhaps you noticed things?' PC Skellon said.

'What I told you is true. I don't know anything.'

Eloise decided she wouldn't mention the phone call. Victoria had hidden it for a reason. What if she got her mother-in-law in trouble? Charlotte was family, sure, but Victoria was Eloise's rock. When Charlotte left, which she inevitably would, Victoria would still be there.

'But?' PC Skellon said.

Eloise felt like they'd cornered her. It was the way they were staring expectantly, leaving her little choice. 'But for a few months he was staying at work later. He seemed less interested in... Well, you know. But like I said, I don't *know* anything. It's just, well, yeah...'

'You believe your husband may have been having an affair,' DI Cartwright said.

Eloise stared down at the table, tears filling her eyes. She wasn't entirely sure how they'd arrived at this ugly destination. But at least she could keep Victoria out of it.

'Yes,' Eloise whispered. 'But I don't know who it could've been. Or why. *Why.*' She let out a shaky sob. 'That's the most confusing question. I don't know why he would do this. We had the perfect marriage.'

PC Skellon and DI Cartwright looked at each other as if to say, *Nobody has the perfect marriage.* Perhaps that was true. Perhaps, if one brought a harsh inspecting light to bear on it, the cracks would show. But when the door shut and Eloise was free to shine and darken where she pleased, she could *make* it perfect.

'We're going to be acquiring a warrant to examine his electronics,' DI Cartwright said. 'Do you have any issue with that?'

There they went again, right to the offensive. 'Why would I? Go ahead; take what little is left of him.'

'Mrs Hawthorne,' he went on, 'if there's anything else you haven't told us, now is the time. Anything and everything is useful to us.'

'There isn't,' she said tersely.

There were things she hadn't told anybody – reasons why Dominic might've sought comfort elsewhere – but she had never spoken of them.

The police said goodbye, and Eloise walked them out. Once they were gone, she leaned against the door, wrapping her arms around herself.

Later, Victoria visited. When she asked to use the bathroom, Eloise sensed something off about her. Eloise wasn't as naïve as

Victoria probably believed, as the world probably believed. She followed her.

That was when everything changed. That was when she made her choice; that was when she birthed a secret she would carry to her grave.

Her husband had cheated on her. He'd tried to ruin her. Eloise wouldn't allow herself to feel guilty. He'd left her no choice.

CHAPTER THIRTY-TWO

PATRICK

When Patrick discovered the corpse, it was the second time Vicky had exploded his world. The first was at their initial meeting when she'd touched his hand and he'd made a flirty comment, his heart pounding from how forward he was being, sweat beading on his forehead with a woman he'd just met... but then she'd reciprocated, and he'd felt an overwhelming sense of victory, of having *done something*. He wasn't the flirty type, but he'd taken a chance with her and it had paid off.

Since then, they'd shared so much. He'd gone so long without having anybody to talk to: about work, about his dreams, about his past, about anything. She listened closely, love pouring from every cell in her beautiful being. She was over twice his age, but how could he give a damn about that?

She was fit for her age, but it was more than that. She was gorgeous inside and out. If Patrick's mother had shown even one-tenth of the love Victoria had in her heart, he would've spent every day trying to make her proud. Each time Patrick pictured Victoria, she was crying, begging him not to go to the police. He knew it would be the right thing to do, but he couldn't do it. Maybe he was mad, but he loved her. It had been months, dozens of meetings, the world would judge their relationship... but he loved her.

After work, with no sleep, he finally rang her. He'd almost done it several times already, but he was a coward. That was the cruel truth. He was terrified of looking at that corpse again. But he was more scared of leaving Victoria to deal with it alone.

He sat in his car as the phone rang on loudspeaker, watching the exit to the warehouse, his colleagues laughing with each other, making it look so easy. He'd always been an outsider; he'd never quite found his footing. But that wasn't true anymore. With Vicky, he'd found something worth far more than casual friendship.

'Patrick?' Vicky answered in a heartbreaking tone, as if she didn't believe it was him.

'I'm here.' It had only been two days, but his voice was unsteady with emotion.

'I thought it was over.' She sobbed. 'I've been waiting for the police to knock on my door.'

'I would never betray you,' Patrick said, disgusted. 'It was a shock, Vicky. But I'd never do that to you.'

'We shouldn't speak about this over the phone. But I know I've got no right to ask you to come to the house.'

Patrick felt like a bully for causing her so much pain. Out of his car window he saw another of his colleagues, a young woman with a bob of red hair who had once rejected him for a date. Patrick had felt like a loser – always had, truth be told – but Vicky had changed that.

'Are you free now?'

'Yes,' she said, the relief in her voice making him feel needed. 'I'll make us some tea.'

'I'll be right there.'

Patrick drove, knowing he was crossing a line. He was

officially becoming an accomplice. But there was some comfort in this. It was he and Vicky against the world. He would help her; he would save her. With Vicky, he wasn't a burden. He wasn't in the way. He mattered.

Parking up outside her large house, he thought about what she'd said about selling it. When this was all over, they'd have a life in Cornwall together. Their love would be all the fiercer for her age; it would make every day special, every moment vital. Their age gap would enhance their romance in a way most people would never understand.

She greeted him at the door, looking youthful and fit and beautiful. He was often shocked by her age: sixty-eight, but she was strong, capable. She was everything he could've dreamt of in a life partner. Her hair was down, messy and gorgeous around her shoulders.

He lost control the moment he laid eyes on her, taking her hips and pulling her against him. He loved how firm her body felt. How practical. He imagined them taking long walks through the countryside together once this was all over.

She moaned and pulled him into the house, turning and pushing him against the wall. He gasped as something released in him: two days of longing, two days of hunger. She pushed her hands against his chest, looking up with glistening eyes.

'I don't want to do anything if this is the end,' she said. 'I can't. Oh, Patrick. It'll hurt too much.'

He tucked a strand of her hair behind her ear. 'I never should've left you. I panicked.'

She rolled her eyes. 'Do you think I blame you for that? How could you *not* have panicked? When Dominic brought the poor dead girl here and threatened me to hide her, my world fell apart. I don't know what to do. I don't know...'

She began to hyperventilate. Patrick wrapped his arms

around her and gently stroked his hand through her hair. 'Shush. It's going to be all right.'

'How could it possibly? I feel awful for the girl, but I've kept her there so long, trying not to think about her, trying not to acknowledge the situation. It's become this stain on my life, but I've blocked it out. I can't ignore it forever.'

'You don't need to worry about it anymore,' Patrick whispered. 'It's a blip, Vicky. Just a blip. I want that life we talked about. I want Cornwall. I want freedom. I want *us*. Let me help you.'

She sniffled, sinking her hands into his sides desperately. It was like she never wanted to let go. 'Help me?'

Patrick kissed her forehead, then her cheek, then moved his lips to hers. He stared intimately into her eyes. When they were this close, her age melted away. When he was looking only into her eyes, she became a scared child, lost and confused, needing him. 'I tried to stay away, but it felt like dying. That's the sort of thing those blokes say in cheesy romcoms, but it's true. I need you. So, let me help you.'

'I still don't know what you mean.'

He wasn't sure if he was up to this. He might have to have a beer or two or three just to work up the courage to go into the cellar again. But he'd do it for her. 'You won't be able to sell the house with...' He swallowed. 'With *her* down there, will you?'

'No,' she whispered. 'We won't be able to begin our lives together.'

'Cornwall, just me and you.'

'Just me and you,' she repeated. 'But what are you going to do?'

The feeling of being mature, of being in control, left him. 'What do you think I should do?'

'Well...' Victoria sniffled, fighting off a sob. He hated seeing her like this. 'You're right; we can't begin our lives until she's gone. Which means she has to go…'

'Then that's what I'll do.'

'I'm going to be in serious trouble if anybody ever finds out about this.'

'Hush.' He held her tightly, stroking her hair again. 'Nobody's going to find out. It isn't your fault. You were doing what you always have, trying to be a good mum. I'd never let anything happen to you.'

He meant it. Their love was worth fighting for. He was still filled with terror, but he'd push past it. For her. For them. For their future. He'd do what he had to do and then bury it so deep, he'd never think about it again.

'This will be over soon,' he said. 'Then it'll just be me and you.'

She looked up at him, tears in her eyes, then grabbed his shirt and pulled herself in for a kiss.

CHAPTER THIRTY-THREE

CHARLOTTE

When Charlotte woke, she experienced that familiar wave of guilt and self-hatred. Drinking too much was a tricky and confusing thing. When she was enjoying her first sips of the expensive wine, she felt as if she was at the beginning of some grand adventure. She felt like she was ramping up to something... and then she woke, and it all seemed dreary and depressing. She sat up, rubbing her eyes. It was getting dark. How long had she been asleep? No, not asleep. Call it what it was: *passed out*.

She took a shower, then splashed cold water in her face and stared at herself in the mirror. This had to stop. This was sad. This was weak. All her high ideals of self-love and self-care were draining away. She wanted to punch the mirror to shatter her reflection. Just like Dominic had.

It was work, she felt sure, the lack of it, the lack of routine. But that was just another cop-out. She couldn't even use self-medicating as an excuse. What was she running from? Nothing; there was no reason. Except for a vague hollow feeling – and she felt sure many people experienced this – she had no reason to blot out her emotions.

She found Eloise sitting at the kitchen bar, tears streaming down her cheeks, staring down at a leather-bound diary.

'E?' Charlotte rushed to her sister, putting her hand on her shoulder.

Eloise reached up and desperately clawed onto her with so much intensity, Charlotte believed for one somehow beautiful moment they might bridge the gap that had existed for their entire lives.

'I found it in Dominic's wardrobe,' she said, gulping as she tried to fight off another sob. For a brief moment, Charlotte thought about how theatrical her sister seemed. 'He talks about... An affair. He claims the guilt is driving him insane. That's why he was drinking so much. He was running away from the pain. The pain of his betrayal. He wants it to end; he says he's thinking about doing something drastic. Hurting himself. Ending it all.'

Charlotte sat down, taking Eloise's hands, ignoring the niggle that Eloise seemed to be putting on a show. Charlotte was being overly suspicious: an occupational hazard. 'This is awful. I'm sorry.'

Eloise looked sideways at Charlotte. 'What?'

Charlotte flinched. 'What?'

'I feel like there's something you're not saying...'

'You said you found it in his wardrobe.'

'Yes.'

'I'm just shocked you didn't find it before now. I know you like to lie down in there with his suits.' Her suspicion bled out despite her desire to be a supportive sister.

'I wasn't looking. It was in one of his jacket pockets. He probably didn't even remember it was there. Or maybe he thought I'd find it eventually. He talks about hurting himself. Do you think he cut his own brakes?'

'I don't know. The police haven't said exactly how it happened?'

'No, but they've implied things.'

'Implied things, E?'

'They've said things that make me think there was a specific method used that would've been easier for somebody of my expertise – well, lack of it. They're trying to say it's me, but they're wrong. Obviously.'

'Obviously,' Charlotte said fiercely.

'What if it was Dominic? He was no mechanic, but he could've done his research. Maybe he wanted this to happen. Maybe he wanted to end it. Not just for him, but for his mistress too, and that was why she was in the car that night. Maybe the guilt got too much.'

Charlotte touched her shoulders. 'Just slow down. Do you think Dominic's capable of that? Not only hurting himself, but an innocent woman?'

'She wasn't fucking *innocent*,' Eloise said viciously. Charlotte was taken aback. When Eloise softened her tone, Charlotte once again felt like this was a show. She tried to bury the feeling. Eloise needed her support, not her doubt. 'I'm sorry. This is just a lot to take in. And no – I don't think Dominic would hurt anybody. But it's right here in black and white. He talks over and over about ending it, the guilt becoming too much. Perhaps that's why he drank that night. To get the courage up. Perhaps he was waiting for a rainy night, knowing his brakes would fail. Perhaps he could justify it in some messed-up way. It wasn't his fault; it was the road, the rain, fate.'

As Eloise ranted, Charlotte couldn't stop her thoughts from whirring. A journal in which a comatose man talked about wanting to end his own life? Discovered just then, when the police were poking around? It all seemed too convenient to her, and yet, she refused to put her sister on trial.

'I really don't know, E,' Charlotte said after a pause.

'I can't believe it,' Eloise whimpered. 'All this time, he was seeing somebody else. Maybe that was why he never wanted a baby. The horrible part is, it all makes sense now. There were so many signs I missed. He stopped being interested in sex. I had to throw myself at him just to conceive our child, and even then, it was like he was forcing himself, doing his marital duty rather than enjoying it. He was distant. He stayed later at work. Once, when he came home, I was sure he'd been crying. His eyes were red. He said it was hay fever. But maybe it was guilt.'

Eloise flipped the page, then shoved the book into Charlotte's hands. 'Look.'

Charlotte read the entry, the handwriting jagged as though the writer had been in a hurry... or under the influence. *The pain in me knows no end. What's wrong with me, doing this to my beautiful wife? I want to end it all, but I'm too much of a coward. Maybe I'll put it into the hands of fate...*

'The hands of fate.' Eloise sobbed. 'No guesses for what he means by that. I wish he'd just *told* me.'

'He knows you'd never take him back,' Charlotte said, thinking that this only applied if Dominic had, in fact, wrote this. Where was Charlotte letting instinct lead her... to the idea that Eloise had written this? Or something more disturbing?

'I don't think he cared about that,' Eloise said. 'He only cared about her. About his girlfriend. He had a whole other life going on right under my nose and I knew nothing about it.'

Charlotte's head spun. She thought about how angry Garry had become when challenged about witnessing the LPA; she thought about the looks flashing across Victoria's face when they'd first met. But she was also conscious of the notion she might be letting her professional concerns seep into this domestic part of her life. Her desire to work, and work hard, might have been bottled up for too long. And now it was attempting to burst free.

'Do you think I should tell the police?' Eloise said. There was something in her tone that made Charlotte think she was seeking her approval. 'They have to know, don't they?'

Eloise struggled not to break down again. Charlotte massaged her sister's arm, attempting to stifle her solicitor's speculations. After all, they were grounded in... what, precisely? A feeling? A notion? A few sour looks and an instinct that all was not as it seemed?

'Uh...'

'What?' Eloise demanded.

'As long as you're absolutely sure that Dominic wrote it.'

'What are you talking about?' Eloise said in disbelief. 'Who else would've written it? It matches Dominic's handwriting; I found it in his jacket. Nobody else has been here except for me, you, and the police. Unless you think somebody broke into this house and planted it? But I have security alarms.'

'I don't know,' Charlotte said, sounding like a broken record even to herself.

'I know what you're thinking, but please, don't say it. Don't even think it. I don't want to hear it.'

'I'm not saying anything.'

'She's supported me every single day. She loves her son.'

'I didn't accuse her, did I?' Charlotte said tersely.

'You were thinking it,' Eloise replied. 'She's the only other person who could've... God, what? Planted it for me to find?' Again: a touch of the theatrical.

Charlotte had a sinister and ugly thought. If Eloise was involved somehow, would Charlotte abandon her? Or would she pretend not to see? Would she still be there for her?

'I didn't accuse her,' Charlotte repeated, letting far more anger into her voice than she'd intended. When Eloise's eyebrows furrowed and her lip began to tremble, she looked like a little kid. Charlotte put her hand on her shoulder. 'E, I'm sorry. I think I'm still a little drunk, not that that's an excuse. I'm sure you're right. I'm letting myself get paranoid. I'm seeing things which aren't there. And yes, you should probably tell the police.'

When Eloise sighed and smiled, Charlotte had the distinct, ugly feeling she had been manipulated. 'I know it's difficult for you being here,' Eloise said. 'You know you don't have to stay, don't you?'

'I'm your sister. I'm going to be here for you.'

She said the last part almost desperately, wanting and needing it to be true, even as a little voice in her head told her she was almost at the end of the line; it was almost time to accept she had made every difference she was going to make. She buried that annoying, cynical voice.

'I love you,' Eloise said. 'I've always loved you, even when we were kids.'

That sounded like an accusation. Eloise had loved Charlotte, but could Charlotte say the same in return? It was only recently she'd tried to rebuild some kind of connection: a connection that might lead her to ignore things she should've seized upon, to silence voices which should've been allowed to scream.

'Let me make us some cuppas,' Charlotte said.

'Sure, and while you do that, I'll ring the detective.'

A MOTHER'S MUSINGS: IF NOT NOW, WHEN?
19/01/25

Victoria Hawthorne

Those of you who have been readers of my blog for some time will know I have often hinted at my less-than-idyllic childhood. You will know that my mother is still alive, but I haven't spoken to her in almost forty years. You will know that when my father died, I did not mourn him. You will know that something happened to me, but I have never stated in clear terms what this is.

Last night, for the first time in a long time, I had a dream about those early, scarring, scary days. I woke covered in sweat, gasping for air, hardly able to breathe or function. It's like all that stowed-away misery was trying to burst out of me. I think it was a sign; I am compelled to share the truth.

I am compelled because I am a mother bear more than anything. I am claws and teeth and protective instincts. I am a woman who did everything in my power, from the day my angel was born, to never inflict pain upon my child.

Sometimes, when my Dom Dom was young, I would look at him and think: how did my parents do that to me when I was his age? How could they live with themselves?

Okay... (imagine, if you will, that I am taking a big breath to summon the courage needed to face these demons) to make it clear: both my parents abused me physically and... And in the other way: the vilest manner. Perhaps I thought I was stronger than I truly am when I sat down to type this post. But I'm sure you all know what I mean. They did things to me no adult should ever do to a child. They took my innocence, both of them, sadistically and enthusiastically and repeatedly. They made a prison of my bedroom.

Oh, my fellow mama bears, just think of it. *How?* Think of those nights spent with your babies, holding them as they try to fall asleep, your bodies pressed against theirs. How could anybody even dream of taking that someplace else, someplace bleaker, someplace evil? Those intrusive thoughts would sometimes strike me as I held my baby...

I'd lie in bed with him, and I'd think this was when they would do it. Instead of savouring the love and the closeness, their thoughts would set ablaze with unspeakable sick desire. My mother or my father would cackle and call for the other, and then *it* would begin, the unacknowledgeable *it*. I can't type it, but you know what *it* is.

It would last for hours, and though it hurt my body, it hurt my heart and my soul so much more. Sometimes I would dissociate, and my young, innocent thoughts would surge into the future. I'd think of the day I had my own child. I'd make silent promises that I would never hurt my son or daughter. I would protect them no matter what. I would die – indeed, I would kill – before I allowed this species of dread to touch them even for a moment.

I am by no means a perfect person, but there is one

thing that will always make me proud. My Dom Dom never knew abuse. My Dom Dom never tasted terror. Mother, if you're reading this, I hope this is the message you take away with you.

I ended the cycle.

To those of you who decided to read this post, thank you. I know it can't have been easy. I consider each and every one of you my friends. Perhaps it will seem arbitrary to some. I've kept quiet on the specifics for so many years, only to allow a nightmare to prompt me. But if not now, when?

[The blog post is accompanied by an image: In black and white, Victoria sits in the corner of a cellar, on the floor, her arms wrapped around her knees. Her hair falls over her face, hiding it. She wears only a shirt, her legs bare.]

Comments (2,052)

HopefulMama38

I'm so sorry you went through this. Your strength in sharing your story is incredible. As a mom, I can't imagine treating a child that way. You're breaking cycles, and that's so inspiring.

LovingLife82

This brought me to tears. My father was abusive, and I've carried so much shame for years. Hearing your story makes me feel like I can finally start to let go of some of that pain. You're helping so many of us by being so open.

TiredButTrying

Thank you for this post. I'm trying so hard to parent

differently than I was raised. Some days I catch myself reacting the way my parents did, and it breaks my heart. Your blog is a reminder to keep fighting to do better.

SarahLouTX

Wow, this hit home. My mom was verbally abusive. I've spent years in therapy trying to undo the damage. I'm in awe of how you've managed to come out the other side and use your voice to help others.

MomOfFourAndMore

I don't usually comment, but I had to say thank you. Reading this made me think of my sister, who went through something similar. I'm sharing this with her – I know it will mean a lot to her.

Bethany_RN

Your words are so raw and real. I'm a nurse and see firsthand the impact of childhood trauma on adults. Your ability to put this into words is a gift, and I'm sure you're helping so many people by sharing your truth.

Max_Was_Here_And_Will_Always_Be

I'm sorry, but I don't buy this. There are way too many people crying "abuse" these days.

Replies—

HealingWithGrace

This has to be a joke. Who do you think you are? Do you seriously think a woman would invent something like this? I bet you lead a very small and sad life.

ResilientRoots77
Look, ladies, we've found the troll!

ShatteredButStrong
Calling her a liar is perhaps the most sickening thing you could do. You'll never know how difficult it's been for us to press ahead and come out the other side of the misery we've suffered. I'm not going to tell you what I think of you, Max, but let me just say this. I hope you're single.

Click here to read more comments

CHAPTER THIRTY-FOUR

CHARLOTTE

Charlotte was at her wits' end. She had never realised before how vital work was to her ability to function as a regular human being. Christmas and her descent into boozing and binging had brought that home, and without work to focus on, her mind was a mess. Eloise didn't know about her stint in rehab. Otherwise, Charlotte was sure her sister would've been far less generous with the expensive and frankly delicious bottles of wine.

Charlotte had decided to do something probably drastic, but she was running out of time. Soon, her absence of work would be over. Perhaps she *could*, technically speaking, stay in Weston-super-Mare longer. If she was the sister she had been trying to become, she might tell her employer to stick her well-paying and rewarding job where the sun didn't shine. She had business in the West Country. She wouldn't leave until it was solved.

But the truth was, she missed work badly. She missed how it made thinking about anything else impossible. She missed sixteen-hour days. She was going insane sitting around Eloise's large house, listening to her sister cry about Dominic's affair, watching Eloise and Victoria clutch onto each other like aristocratic heroines in a Victorian melodrama.

Had Dominic truly cut his own brakes? Had Eloise's husband done this to himself and his secret lover? Or was her sister somehow involved, perhaps even working with Victoria – for what, exactly? Why? Charlotte hated herself for the thought. But if she distanced herself, looked at it like she'd look at any other case in her working life, she couldn't rule it out. She also knew that stranger things had happened than a cheating husband leaving behind a journal in which he ranted about his guilt and desire for self-destruction.

Charlotte massaged her forehead as she drove down the motorway. She'd told Eloise she had to return to London for the evening for a meeting, but that was a lie. Using a contact she'd known for years through her solicitor work, she'd got hold of Victoria's mother's address. Cecilia Basset lived in Cornwall.

What was Charlotte doing, exactly? She couldn't shake the feeling that something was off about Victoria. She had recently posted some serious allegations online. Were they true? Charlotte wanted to know just how far Victoria would go to paint herself as the victim, even if the idea that somebody would make something like this up disgusted her. Also, Charlotte was inclined to believe all women. But *this* particular woman was just... off somehow. That blog post seemed almost too perfect. And the photo, the staged photo she'd taken, it was too much.

The post had reeked of somebody trying to farm as much pity as she possibly could. It stank of a guilty conscience... or masking an uglier side she refused to show the world. It was titled *If Not Now, When?* as if its appearance at that particular time was just happenstance, prompted by a dream, but that seemed flimsy. It was an example of attention-seeking, but it was also more than that. It was like Victoria was overcompensating. *Look at me; I am a good person; I am a victim. How could I possibly scheme or manipulate or hurt anyone?*

Even as she thought this, Charlotte felt guilty. She felt like she was betraying her sex, betraying the cause, but she couldn't ignore the fact the post reeked of crap.

Eloise wouldn't listen to Charlotte when it came to anything Victoria-related. As far as Eloise was concerned, Victoria was the doting, caring mother-in-law. Victoria was the mama bear she'd always wanted. Eloise liked to claim not everything was about childhood, but clearly, this was. Eloise wouldn't have stubbornly attached herself to Victoria if their own mother had shown just a little bit of love.

Charlotte arrived as the sun was setting. She sat in her car outside the converted Victorian house, which had been turned into four flats. Her head was pulsing, the urge to crack open a bottle of wine far too strong. She despised herself for this, but damn it, she was doing her best, wasn't she? Never mind that if Eloise knew she was there, she'd hate her for it. Even if Charlotte learnt that Victoria was a liar, what then? Could she tell Eloise?

It would give Charlotte something secure to latch onto. It would mean that all this wasn't merely based on a vague, angry hunch.

She climbed from the car and walked across the street. As she pressed her finger down on the buzzer, she thought about leaving. A voice crackled over the intercom quickly, before she could give into her doubts.

'Hello?' a woman said defensively.

'Hello, Miss Basset. My name is Charlotte. I'm Eloise

Hawthorne's sister. Your daughter is my sister's mother-in-law. I want to speak with you about Victoria.'

'What?' Miss Basset demanded. 'About Vicky?'

'Do you know that she has a blog? Have you seen her latest post?'

'Are you a journalist?' Miss Basset said, sounding confused.

'No, Miss Basset. I'm Eloise Hawthorne's sister.'

'Don't take that tone. I'm not slow. You could be her sister *and* a journalist, couldn't you? Or is sister a full-time profession?'

Charlotte thought about the post, the accusations. If they were true, this woman was pure evil. Her behaviour wasn't exactly dissuading Charlotte. But being snappy didn't equate to being an abuser.

'I'm a solicitor,' Charlotte said. 'I'm not here in a professional capacity though. I just want to know if Victoria is the person she pretends to be. Could you please let me in so we can speak? Or perhaps we could go for a coffee someplace?'

'I don't go out much.'

'It could be my treat, Miss Basset.'

'Just get up here. But if you're some scammer, know this: I've got nothing worth stealing. If you're one of Vicky's mad fans, and you're here to hurt me, then go ahead. I'm not long for this world anyway.'

Sadness tightened in Charlotte's chest as the door buzzed open. She walked up a flight of rickety stairs, noticing the damp on the walls, the thinness and threadbare quality of the carpet. When she knocked on the flat door, Miss Basset yelled, 'Yes, yes, come in.'

Charlotte entered a surprisingly neat flat. It was old, parts of it clearly in need of repair, but it was regularly cleaned and had a faint, not unpleasant vanilla scent. Miss Basset was sitting in the living room, watching a game show on an old television.

She looked up tiredly, her face incredibly wrinkled, her eyes moist. 'Told you there isn't much worth stealing. I'd offer you a drink but that'd mean standing up. My knees aren't what they used to be.'

'I can get us some tea, if you like?'

'All right, fine. Why not? Milk, two sugars.'

Charlotte went into the kitchen. It hadn't been modernised since the seventies or eighties, it seemed. She found the teabags, boiled the kettle, then carried two ancient mugs into the living room.

Miss Basset had turned off the television. 'Are you here about Vicky's blog then?'

'Have you read her most recent post?'

'No, but my neighbour, Tony, he told me about it this morning. Apparently, her father and I did all manner of awful things to her. Apparently, I was just as bad as him. Apparently, my daughter is the biggest victim who has ever lived, a woman deserving of all the pity in the world. Do I have it about right?'

'More or less.' Charlotte took a sip of her tea. 'Is she lying?'

'Lying and Vicky... that's a tricky question.'

'How so?'

'Does a bird, when taking flight, think about each movement of its wings? Does a rat contemplate the twitch in its tail when scurrying across the floor? Does a dog spend time dwelling on its bark when the postman comes?'

'You're saying lying comes naturally to her.'

'The way she sees it, lying isn't what she does. She creates her own bloody... *world*.'

That was why Victoria and Eloise got on so well. Charlotte didn't share this with Miss Basset, but it made sense. How many times had Eloise talked about creating her own reality? Most of the self-help podcasts she listened to were about that, or a variation on the same theme.

'So, she was lying in her most recent blog post?'

Miss Basset sighed. 'It doesn't matter what I say. These days, people can put anything they want online. It makes no difference. People will believe what they'll believe.'

'What if I'm ready to believe you?'

'What's Vicky done to you to get you to visit little old me?'

'She gives me a strange feeling,' Charlotte said. 'And it's like she's cast a spell on my sister. For Eloise, Victoria can do no wrong. It's unhealthy. She won't hear a bad word said about her, and Victoria plays on that. I haven't got long to set this right.'

'Why not?'

'I've got… work.' Charlotte sighed. The excuse sounded flimsy when she said it aloud. 'I've got my own life.'

The real answer would've been: *I need to get back to London and make my life as busy as I possibly can so I can stop climbing into a bottle.*

'You're asking me if I abused my own daughter?'

'Yes.'

Miss Basset coughed out a laugh. 'Dear, if I was the monster Vicky says I am, do you think *asking* me would do any good? I would lie, wouldn't I? It's a step down from what I have apparently done already.'

'I want your side of the story.'

'There's no side to the story. There's only the truth.'

'Give me that then.'

Miss Basset slurped on her tea, her hands trembling as she placed the mug on a coaster. 'It's not something I enjoy talking about.'

'She's told the whole world that you and your husband took turns abusing a defenceless child, Miss Basset. Are you fine with that?'

'Of course not, but there's not much to be done about it, is there? I won't be around for much longer. Whatever's going to happen, will happen. Vicky knows the truth, deep down in her heart. At least, I hope she does. I hope her lies haven't burrowed so deep they've changed her. Now that I think of it, though, Vicky would be capable of that.'

'Of making her own reality. Believing in it.'

'Yes,' Miss Basset said. 'Exactly. She was always like that. Apparently, what happened to her, to us, it wasn't special enough.'

'What happened?'

Miss Basset blinked, her eyes welling. She took a tissue from the sleeve of her cream cardigan and dabbed at her face. 'Her father used to... hit me,' she said falteringly. 'It wasn't as uncommon as one might have hoped, but it was still monstrous.'

'Of course it was,' Charlotte said fiercely. 'Any time, any place, it's unacceptable.'

'I was scared to leave him. You know, the old cliché. The battered wife.'

'I understand.'

'But then, when Vicky was around fourteen, I discovered that her father had been abusing her. I caught him sneaking into her bedroom, that foul, foul man. That gave me all the motivation I needed to leave him. I screamed at him to get out that night. I would've killed him if he'd stayed. Or drove him to the point where he would've killed me.'

Charlotte was afraid to talk. It was like Miss Basset had slipped into the past, was reliving what had happened to her.

'He left, and I was going to ring the police. But Vicky stopped me.'

'Victoria didn't want him arrested?' Charlotte said, when Miss Basset paused.

'The poor girl.' Miss Basset sniffled. 'He'd filled her head with lies about what she owed him, about her obligation to keep him out of prison. He'd convinced her they were in it together.

It was heartbreaking. I'm ashamed to admit I let her convince me. I didn't ring the police, but only with the promise that she would never see him again. He fled to the other side of the country, then did us both a favour and died.'

'How were things between you?' Charlotte asked.

'They weren't,' Miss Basset said. 'I had to work. Vicky ignored me when I came home. She left as soon as she could. Years later, during our infrequent meetings, she would begin dropping hints about this other version of her childhood. Finally, she came right out and said it. I was livid. We had an argument that almost turned into a physical fight, and she left. That was the last time I ever saw my daughter. She refused to have anything to do with me.'

'But why?' Charlotte said, though she believed Miss Basset.

'I don't know for sure. I think, perhaps, it was easier for Vicky to deal with a more extreme version of what she experienced. If a bad thing had happened to her, she wanted it to be the *worst* thing. She wanted to be special. It didn't matter that what had happened was already the worst thing; it didn't matter that she'd suffered more than any girl ever should...'

Miss Basset broke down, sobbing violently.

'Miss—'

'Just go,' the old woman croaked. 'Leave me in peace...' She sucked in a breath. 'What use is it talking of this? She is who she is. I didn't hurt her in the ways she claimed, but I hurt her by not noticing sooner, by not leaving that violent man the moment he laid a hand on me. I should've known his sickness would spread.' She spoke through choked sobs. 'I... should've... *known*...'

When Charlotte tried to touch her shoulder, Miss Basset screamed, '*Go!*'

Charlotte left the woman, her sobs echoing down the hallway. She was perfectly aware that Miss Basset could've put on a performance just as easily as Victoria did, but she believed the old woman. If Victoria would lie about something like this, there was no telling where she'd stop, or if she ever would. She was willing to sacrifice her own mother's reputation to garner sympathy online... sympathy she perhaps needed to assuage the guilt she felt at manipulating her own son with the LPA, of stealing her daughter-in-law's agency by holding power over her husband. She needed the world to know she was a precious, put-upon flower so that she could tolerate her own thorns. But Charlotte also knew that if she went to Eloise too soon, she'd push her sister deeper into Victoria's possessive and creepy embrace.

What was her next move then?

She didn't even know if she had one. It was Miss Basset's word against her daughter's. In the end, this proved nothing to nobody except Charlotte, and all Charlotte had was a solicitor's sense and a hangover that was making her head pulse as it demanded her attention.

CHAPTER THIRTY-FIVE

VICTORIA

Victoria had been shocked when, the day after Dominic had dug a large hole in their garden and dragged his own father into it, he had woken and said, *'Mother, is Dad still at work?'* He'd looked at her with glazed eyes, prepared to accept whatever reality she thrust upon them. What else was she supposed to do? Remind him of what had happened the night previously? Remind of him of how she'd hidden upstairs, refusing to acknowledge the corpse, while he made it disappear?

'I believe so, my darling,' she'd said.

'Right,' he'd grunted and that, she thought, was that. When Victoria had a concrete patio laid over the buried body, Dominic had never remarked upon it. When Victoria, despite moving to Weston, had rented out his childhood home with strict instructions to leave the garden unaltered, instead of selling it, he'd made no comment. Until his mind cracked.

Victoria snapped to the present when Patrick turned his car up the hill that would lead to the woods entrance. It was night, the sun long since set. The woods was a terrible choice to dispose of a body, but Patrick wasn't exactly thinking straight.

The poor man was convinced that, after he'd done this dark deed for her, they were going to elope into some romance-novel happily ever after together. Perhaps they even would, if she could persuade Eloise to join them with her grandchild. She couldn't lie; she appreciated the fact that, just like decades previously, just like her Dom Dom, Patrick was handling the cold deadness she simply couldn't face.

As their cars chugged up the hill – as far as she was aware, Patrick had no idea she was following him – Victoria thought about that night, her husband's death. The odd thing was, even now, she wasn't sure which of them had murdered Joseph. The night was a blur of chaos and agony, as much as her own childhood was. Sometimes, she remembered the sensation of the knife slipping into his surprisingly soft flesh. But other times, she was certain it had been Dominic.

Had she done it? Had he? It wasn't as if Dominic was any help. His mind, when it came to that night, was as confused as hers. But now that Victoria had seen the footage of what she'd done to Janine, she wondered if she had done it after all. Because no matter how hard she tried, she couldn't remember murdering Janine. It had been like watching somebody else. Which meant anything could've happened that night with Joseph. Her son could've protected her; she could've protected herself. There were only two unassailable facts of that night: Joseph was killed, and Dominic handled the corpse.

In his twenties, when Dominic had experienced his first breakdown, she'd convinced him that it was she who had murdered Joseph. The poor lad had wanted to go to doctors, then police; he'd even talked about making it public. Victoria had locked herself in with him for days, speaking for hours at a time until her throat was raw, succeeding in reworking the entire night into something they could both live with.

Victoria had killed her husband; that was the story. But

when she listened to those whispers of memory, strained past the layers of self-deceit and the coping mechanisms that stood like scaffolding in her mind, she saw a different image. She saw her son with a sharp blade in his hand, plunging it over and over into his father's chest, looking up at her with tears in his eyes, sobbing as he did it.

'For you, Mummy,' he said in a childlike voice. 'I'm doing this for you.'

Sometimes, she was almost certain this version was *the* version, because that was what Dominic said during his breakdown in his twenties. He'd told Victoria, 'For you, Mummy. I did it for you, didn't I?'

Maybe it had been him, then. But what Dominic refused to understand, and what people like him refused to accept, was that it didn't matter who'd done what to whom. All that mattered was what they'd agreed, and that was simple: take it to their graves. During his breakdown, Dominic had become convinced he'd taken his father's life; he couldn't live with it. He wanted his so-called suffering to end.

Victoria, ever the mama bear, had taken that burden for him. Finally, he'd settled down. He'd continued to pretend, or perhaps even believe, that his father had disappeared when he was a teenager. Life had gone on; he'd started his businesses, eventually met Eloise, moved to Weston. She'd continued her work in art, then started her wildly successful blog.

She sighed when Patrick stopped outside the woods entrance, probably suspicious about the three cars parked with their lights on. She waited down the road, her lights switched off. What was he playing at? He needed to get a move on. Victoria wanted this to end. It had to be over. Soon, there would be a new, beautiful baby in her life, a child who'd get the best of Victoria.

Perhaps she had to face it: she had not been the best mother.

She'd been too full of emotion and too desperate to hold on to her baby boy. Joseph had made *some* good points, but if those memories were true, if Dominic had reverted into some psychotic childlike state and killed his own father, and Victoria had taken responsibility for it, was she really that bad? She had given her child a version of the story he could swallow. But Dominic refused to accept how lucky they were. They had each other; they had their freedom. Why wasn't that enough?

With her grandchild, she would be different. They would never know about her childhood. She would never drink around them. She would never inflict her issues upon their young and fragile mind. She would be so much better, so much sweeter, so much more like the version of herself she projected on her blog. At the end of the day, that was the real Victoria anyway.

She wondered if Eloise knew the truth about her nature, or some of it at least. The other day, when Eloise had caught her, when Victoria had been convinced it was all over, Eloise had shown a side of herself Victoria had never expected. When Dominic cheated, he'd made a terrible mistake. It was the mistake so many men made, assuming the loyalty of their patient wives would last forever. Eloise had taken her marriage vows more seriously than any woman Victoria had ever met or heard of. She would've done anything for Dom Dom if the silly boy had been able to resist Janine – which should've been easy considering Eloise was an angel and Janine was, well... Janine.

Patrick finally backed up. Victoria slumped in her seat, letting him drive past. She caught a glimpse of his terrified expression as he drove down the street. Waiting for him to almost be out of view, she started her car and continued following him.

Dominic had it all: a perfect wife, a perfect home, a doting mother, a baby on the way, a successful career, money in the bank, even a mistress to keep him busy. The silly, misguided boy. Why hadn't he been able to leave well enough alone?

But no. He had to press the issue. Just like in his twenties, when his early forties rolled around, he'd demanded to meet with her. Apparently he'd watched a film and it had triggered a memory. He'd shown up on her doorstep with red eyes and tragedy etching his every feature. It hurt her to even think about it.

'We killed him,' he said. *'I'm done pretending.'*

She'd brought him inside, tried to make him see reason. They didn't have to think about this anymore. Their lives were bright and hopeful. But some people refused to leave the past alone: picked at it like a scab, turned it into a wound, made it bleed, *wanted* it to bleed.

Patrick turned towards the back road that led to the motorway. Victoria sighed; this was becoming a long night.

She'd managed to keep Dominic quiet for some time, begged him to reconsider, begged him to try and live while carrying this secret. But as days turned to weeks and months, his outbursts became even worse. He began to drink more.

'How can you live like this?' he'd roared at her once, towards the end. *'How can you pretend everything is normal? You didn't block it out, did you? You remember that night. You remember what I did. What you did. It doesn't even matter. You or me, it's the same. We did it, Mother. Poor Dad. Wuh-we did it...'*

She'd tried to hold him, whispering, *'You didn't do anything. It was me. It was Mama Bear.'*

He'd slapped her across the face. Hard. She could still feel the sting. *'Don't call yourself that, you sick bitch.'* He began to shudder and sob as though he was the one who'd been slapped. *'I have to tell people. They have to know. I have to.'*

Again, she'd managed to talk him down, but the argument

had made her realise it was only a matter of time. It wasn't going away. He was going to ruin their lives: his, hers, Eloise's. Victoria's blog, her fame, her respect, the soaring rocket ship that was her new-found career, it would all turn to ash. She would go to prison as an accomplice. Or perhaps she would go to prison for murder. The police's test would give them the answer their shattered minds were incapable of, but that would be small consolation while rotting in a cell. At her age, either sentence would most likely mean death behind bars.

Victoria knew that things were going to get out of hand. One weekend when Eloise had been at a writer's conference in Bristol, Victoria had watched Dominic leave his house and park outside his girlfriend's flat, with far less security, fewer lights. It was past midnight, and when he went inside, Victoria turned on her head torch and slipped beneath the car.

She had practised loosening brake lines on her own vehicle. In ten minutes, using a 10mm wrench, she had torn the nut just enough to cause a slow leak. Knowing how stressed Dominic was, she doubted he'd notice until it was too late. She cried when she thought of this. It wounded her on a level so deeply, she wondered if she'd ever be able to live with herself again. But what other choice did she have? Let him destroy everything?

Patrick led her down a country road, stopping in the middle of nowhere. Victoria pulled her car up and killed the lights. Was this the moment: the end, the new beginning?

Perhaps Patrick was getting himself mentally prepared to dispose of the thawed corpse.

Her mind went to the phone call of the night of Dominic's crash.

'Hello? Dominic, is that you?'
'Who else would it be, my loving mother?'
'Have you been drinking? You sound drunk.'

'Drowning my sorrows is the only way to handle this.'
'Handle what? What are you talking about?'
'What you did, my sweet mother: what we did.'
'Please, not this again. It's ancient history. You need to let it go.'
'I tried. I failed. I can't just let it go.'
'What else are you supposed to do? You can't hold on to—'
'I can't keep it locked up anymore. People need to know.'
'You can't.'
'Scared of ruining your blog? Your celebrity?'
'Please, just come to me, my sweet boy. We'll talk about this.'
'What? Now?'
'Yes, please—'

He'd dropped the phone, but hadn't hung up. Victoria had heard a loud crashing noise as he punched the mirror, then ended the call, waiting anxiously. When he hadn't arrived, she'd driven the route she knew he was going to take, wondering if his brakes would finally give out; it was the weather for it. Just as she'd hoped, just as she'd dreaded, she found him... Dominic, so corpse-like, so *clearly dead* that she'd left him there. But he was a fighter, just like his father had once tried to teach him, a scared lad trying to look brave as he raised his boxing gloves and told his dad he could do it. Somehow, despite looking like a corpse, he'd clung to life.

She wiped her cheek; he would've lived such a perfect life if he'd managed to keep his head. Why couldn't he have just let it go?

Finally, Patrick left the car and was walking around to the boot. From the way he moved, she could tell he'd been drinking. He was a clumsy criminal; he didn't even spot her at the end of the lane, watching him.

She sighed, starting her engine. There was no use hanging

around there. Perhaps following him at all had been a mistake. But she had to see: to make sure he wouldn't wimp out. She drove away.

Surely he couldn't mess this part up, just digging a hole and then forgetting about it forever. She hoped, for his sake, he was capable of that.

CHAPTER THIRTY-SIX

ELOISE

Eloise felt like she was in a dream as DI Cartwright told her the news. Patrick, the man who had found her husband on the night of the crash, the man who had been so kind to her that first night, had been found attempting to dispose of a body: a woman's body, a body Eloise's husband had touched and made love to and cherished more than he'd ever cherished hers. The police had found texts from Dominic on her phone when they'd searched her flat; the texts had come from a pay-as-you-go phone, but he'd signed them with his name.

Charlotte reached over and touched her hand. 'It's okay, E,' she said softly.

Eloise clung desperately onto her sister, holding tight, attempting to believe the deceitful words. That was what her life had always been; that was what her marriage had been. Deceitful.

'Has he said anything?' Charlotte asked.

DI Cartwright sighed, massaging his jaw. 'He's refusing to give any comment at all.'

'What does he have to do with any of this?' Charlotte asked.

DI Cartwright shook his head. 'At this stage, it's unclear.'

'What now?' Eloise said.

'I'll let you know if we need anything else,' DI Cartwright replied.

Charlotte stood. 'I'll see you out.'

When they left the room, Eloise stood and looked at herself in the mirror; she composed her face. Everything had changed when Victoria revealed the affair. Perhaps she could've doubted it before, but not after the police had revealed the presence of another woman through the CCTV... and not when Eloise looked back through her mind, studied his behaviour, his absences, his lies. Anger surged through her, her features shifting. She looked like a demon. She didn't care. She wished Dominic was awake so she could make him pay.

Dominic made his choice. He fucked another woman. There was no coming back from that. What about the woman – Janine? How had she died? Eloise, with a pit in her belly, had an idea. But if she was right – if Victoria had been somehow involved – she couldn't resent her mother-in-law. Dominic wasn't the only one who'd made a choice when he participated in an affair.

When Charlotte returned, she said, 'Do you want a drink or something?'

'It's not even midday.'

Her sister sounded wounded. 'I wasn't talking about booze, E. I'm trying to help.'

Eloise sighed, then forced her face into a socially acceptable mask. The journal – the body – the sickness of it... She had to stay strong. Turning, she shuddered. 'I'm sorry. Yes, please. A cup of tea.' She slumped onto the sofa.

When Charlotte was gone, she texted Victoria. *Come over. The police have been.*

Eloise and Charlotte were sitting in awkward silence when Victoria arrived at the house. Charlotte looked out of the front window when the doorbell went. Her posture tightened. She was about to say something when her phone rang; she quickly rejected the call.

'Was that your boss again?' Eloise asked.

A look of guilt flashed across Charlotte's face.

'She wants you to go back to work,' Eloise said.

'Yeah, E. She does. But that doesn't mean I'm leaving you.'

'You want to go back to work too.'

Which might be for the best. Charlotte wouldn't understand, and so Eloise would never tell her the full truth. She had been able to accept the steps Eloise had taken to secure a baby for herself, but this was far more serious than pricking a condom. If Eloise had told Charlotte the journal was fake, any support would be as dead as Eloise's marriage. Charlotte could only condone so much. She wouldn't understand. 'I don't know,' Charlotte muttered.

'It's fine; you don't have to lie. Can you let Victoria in? I'm going to make her a cup of tea too.'

Eloise went into the kitchen, putting her thoughts into the future, into sunny visions of sitting in the garden with her baby in her arms, with Victoria sitting at her side, both of them ready to do better, be better, to be the women the sweet child deserved. They were so close.

In the living room, the atmosphere was tense. Charlotte was doing a terrible job at hiding the disdain she clearly felt for Victoria.

'Have you told her?' Eloise asked.

'The police have already visited,' Victoria said with a croak in her throat. 'Oh, Eloise – it's awful, that sick man... Huh-he—'

Victoria broke into pained sobs. Eloise rushed to her side and put an arm around her mother-in-law, holding her tightly, stroking her shoulder. Charlotte watched the scene with poorly concealed judgement in her eyes, as though she was mentally picking holes in it.

'I knew something was wrong,' Victoria said, wiping her cheek. 'I knew I was being a silly old crone, thinking a man of his age would be interested in me.'

'Wait – what?' Charlotte said sharply.

Eloise leaned away from Victoria. 'What do you mean?'

Victoria stared at Eloise bleakly, convincingly. 'He reached out to me through my blog. He said the experience of finding Dominic had stuck with him. He wanted to help in any way that he could. I believed him. I didn't have any reason to think… to think *this*…' She shuddered. 'The whole time, he was secretly laughing at me…'

She broke down again, her entire body shaking as if she couldn't contain the agony. Charlotte's foot began to tap frantically on the floor. She was biting her lip, trying not to say anything, but in the end, she couldn't stop herself.

'So you and this man knew each other,' Charlotte said coldly.

'It sounds like he tricked her, Charlotte,' Eloise said, disliking the look on her sister's face. The news had taken Eloise off-guard too, but it all but confirmed her suspicion that Victoria was somehow linked to Janine's death. The connection was too much of a coincidence otherwise. The rot went deep in this messy tale. Eloise just wanted to move on.

'How could you possibly know that, E?' Charlotte demanded. 'We don't know anything. In fact, all I know is this: this is bloody suspicious!'

Victoria slowly looked at Charlotte with red-rimmed eyes. 'Excuse me?'

'Well – it... it is.' Charlotte was tripping over her words. 'What else would you call it? What else am I supposed to think?'

'Charlotte...'

'So, this man, this stranger, who was miraculously found disposing of your son's girlfriend's body... he just also happened to have been *your* boyfriend, Victoria?'

Victoria dabbed her cheeks. 'Are you accusing me of something?'

'There are too many bloody coincidences,' Charlotte said, and Eloise agreed. But she would never say that aloud. 'I'm sorry, E, but you have to be able to see that.'

'What are you saying?' Eloise asked.

Charlotte folded her arms. 'I think you're a liar, Victoria. I think you've been lying for so long, you hardly know what the truth is. I think you were involved with Janine – and maybe even Dominic too!'

Victoria gasped. 'How dare you! I have lied about *nothing*!'

'A pathological liar. It started when you were a girl.'

'When I was a... girl?' Victoria spoke slowly. 'What on earth are you talking about?'

'I saw your blog post, read all that stuff that apparently happened to you as a girl. I visited your mother—'

'Charlotte!' Eloise gasped with genuine shock, which was perhaps rich considering everything that had happened. 'Why would you do something like that? Listen to yourself; just think about what you're saying. Victoria is his mother. She loves him more than anything.'

'Something's been off from the start,' Charlotte said. 'She's got you wrapped around her finger, E, so you can't see it. But I can. Do you know what her mother said?'

'My mother has gaslit me since I was a small child,' Victoria said, choking down another sob. 'But please, enlighten me.'

'She said it was all *crap*. Your father wasn't a good man. There was abuse, but not like you said, and your mother was never involved. You've always needed your story to be more extreme than it really is. You've always needed to feel more special than you really are. Everything has to be over the top. If you lied about something like that, what else would you lie about?'

Victoria hunched over, burying her face in her hands, collapsing in upon herself as grief tore through her. Eloise rubbed her mother-in-law's back, glaring at Charlotte.

'Are you drunk or something?' Eloise said. 'What's wrong with you? Listen to yourself; you're accusing her of lying about her son, her parents, her entire life, *and you don't even know her*. She's done nothing to make you so suspicious. Instinct, you call it. Do you seriously think that's enough?'

'She may have blinded you, E, but she hasn't blinded me.'

'Stop calling me E. Stop pretending you care. When you're gone, Victoria will still be here. When you've forgotten about this very, very, *very* recent desire to be a good sister, to be part of a supportive family, *she will still be here*. Don't you get that? Can't you fit that into your head?'

As Victoria continued to cry, Charlotte jumped to her feet. 'I don't buy those crocodile tears for one second. This is all – it's all – it's just too... Bloody. Convenient!'

'Convenient?' Victoria screamed, leaping to her feet, her cheeks glistening with tears. 'There's nothing convenient about losing my baby. There's nothing convenient about being *toyed* with by that sicko. There's nothing convenient about any of this. All I've ever wanted is to be happy, and that sick man took that away from me. And now you're blaming me. Do you have any idea how painful that is?'

'Your mother—'

'My mother is a liar. It's all she knows how to do. All she's ever known how to do. To believe her over me... over somebody your own sister trusts and loves, it speaks to your nature.'

Charlotte laughed in disbelief. 'My nature? What are you banging on about?'

'You're distrustful. I'm sorry, Charlotte, I truly am. But to think like this, so cynically, you must be broken on some level.'

Charlotte glared at her, then looked at Eloise. 'Are you seriously going to listen to this crap?'

'Show me the evidence,' Eloise whispered, hating that it had come to this. But what she had said was true: Charlotte would go, Victoria would stay. Eloise had to think about her baby's future. 'Charlotte. I love you. And I think you love me, in your way.'

'In my *way*?'

'But the police found Patrick getting rid of a body. He's clearly a damaged individual who took advantage of Victoria's kindness. I just don't understand why you're being like this. Because of instinct? Do you seriously think that's good enough?'

'Just because I can't prove it,' Charlotte said, 'doesn't mean I'm wrong. There's information I don't have access to. There must be something else. I'm trying to help you, E.'

'You're trying to help yourself,' Eloise said. 'You came here for me. That's what you claim. To support *me*. But ever since you got here, it's been about you: about your *instincts*, about trying to make this into something it isn't. You want to crack some big case, to be better than Victoria, better than the police, better than me. You're just like Mum and Dad—'

'Please, just listen—'

'Everything is about you, you, you. Our whole family is selfish, and now, I've found somebody who's selfless, who really loves me, and you're trying to ruin it.'

'E—'

'No!' Eloise screamed, despising herself on some level, but

knowing it was necessary, knowing she would have to endure hell for some time longer if she was ever going to reach her heaven. 'I'm sorry, but I think you should leave. Victoria doesn't deserve this.'

Charlotte shook her head slowly. 'You're seriously picking her over your own family.'

'Charlotte, don't you get it? She *is* my family, the closest I've ever had to one anyway.'

Charlotte's eyes glistened. Eloise killed the pity trying to swell in her heart. After a long, lingering look at Victoria, Charlotte left the room, then the front door slammed.

Victoria turned to Eloise, dabbing at her cheeks, a smile slowly spreading across her face. 'That was very good.'

'Stop smiling like that,' Eloise said. 'It makes you look like a fucking psychopath.'

She stormed from the room.

CHAPTER THIRTY-SEVEN

CHARLOTTE

Charlotte sat in her car outside the police station, trying to figure out what she knew exactly. Not what burnt in her gut; not the instinct that drilled into her head and made a home there. What did she *know* about Victoria? She knew that Victoria had viciously lied about the most evil thing which had supposedly happened to her; she knew that Victoria had known the man who had, in a coincidence that would make a soap opera look like high literature, disposed of her son's mistress's body. She knew that Garry, the witness to the LPA, had become weirdly aggressive when challenged on it.

None of this was evidence, not even circumstantial. All of it could be explained away by other factors. Perhaps Garry had had an argument with his partner that day. Perhaps Victoria's mother was the liar, the monster Victoria painted her in her blog posts. Perhaps—

Her mobile rang, interrupting her thoughts. It was her boss, Shelly. Charlotte debated ignoring the call, but she'd already done that several times. Charlotte had been – Charlotte *was* – determined to be a good sister to Eloise, but if Eloise was going to side with Victoria no matter what Charlotte said or did, she wasn't sure what she could do.

'Hello,' she said, putting the phone on loudspeaker. Her hand fell to the hatch in the car door. There was a small bottle of vodka there, the kind you get in hotel rooms. She moved her finger around the tiny lid.

'Charlotte, hey,' Shelly said. 'Am I going to be seeing you on Monday? I know I was harsh with you before, but obviously, you get why I had to be that way, don't you?'

There was a tone of reconciliation in her employer's voice, a tone Charlotte found far too tempting. She was going to let her transgressions pass. Charlotte took her hand away from the bottle. 'I messed up.'

Shelly laughed gruffly. 'Yeah, just a little. But if you're less messed up now, and if you're not going to mess up again, we could really use you. I've got it on good authority we've got two big cases about to kick our doors down. It'll mean long hours, a proper project for you to sink your teeth into. I was thinking of what you said to me that day.'

"That day" needed no explanation. It was the day Charlotte had drunkenly stumbled into the office, somehow thinking she could hide her state.

'You said work is the only thing that's ever made you feel like a real person,' Shelly went on. 'Well – it's time to be a person again, Charlotte. I know your sister is going through a lot, but you can't hide forever.'

'Actually, my sister has been leaning on her mother-in-law quite a bit.'

'She has you when she needs you, but you're not her only support structure. That's excellent.'

Charlotte stared at the police station, at two men in suits, presumably detectives, walking through the entrance, and at a uniformed officer leaving. She knew they had sky-high caseloads. She knew they had pressure from their superiors to close cases with the best means available to them, which meant pursuing the most likely leads. She knew that if she went in there talking about aggression from Dominic's friends, or *bad vibes* from Victoria, they wouldn't listen.

'Charlotte?'

'I promised myself I'd be a good sister,' Charlotte whispered.

'You *have* been a good sister.'

Charlotte ground her teeth, not sure if it was true. Their family had been marked from the start by a banal sort of disconnection which had scarred them all in ordinary and undramatic ways. It had torn rifts within them that had disconnected them subtly from everybody else. It wasn't as though their parents had hurt them. Or perhaps it had been a form of emotional neglect. Whatever the case, Charlotte knew something for sure, and it was depressing. Work was her family. Her job was her child. Without it, she drifted. That was why Christmas had ruined her. Without her family, she had become untethered.

'When you're sober, you're the best we have,' Shelly said. 'You've got a bright future. One day, you'll be making calls like this, rallying troops of your own. Please, let's put this behind us. It's time to move on. It's time to do what you do best.'

Charlotte felt an unexpected tear slide down her cheek. She wiped it away, looking at herself in the rear-view mirror, at her red eyes, at her puffy red cheeks, at the state she'd allowed herself to fall into. She wanted to put Eloise first, but what about Charlotte? What about her health, her sanity? If Eloise didn't want to be helped, what was Charlotte supposed to do: stay there as a spare part, watching as Victoria and Eloise grew closer, stubbornly convinced of something she couldn't prove?

'Do you consider us friends, Shelly?' Charlotte asked.

'Of course I do.'

'Sometimes...' She stopped herself; she'd been about to say, *I don't think I have any friends, or anybody at all.* 'I think you're right. I need to come back to work. I need something to focus on. I need to make a difference.'

'That's absolutely brilliant to hear you say. So, you'll be in on Monday?'

'Yes.' Charlotte wiped another tear away. 'See you soon.'

Ending the call, she left the police station and returned to Eloise's big house on the hill, taking a moment to drink in the grandeur. The gate was open. Charlotte parked in the courtyard and looked through the front window. She saw Victoria and Eloise embracing. Eloise was crying, her shoulders trembling, as Victoria massaged her back. They looked like the perfect pair. They looked determined to make it through their hardship together.

Charlotte went to the front door, finding it open. Eloise must've heard the door. She came into the hallway. Victoria remained in the living room.

'I know you told me to go,' Charlotte began.

Eloise rushed to her, touching her hands. 'No, it's fine. I'm sorry. I shouldn't have shouted.'

'You were angry,' Charlotte said, conscious of the fact her sister didn't invite her in, offer her a drink or anything.

An intense flashback struck her. When they were kids, Eloise had begged Charlotte to go to the cinema with her. Charlotte had told her no several times, but when her plans had fallen through, she'd finally relented. But by then, Eloise had found a boy to go with. They'd stood just like this outside her bedroom, Eloise too nice to outright tell her to leave, Charlotte feeling unfairly stung and rejected. The same energy emanated from her sister now.

'My boss wants me back in work,' Charlotte said.

Eloise smiled. 'That's great. That'll be good for you.'

Charlotte glanced at the living-room door, lowering her voice. 'But what about you? I'm not sure I want to leave you.'

'I'm going to be okay,' Eloise said. 'I've got my baby. I've got Victoria.'

There was a subtle challenge in Eloise's voice when she said her mother-in-law's name. It was like she was baiting Charlotte to say something. But what could Charlotte say that hadn't already been said?

'I'm only a phone call away,' Charlotte told her. 'Please don't forget that. And I'm going to be checking up on you often, so you better get used to lots of annoying calls and messages. I want to FaceTime, too. I don't want us to drift apart, E.'

Eloise clutched Charlotte's hands tighter. 'I've made my peace,' she said, which sounded strangely ominous. Her peace with what? With her twisted mother-in-law? 'I want you to be happy. I want my child to be happy. And, if possible, *I* want to be happy. I think we can do it.'

Charlotte pulled her into a hug. After all this time, it still felt stiff and slightly forced. She felt a pang of pain as she thought about all the hugs Eloise had tried to coax out of Charlotte when they were growing up, all the times Charlotte had brushed her off, the distance between her and her sister and their parents. Suddenly, an overwhelming sense of tragedy gripped her. She felt like she might burst into tears. Could broken people ever be fully healed? Was Charlotte even broken, or was she, like Eloise had joked without really joking, being dramatic and narcissistic?

'I love you, E,' Charlotte said, wishing it didn't sound so damn hollow.

'I love you too.'

Charlotte took her sister's shoulders and put her at arm's length so she could look at her. 'I meant what I said. If you ever need me, you ring, understand? Don't hesitate. I'm always going to be here for you.'

Later, Charlotte would wonder if she imagined the expression that flashed across her sister's face. Her lips twitched into a bitter smile. Her eyes gleamed with something like pity. It was as if she found the thought hilarious. As if Eloise would need *her*. But then it was gone, and Eloise was back to her usual soft self. The transformation would return to her for weeks, scaring her on a deep level she refused to acknowledge.

'I know,' Eloise said. 'The same goes for you.'

That was that.

Soon, Charlotte was driving back to London. As she left the West Country town behind, tears flowed down her cheeks. She thought about the beach and the setting sun kissing it orange, and the old islands, watching the wind-beaten promenade, and the families she had seen walking in and out of cafés. She thought about a little girl she'd seen pick up her brother after he'd fallen, brushing his shirt off, and the fleeting memory hurt her more than she understood.

There was nothing she wanted more than to turn back time and behave as that little girl had done. All it would've taken was a nudge from her parents, a comment about the importance of being a good sister, a determination that family meant something, anything, and was worth holding onto. Then she wouldn't feel this lack, this colossal void inside, that felt like a piece missing inside of her, something she filled with booze or casual sex or work.

Anybody who had a family that tried, despite their imperfections, despite their struggles, who sincerely tried, who shook away their own concerns and put their ties first, should sink to their knees in gratitude. Or perhaps Eloise was right; perhaps Charlotte was dramatic and self-indulgent. Perhaps not everything was about childhood. Perhaps she should just let go.

Whatever the case, as Charlotte left Somerset, she made a promise to herself. If she ever became a mother, she would make her children know how much she loved them and how important it was that they loved each other.

A MOTHER'S MUSINGS: MY HEART IS BROKEN

25/03/25

Victoria Hawthorne

The day I have feared for so long has finally arrived. Eloise and I have made the unfathomably difficult decision to turn off my sweet Dom Dom's life support. The doctors tell us, at this late stage, any chance of him waking up is incredibly unlikely. I don't want him to suffer, and the truth is, my loyal, dear readers, I don't want sweet Eloise to suffer either…

Or myself. Yes. Because that is one of the most essential truths of motherhood, the fact we so often try to deny. Sometimes, we need to feel safe too. We need to feel taken care of. We need to feel like we can finally, just for a little while, breathe freely.

I love you, Dom Dom. I'm sure that we will be reunited one day.

Wow, this is "A Mother's Musings" most viral post. If you would like to become a follower of this blog, click here.

[The blog post is accompanied by an image: Victoria and Eloise sit on either side of Dominic in the hospital bed, each holding one of his hands, their cheeks glimmering with tears and their expressions profoundly sad.]

CHAPTER THIRTY-EIGHT

ELOISE

The tears were real; the tragedy tearing through her heart wasn't feigned. But she wasn't mourning the man her husband had shown himself to truly be. She was mourning what they should've been, the version of them she had stubbornly strived towards even as he had tried to drag them down into the gutter. She sat in Victoria's car, sobs exploding from her, as Victoria gently cradled her hands and whispered words which Eloise didn't hear.

Rain pattered against the window, and people exited and entered the hospital; they looked like wraiths, not even human, not living and not dead. Victoria was crying too, but with far less passion. Why would she force it? Nobody was there apart from Eloise, no onlookers, no cameras, nobody for whom to put on a show.

They stayed like that for a long time, until eventually Eloise managed to regain some semblance of control. She wiped her cheeks, looking at her mother-in-law.

'I think I'm ready to speak about it,' she said.

Victoria bit down. 'We did the right thing.'

'*We* weren't going to do anything. You were going to try and do it all behind my back. If I hadn't caught you, you would've tried to move me into place like a chess piece. You must've seen me as some small, naïve, scared little thing. Easily manipulated, but I tricked you, Victoria. I only showed you the version of me I wanted you to see.'

A look flashed across Victoria's face, but it passed a moment later. They were bonded beyond doubt. Eloise had made her choice. No, that wasn't right. Dominic had made the choice for her. By cheating on her, he had sealed his own fate. She could forgive almost anything from her husband, but not choosing another woman over her. That was unacceptable. Charlotte might've mocked her for taking her marriage vows seriously, but she did. Deadly seriously. *Forsake all others...* Eloise hadn't even looked at another man after taking those vows.

'We should leave the past behind us,' Victoria said. 'We're alike, Eloise, more alike than twins in many ways. We understand that we choose what world we live in. Don't you see, sweet girl? That's a superpower.'

When Eloise walked in on Victoria hiding the fake journal in the walk-in wardrobe, Victoria had quickly explained, seemingly unable to keep all the deceit stowed inside of her. Or perhaps she had sensed something in Eloise; perhaps she had anticipated that Eloise might be persuaded.

'When I caught you,' Eloise said, dabbing her cheeks again, 'did you tell me the truth because you thought you'd come to the end of the road, or because you knew I'd be on your side?'

Victoria chewed her lip.

'Don't tell me what you think I want to hear,' Eloise said harshly. 'Tell me the truth.'

'The truth. That's not a simple concept, Eloise. We both know that.'

'Don't get poetic. Just tell me.'

'It's been two months since you found me hiding that

journal, since Patrick was discovered trying to bury Janine's corpse. All that time, you haven't asked me for the full story. I told you I faked the journal – I told you I needed to give the police an explanation. I expected questions then.'

'Sometimes, it's easier to live in the make-believe. We both know that.'

Victoria wrapped her arms around herself, looking surprisingly vulnerable, and offered a nod. 'If I tell you the truth, you'll call the police.'

'I already know the truth, I just need to hear you say it. And we're long past me turning you in.'

'Why don't you tell me your theory?'

Eloise groaned. 'Are you playing games with me, Victoria? Today of all days? I put on a show for you. To Charlotte. To the police. I pretended that journal was real.'

'And then you stopped mentioning it. I thought we were going to leave well enough alone.'

'I will. After you tell me.'

'What do you think you know?'

Eloise slammed her hand on the dashboard. 'You killed Janine.'

Victoria stared out the rain-spattered window, then gave a short nod.

'You were there that night – there to take Janine – because *you* were the one who cut Dominic's brakes.'

'It's not what you thi—'

'I don't want to hear it. The truth. *Now.*'

'Dominic killed his father. I helped him cover it up. He was going to reveal the truth. He was going to ruin our lives, Eloise. I couldn't let him do that.'

Eloise let out a breath as the news thundered into her. She almost wished she hadn't asked. But something about her husband's death had triggered her need for the full story. 'I could've forgiven him for almost anything, you know. Almost.'

For a long time, they sat wordlessly as rain hammered against the car.

Finally, Victoria spoke. 'When I learnt you were pregnant, that changed everything. I knew I had to do the best for my grandchild. I knew I couldn't let Dominic wake up. He'd tell the world about his dad. He'd ruin everything. Do you want your baby growing up knowing his father killed his grandfather?'

'No,' Eloise allowed.

'I had to take action. I wasn't sure it would work. Even now, the police might figure it all out. We're hanging on dangerous threads. Charlotte with her poking around – poor Patrick might forget about his loyalty to me. There is so much still up in the air.'

'I want to return to my question,' Eloise said. 'Did you tell me about the journal because you knew I'd help – because you saw something in me – or because you thought you'd hit the end of the line?'

Victoria sighed, brushing down her hair. 'When you caught me, I was... well, I was caught, Eloise. The game was up. What could I possibly say? My only option was to tell you the truth.'

'It was a tactical decision then. It was strategy. It had nothing to do with the way you felt.'

'I suppose you might put it like that. Though that makes me sound rather callous.'

'We're both callous. Let's not pretend otherwise.' When Victoria remained silent, Eloise said, 'You could've invented some lie. You're clever enough. Instead, you told me that you'd written a fake journal. That you were planting it. That you wanted to trick the police into believing Dominic had taken his own life in a rather roundabout fashion. And somehow, you knew I'd go along with it. How, Victoria?'

'I think you know,' Victoria said, recoiling slightly.

'Maybe I need to hear you say it.'

Victoria swallowed, seeming frightened, and Eloise allowed her to be frightened. After a pause, she said, 'It was the look on your face when I told you about the affair. Pure hatred. I knew then that you were done with Dominic. I knew then that, if it came to it, you would choose a future without him rather than a future with him.'

'Because it was a look you recognised. A look you've seen in the mirror. We're as sick as each other, aren't we?'

'We're not sick. We're just not like other people.'

Eloise looked at her mother-in-law. For a brief moment, she saw the Victoria she'd always known, the scared child behind her steely gaze, her age and tiredness pressing through her firm figure.

There was another long silence, Eloise's thoughts returning to the moment she'd walked into the wardrobe and caught Victoria hunched over with the journal in her hand, the look of guilt, then cunning on her mother-in-law's face. Eloise still wasn't sure if the emotion which had bubbled out of Victoria was real or fake. Probably, Victoria didn't know either.

She smoothed her hand over her belly. They both had issues that went deeper than their bones and their DNA and their histories and their souls – if such things existed.

'I tried to make Dominic understand that our marriage had to be special, had to be perfect,' Eloise said, trembling again, grief gripping her. 'There were times I stepped over the line. There were times I was less than... wifely.'

'You don't have to tell me anything.'

'You just told me he killed his father. You need the full story too.'

'But that's just it, Eloise. I don't. I'm ready to live *our* story, the one we *choose*.'

'There were times I hit him,' Eloise said, ignoring her. 'He once teased me about leaving kisses in texts, made me feel small for doing it. He mocked me. *Kiss, kiss, kiss*... so, when his back was turned, I shoved him so hard. He collapsed against the counter, bruised his hip. There was another tim—'

'Eloise, it's over now.'

'Another time,' she went on stubbornly, 'he threw a bottle of Dom Pérignon against the wall. He made me feel so scared. I collapsed against the wall, and he stood over me, sneering. He called me his *precious prize*. He called me his *precious petal*. But he didn't mean it. He was trying to hurt me. I lost it. I didn't mean to. I never meant to. But I hit him, not once, not twice. I don't even know how many times. It was like I blacked out. I just wanted him to be the man, the husband he was supposed to be.'

Victoria took Eloise's hands, massaged them gently. 'Whatever you did, whatever he made you do, it doesn't matter anymore. Don't you get it, sweet girl, sweet child? I'm your doting mama bear. You're a grieving wife, a woman who's going to give everything to her child. That's all we can ever be.'

'I just wanted him to understand,' Eloise said, tears blurring her vision as she stared at the rain-streaked window, like it was her tears distorting the world, not the raindrops. 'We couldn't be like everybody else. We had to be better. We had to try, always, even when nobody was watching. I thought he was finally getting it. I thought he understood.'

'He was never going to understand. He wasn't like us. He couldn't keep the facts straight in his head. He was too concerned with the truth.'

'How do you deal with the guilt?' Eloise asked.

'You build a box in your mind. You make it strong, unbreakable. You put all the bad things in there and you lock it, and you never look in there, no matter what. I don't need to explain this to you.'

'This is the last time we'll ever speak of any of this,' Eloise said. 'What you did; what I did. What I am; what you are. We're never going to discuss it again. From now on, it's like you said. I'm a grieving wife, an expectant mother, determined to give my child every last shred of love left in my heart. And you're a doting mama bear. That's all.'

Eloise stroked her hand over the bump, closing her eyes, breathing steadily, affirming in her thoughts, *My world is what I make it, I am stronger than I realise, I can do whatever I set my mind to.*

Victoria moved her hand to the bump too.

When the baby kicked for the first time, Eloise opened her eyes. Victoria was beaming. The past slid away like raindrops against a car window, out of sight, out of mind.

CHAPTER THIRTY-NINE

VICTORIA

Months later, Victoria popped home to collect the overnight bag she'd had prepared for several weeks. She had taken great care packing it, a smile on her face as she thought about sitting at her daughter-in-law's side in the hospital, waiting for her grandchildren to come into the world. That was *children*, plural; the scans had showed a boy and a girl who were so beautiful in their grainy black and white, Victoria had posted a photo of them to her blog... her blog which she had, after her son's tragic but necessary passing, turned into a wildly successful podcast on which Eloise routinely featured.

Eloise had started her own blog, too, talking about her grief, her modelling days, her plans for motherhood. An agent had become interested in her books as a result. After the conversation in the car, they had never again breached the walls of their preferred selves. They had never – and would never – discuss it. Eloise was superior to Dominic in that way. She was able to build walls and maintain them, appreciate them even, while Dominic had struggled and obsessed and wouldn't leave them alone. He had studied them for cracks too often and, in studying, caused them to crack.

The most miraculous thing was that Patrick hadn't said a word to the police. Victoria had been prepared for him to point the finger at her. It was the natural thing for him to do. But no accusations had come. His tragic loyalty had somehow held. Victoria was grateful but also pitied him for it.

Murder flashed across her mind when she saw DI Cartwright, that alcoholic-looking police officer, smoking a cigarette outside her house. He'd come to visit her soon after Dominic's death. *'I can't prove it,'* he'd said, *'and you may have everybody else fooled, but I see you, Miss Hawthorne.'*

Bringing her car to a stop, she wondered if there was some new development. Why else would he be there? Had Charlotte said something? Charlotte was back in Weston for her niece's and nephew's births. So far, they'd managed to maintain a mask of civility.

Victoria left the car, painting a confused expression onto her face. 'DI Cartwright,' she said. 'I hope you don't find this offensive, but I'd hoped we'd seen the last of each other.'

DI Cartwright ran a hand over his stubbly jaw. 'I spoke with our mutual friend the other day.'

'You'll have to be more specific, Detective.'

He nodded as if to say, *Sure I will.* 'Your ex-boyfriend.'

'You mean the man who ingratiated himself into my life as a perverse way to get closer to my tragedy?'

'Ah, yes. Patrick, with no other evidence to support the claim, was an opportunistic lunatic who just so happened to kidnap an injured woman to do who knows what with her. And this *after* he'd rung the police to report your son's state.'

Victoria said nothing. God, it was flimsy.

The detective grinned again. 'He's going for the "no comment" record, seems very determined to stick to it. But it's in the eyes, Miss Hawthorne. You can see when they're close to breaking.'

Victoria shook her head. 'Do you have anything substantive you'd like to say? This is a very big day for me. I'm going to be a grandmother.'

'A sabotaged vehicle – a comatose man – no explanation forthcoming – and that man just, *poof*, appears... along with a journal which conveniently states the comatose man was determined to end his life in the most elaborate way imaginable.'

'Please, don't speak about my son, not you – who won't let him rest in peace. And if I'm not mistaken, *that man* is going to be sentenced.'

'Maybe... if he keeps the "no comment" crap up. Or maybe you were being far too clever trying to frame him.'

Victoria almost swore. Frame him? No. Somebody had seen him. Perhaps the silly man had even turned his headlights on to help with digging the hole. She hated herself for not having the strength to handle it on her own.

'Have I said something to upset you?' the detective asked, a smarmy smile on his face.

'Everything you're saying is unthinkably evil to me.'

'A man gets lonely without visitors. Guess how many Patrick has had.' The detective made a zero with his finger and thumb. 'You know, of course, how suspicious it would look if you were to become his regular visitor... and his resolve suddenly became hard as nails again, wouldn't you?'

Yes, she'd thought about that. The only way to keep him loyal was to visit, something she couldn't do under any circumstances. 'Have you been drinking, Detective?'

He smirked. 'If you truly were affronted by my uncivilised behaviour, you'd contact the station. But you won't do that, Miss Hawthorne. You don't want to draw attention to the only man committed to unmasking you.'

Victoria wanted to do feral and appalling things to him. The urge burnt in her gut as it had many times before, as it had since she was a girl, as it had even before her father had done his wicked things. Her earliest memory was of this feeling, this irrepressible need to do something bad to relieve some of the pressure. People didn't understand how torturous it was, living with a tension that wouldn't leave her alone.

'Do your superiors know you're here? This is absolutely unacceptable. I'm trying to put all this behind me.'

'My superiors want me to leave this alone. In fact, if you reported this incident, I might get in trouble. But you won't do that.'

'Are we done? I'm very busy.'

'I think you tell yourself you're a good person. But do you know what I think about sometimes, at night, when I can't sleep? The Legal Power of Attorney. You got your grubby hands on that three years before any of this happened. Which means you wanted your son to crash, your precious Dom Dom. You wanted to switch off his life support. I bet you had dreams about it, Miss Hawthorne. Fantasies.'

'This is quite enough. Get off my property or I'll call—'

'The police?' He laughed and swaggered away. She watched him go, thinking what it would be like to plunge a knife between his shoulder blades. He turned, spotted the look on her face, then laughed again like it meant something.

He didn't know anything. He couldn't prove anything. But he'd hit a sore point when he mentioned the LPA. He was right. She had established that as a possible contingency plan. It was better if she was in control anyway; Dominic hadn't even put up a fight. Eloise, even after the affair and her belief that she was just as tough as Victoria, might've lacked the resolve to do what was necessary when the time came.

The investigation was closed. Patrick hadn't spoken, not a single word. He'd let them pin it on him. He'd stay strong... forever though? Would he? Had she stolen his heart that much?

Could their brief fling sustain him for one year, two, three? What was she going to do – somehow kill him *in* prison?

Victoria wouldn't let this ruin the day. She leaned against the wall, breathing hard at first, then steadier, as she built another box in her mind and stuffed this experience into darkness.

'She's beautiful,' Charlotte said, tears glistening on her cheeks as she cradled her niece to her chest.

Victoria held her grandson. They sat on opposite sides of the bed, a tired and smiling Eloise lying between them. Victoria sometimes wondered if she'd imagined the confessions Eloise had made in the rain after Dominic's death. This woman, this new mother, was so full of love, it made her skin glow. She couldn't imagine her hurting a fly.

'I'm going to call her Charlotte,' Eloise said.

Charlotte gasped. She looked far healthier than when she'd left Weston, thinner, wearing stylish clothes. She had an air of having done important things and needing to leave them soon to do more important things. 'Are you sure?' Charlotte said.

'Positive,' Eloise replied. 'I just hope she's as beautiful and successful as my big sister.'

Charlotte kissed her niece's head. 'Hello, little Charlotte.'

Eloise looked Victoria dead in the eye. Suddenly, Victoria *could* believe the scene in the car. 'And I'm going to call him Dominic. Isn't that wonderful, Victoria?'

Victoria looked down at the little boy, the perfect cherub. Perhaps Eloise was trying to hurt her with this, but Victoria didn't take it that way. She couldn't think of a better name for her grandson: for her second chance. 'Hello, Dom Dom.'

CHAPTER FORTY

PATRICK

Patrick had tried to be strong for so long. He had done it for Vicky, knowing that revealing the truth would implicate her in this mess. If he told the truth, then they would question her, demanding to know why she had agreed to do something so warped, so unforgivable. She loved her son all right, but keeping a corpse for him? It wasn't Vicky's fault some passer-by had seen Patrick trying to get rid of the body. He'd completely ballsed that up, but it wasn't as if he was an experienced criminal.

Murder. That was what they were pinning on him. With no comment from Patrick, they were branding him as a psycho, some freak who'd happened upon a vulnerable girl and taken her as his personal plaything, ringing emergency services for Dominic to cover his tracks.

Patrick's main concern was protecting Vicky, but he hadn't trusted himself to speak, knowing he'd give something away. So he'd sat there, interview after interview, breaking apart on the inside while remaining stone-faced on the outside.

'*No comment,*' was what he told them, if he said anything at all, but it was becoming real. Soon, it would be time for his sentencing. He was only thirty-three; he had a life to live, things to do, chances to take. Losing his freedom brought it all into painful definition; he hadn't even made use of his freedom when he had the chance.

During the interview process, he had represented himself, though the police officers had heavily advised against it. It was the only way he could be sure that he wouldn't slip up and share something. The solicitor would urge him to stand up for himself, but he couldn't, not if it meant hurting Vicky.

But as he rotted in his cell, awaiting full-fledged prison, he was painfully conscious of the fact Vicky hadn't visited him. He'd tried ringing, but the operator always told him she had refused the call. That was when his mind began to comb over their relationship, and he noticed, far too late, the small flashes of distaste that had crossed her face, the pity in her eyes, the smirks she'd tried to hide.

Maybe his mind was torturing him, but he didn't think so. Without her physical closeness, without her whispers of a bright future together, the ache in his soul began to lessen. His mind cleared. He had never been the most intelligent person – he was ready to admit that – but he felt like he was finally seeing clearly.

She had used him, and he wasn't going to spend the rest of his life in prison for it. He asked to speak with the investigators, stressing he had information that would change their understanding of the case.

Soon, it was time for the interview. DI Cartwright walked into the room, looking tired and impatient as usual. 'You better have something worthwhile to tell me.'

'I do.' It made him ache to think that he'd once planned to say those two fateful words in entirely different circumstances, with a woman he still loved even if he hated her too.

'Strange hearing anything other than "no comment" from you.'

'Vicky isn't who you think she is.'

DI Cartwright sat. 'I'm listening.'

THE END

ALSO BY NJ MOSS

All Your Fault

Her Final Victim

My Dead Husband

The Husband Trap

The Second Wife

Through Her Eyes

Ruin Her Life

The Twins

Nowhere to Run

The Fame Game

ACKNOWLEDGEMENTS

I would like to give special thanks to Betsy Reavley and Rachel Tyrer, who were integral in the plotting and ideas stage for this novel. Their patience and imagination gave me the creative kick up the backside I sorely needed.

To my editor, Ian Skewis, I express endless gratitude. His notes were insightful, and I always felt that he was doing that most noble of editor's tasks: helping me to improve the book I wanted to write, to reach my vision, rather than replacing it with his own. He made the final product far better than it would've otherwise been.

Thanks to the rest of the team at Bloodhound Books: Tara, Hannah, Lexi, Abbie and Shirley.

Writing is a lonely journey at times, and I am grateful to have writers who allow me to vent my ideas, and who share their moments of inspiration and frustration with me, with special mention to Diane Saxon and Patricia Dixon. To all the members of the Bristol and Bath Crime Club, thanks for the laughs and the meet-ups. And to all the reviewers – there are too many to name without unfairly leaving people out, but you know who you are! – I am sincerely grateful for all that you do. The book world, especially with your delightful Facebook groups, wouldn't be the same without you.

My other hobbies keep me sane and busy, so thanks to Weston Rollers and Rising Tide Brazilian Jiujitsu.

Last, but never least, thank you, Krystle. I love you, and I'll never stop being grateful for your belief in me.

A NOTE FROM THE PUBLISHER

Thank you for reading this book. If you enjoyed it please do consider leaving a review on Amazon to help others find it too.

We hate typos. All of our books have been rigorously edited and proofread, but sometimes mistakes do slip through. If you have spotted a typo, please do let us know and we can get it amended within hours.

info@bloodhoundbooks.com